HOMEGROWN

A NOVEL

By: Larry J. Alvarez
© L. Alvarez

How many dirty FBI Agents do you know?

When LAPD Detective, and former Army Ranger, Steve Hudson uncovers not only a silent terror cell but a radical Islamic mole inside the FBI, a counter-terrorism investigation becomes a counter-terrorism, espionage, and treason investigation.

Homegrown is set against a backdrop of current national and international events played out on the streets of urban America.

The threats are real....

HOMEGROWN is inspired by true events which have been fictionalized to protect the innocent, with an insider's view of modern police operations and counter terrorism investigations.

LAPD

Anti-Terrorist Division
Unit Logo

Eye:	The ever-watching eye, always on the look-out.
Shield:	Protection.
ChessBoard:	Represents a game of strategy, intelligence, and timing.
Scales of Justice:	Represents law, order, and justice.
Sphynx:	Protects the city by means of a riddle.
Lightning Bolts:	The different sections which make up ATD: (1) Domestic Squad
	(2) International Squad and (3) Surveillance Teams

LAPD RANK & INSIGNIA

No Insignia

No Insignia

Police Officer I (Probationary / Rookie Officer)

Police Officer II

Police Officer III (Field Training Officer or Other Specialized Assignment)

Police Officer III+1 (Senior Lead Officer or Other Specialized/Hazard Pay Assignment)

Detective I (Investigations)

Police Sergeant I (Patrol Supervisor)

Detective II (Detective Supervisor/Sergeant)

Police Sergeant II (Patrol Supervisor or Assistant Watch Commander)

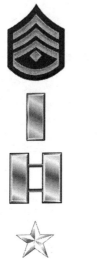

Detective III
(Detective Supervisor/Sergeant
or Assistant Officer-In-Charge))

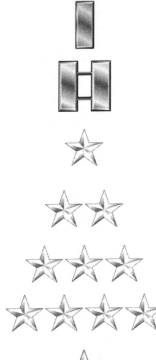

Police Lieutenant (Patrol Watch
Commander or Officer-In-
Charge Specialized Units)
Police Captain
(Commanding Officer
of a Police Division)
Police Commander
(Assistant Commanding
Officer of Police Bureau)
Deputy Chief
(Commanding Officer
of Police Bureau)

Assistant Chief of Police

Chief of Police

Police Commission
(Five Member Civilian Oversight
Board. Appointed by the Mayor)

INDEX OF CHARACTERS

Ziya Gokalp	Woodland Hills Islamic Center Council Member
	Accountant
Habib Khan	Woodland Hills Islamic Center Council Member
	Ventura County Mosque Imam
Abu Mulaika	Student of Qazi; Security Guard
Antonio "Tony" Marino aka Rasheed Shari	Italian Convert and Student of Qazi
Yunnus Banah	Student of Qazi
Nassim al Waqqas	Student of Qazi
Mustafa Sadat	Student of Qazi
Farooq Zahir	Student of Qazi; Playboy Mansion Gardener
Naim Ibrahimi	Former Imam, Woodland Hills Islamic Center
Umar Hayat	FBI Al Qaeda Cell Arrest, Lodi, CA
Hamit Hayat	FBI Al Qaeda Cell Arrest, Lodi, CA
Global Relief Foundation	An Islamic charity suspected of fundraising for foreign terrorist organizations
Mohammed Chehade	Co-Founder of the Global Relief Foundation
Rabin Haddad	Co-Founder of the Global Relief Foundation
Rachel	LA City Zoo Caretaker
Yasmine Erdogan	Mahmood Erdogan's Wife
Gerard Chaudry	Moderate Muslim Businessman
A'amira Chaudry	Wife of Gerard Chaudry
Hussein Nazari	Police Officer and Brother of FBI Agent "DAN"

Reymundo Lopez **aka "Lil Rey"**	Los Angeles Street Gang Member
Phil	Animal Right's Activist
Maria	Playboy Mansion Operations Manager
Hurrah	Brother of Fatima. Killed by Taliban
Ismail Ibn Marzook	Fahim's father

CAST OF CHARACTERS

LAPD Chain of Command

 Captain Jennifer Wade, Commanding Officer Anti-Terrorist Division

 Detective III John Carter "JC," Senior Detective Supervisor

 Detective II Steve Hudson, Detective Supervisor & Case Agent

 Detectives I Ryan Riley, Pedro Gonzalez, & Jimmy Butler

 Police Officer III/ Field Training Officer Franco Garcia

GLOSSARY OF TERMS

A-File	Immigration Application
ALF	Animal Liberation Front
ATD	LAPD's Anti-Terrorist Division
Assalamu Alaikum	A Muslim greeting meaning "peace be to you"
Barfi	A traditional Afghani game played at first snowfall
Burka	A full body garment worn by some Muslim women
Code 2 High	Police priority response without lights and sirens
CRASH	LAPD Anti-Gang Unit, "Community Resources Against Street Hoodlums"
Deobandi	A revivalist movement under Sunni Islam common on Indian sub-continent and spreading through Europe and Africa
DZ	Drop Zone
FATA	Federally Administered Tribal Areas. An ungoverned and lawless area of Pakistan's Northwest Frontier Province
Haleen	A traditional Afghani meal
Henna	A red colored hair dye allowed under Muslim tradition

Hijab	A head scarf or veil worn by some Muslim women
Imam	An Islamic religious figure
Inshallah	"God Willing"
ISI	Pakistan's Intelligence Agency
Jamaat-ul-Fuqra	A radical Islamic organization originating in Pakistan with ties to Al Qaeda and Osama Bin Laden
JTTF	FBI's Joint Terrorism Task Force
Mujahideen	Religious holy warriors
Northwest Frontier Province	A region of Pakistan
Pashtu	Common language of Afghanistan and Western Pakistan
PR	Police radio code meaning the "person reporting"
Qazi	Title meaning "Religious Judge"
Salafi	A movement under associated with strict, literal, and traditional interpretations of Sunni Islam
Sharia Law	A strict moral code and Islamic religious law
Stick	A straight line tactical formation
Sunni	An orthodox version of the largest branch of Islam
SWAT Valley	A Pakastani area divided by pro & anti-Taliban sentiment
Umma	Worldwide Muslim community
Wahhabi	An ultra-conservative branch of Sunni Islam
Waziristan Province	A mountainous region of Pakistan bordering Afghanistan

12th **Imam**	An Islamic prophecy
"650"	LAPD undercover code
5150	That section of the Welfare & Institutions Code which designates a mentally ill person

WOODLAND HILLS ISLAMIC CENTER LINK CHART

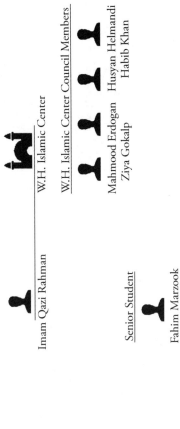

W.H. Islamic Center

Imam Qazi Rahman

W.H. Islamic Center Council Members

Mahmood Erdogan   Husyan Helmandi
Ziya Gokalp   Habib Khan

Senior Student

Fahim Marzook

Students

Abu   Tony   CI   Yunnus   Nassim al   Mustafa   Farooq
Mulaid   Marino   Karim   Bannah   Waqqas   Sadat   Zahir

CI's
Romeo & Juliet

FBI Special Agent-JTTF

Dawud Ali Nazari "DAN"

What has one voice, four legs in the morning, two legs in the afternoon, and three legs in the evening?

PART I : ONE VOICE

20 December, 1989, 0058 hours.

"Two minutes!"

The preparatory command was yelled and then echoed to the sixty-four paratroopers over the roaring engines of the C-130 Hercules troop transport aircraft. The cold night air whipped through the cabin as Sergeant **Steve Hudson** conducted one last mental checklist and inventory of his sensitive equipment.

Several hours earlier, the soldiers of the 75th Ranger Regiment, 1st Battalion, Alpha Company, had received an alert notification. Due to the secretive nature of the upcoming mission, a strict form of isolation from the outside world was imposed.

Rangers from all three companies of 1st Battalion, as well as 3rd Battalion, Charlie Company, were charged with securing the Omar Torrijos International Airport in Panama, clearing the airport's runways and establishing defensive blocking positions.

Forty-five minutes later, soldiers from the 82nd Airborne Division were scheduled for an airborne insertion. Their mission was to prevent the Panamanian Defense Forces and the Panamanian Air Force from interfering with American operations.

"Stand up!" was the next in a series of simple commands designed to get all the paratroopers through the rear aircraft doors and onto a predetermined drop zone (DZ).

"Hook up!" This command instructed jumpers to attach a fifteen-foot nylon static line to a metal cable running the length of the troop carrier compartment.

Despite forty-seven successful jumps, Sergeant Hudson had always been afraid of heights and didn't particularly like jumping out of airplanes.

However, it was a requirement for Rangers to be airborne qualified. Hudson liked being around men who liked to jump out of airplanes. There was a certain blend of bravado and camaraderie in serving among the ranks of one of the world's elite special operations units, the U.S. Army Airborne Rangers.

No one knew what awaited them in the darkness less than a thousand feet below. No one was talking. Everyone was in their own final thoughts, with all eyes glued to the solid red light on the back wall next to the jump door.

Hudson was in the middle of a silent prayer to Saint Andrew, the Rangers' patron saint. He wasn't much for religion, but like most men, he had a tendency to turn towards faith in times of uncertainty. Missions like this one could very easily and very quickly turn deadly. Suddenly, the solid red light changed to solid green.

"Go! Go! Go!" Hudson stepped out of the door into the black night sky in textbook form: Chin down, eyes open, arms by his side, as he started his four second count. The roar from the aircraft engines was deafening as his body experienced the usual whiplash from being propelled out of the aircraft, coupled with the engine backwash.

From the beginning, nothing went as planned. The mission, "Operation Just Cause," had been compromised and so AC-130 gunships had been forced to begin the campaign to capture Dictator Manuel Noriega fifteen minutes early.

Since Panamanian defense forces had been alerted, the element of surprise was no longer on the Rangers' side.

As Hudson's chute deployed, he observed the flashes and sounds of gunfire erupting around the city. He was trying to make out the rapidly approaching DZ below him when he realized that Panamanian forces had scrambled a hastily formed defense on the air strip below the Rangers.

"Oh, Shit." Hudson mumbled. "It's a hot DZ! It's a hot DZ!" he called out to his squad.

Hudson hit the ground and instinctively performed a hasty parachute landing fall in the high grass, roughly thirty-five yards in front of a Panamanian machine gun nest.

Hudson's rank of sergeant had allowed him to check out a Colt .45 caliber semiautomatic handgun from the armory, in addition to his normal armament. The soldiers' M-16 rifles had been packed in a jump case which dangled below them alongside their rucksacks.

The pistol was in his hand without his being conscious of having drawn it. Without a clear front sight picture, Hudson acquired his target instinctively, based on all of his previous training, and fired six quick shots.

The sounds of bullets striking metal gave the Ranger sergeant confidence as he concealed himself in the high grass and listened- confident and something much more…active, satisfying in a gut- churning way.

There were no sounds from the machine gun nest. No return fire. Hudson used these few seconds to retrieve his M-16.

"You OK, Sarge?" a private in Hudson's squad called.

"Yeah, let's move on that position!"

They encountered no resistance from the machine gun nest as they leapfrogged toward the enemy post and the Rangers saw that it had been abandoned. As Hudson examined the area, he found a blood trail leading away from the machine gun post.

"Looks like you got one, Sarge."

Hudson longed to follow the blood trail but his duty to lead his men overcame his urge to track-and-kill.

"Mess with the best, die like the rest!", he proclaimed to his team before moving them through the darkness in a choreographed progression to their next target.

EARLY WINTER, 1371, SOLAR HIRJI CALENDAR (1992, GREGORIAN CALENDAR)

THE TEMPERATURE DROPPED AS EVENING fell across the newly fallen first snow of the quickly advancing Afghan winter. The aromas of traditional Afghan cooking traveled through the small house on the outskirts of Kabul. **Fatima** was preparing the winter seasonal dinner of haleen, a dish of wheat mixed with ground chicken and served with oil and sugar.

Fatima's parents were still at the open market where they worked as trade merchants. The last two weeks, Fatima had noticed that her parents were getting home later and later. She knew they lingered to discuss politics, economics and the future of business with the other merchants.

Since the departure of the invading Soviet forces, the Taliban had come to power and instilled a strict form of Islamic Law among the predominately Muslim population. Fatima's twin brother, **Hurrah**, though, was not among those who simply accepted the Taliban's stringent interpretation of the Quran.

Hurrah, who lived up to a name meaning "liberal and free," craved adventure and excitement, much like any healthy thirteen-year old does. He was intrigued by the west and had an appetite for items shunned and condemned by the increasingly oppressive and influential Taliban imams, and would much rather spend his time with his friends or with his western studies then with his parents helping them at the bazaar.

Fatima, the more conservative and responsible of the twins, had easily adapted to her traditional roles and household chores. As she continued preparing this evening's meal, she worried that her parents would return home late again.

As she continued preparing this evening's meal, her thoughts were interrupted by a light knocking on the front door. She knew better not to answer it. With the arrival of snow, Afghans played a game called Barfi. A relative or friend would send an envelope packed with snow. Acceptance of the envelope would commit the received to host a party for the sender and his family. Many Afghans avoided answering the door during the first snowfall to avoid this trick altogether.

Bang. Bang. Bang. The knocking this time exploded with more

authority. That's odd, Fatima told herself. Usually, in the game of Barfi, a child would be sent to deliver the envelope.

Bang. Bang. Bang.

"Open this door," a male voice commanded in Pashto, the common language of Afghanistan and western Pakistan.

Fatima, startled and panicked, ran to find her hijab head covering and face veil, which she would be expected to wear when greeting an unknown man at the door.

The fierceness of the banging urged an urgent response. Fatima wouldn't have time to cover herself completely in a burka, but at least her face would be covered in a display of honor and respect to her family.

Where was Hurrah? Why wasn't he responding?

Bang. Bang. Bang.

Hurrah ran out from the back room and into the entranceway just as the whole house shook. The forceful pounding was replaced by a violent blow to the door that left cracks in the door frame.

Fatima and Hurrah stood paralyzed by fear. Adrenaline raced through their bodies but they were unable to move, as time seemed to stand still. The door, unable to sustain a second blow, disintegrated in front of Fatima.

Members of the Taliban secret police raced into the house, yelling indiscernible commands. A secret police officer charged Fatima and threw her to the floor, causing her head covering to become dislodged. Although not hurt, Fatima was stunned by the sudden explosion of violence. The policemen could be heard ransacking the back rooms.

"Who is Hurrah?" the senior officer commanded.

"I...I...am." Hurrah, trying to be brave, stepped forward.

"You are accused of wearing western clothing in public."

Just then, a policeman reappeared from a back room. He was carrying a pair of Levi blue jeans. He held them up to Hurrah's slender frame. A perfect match.

"Where did you get these?"

Stunned with disbelief, Hurrah was unable to answer.

"By order of the religious courts, under the authority of the Taliban, you are sentenced to death."

As Hurrah stumbled backwards towards the wall, the senior policeman unholstered his Soviet S-4 sidearm.

"Effective immediately." He raised the pistol toward Hurrah and fired one shot into his head.

Fatima watched in horror as blood spattered the wall and Hurrah's lifeless body crashed to the floor.

"Noooo!" Fatima shrieked.

"You are saved, as I will not condemn a virgin to death," the senior official said.

Although Sharia law doesn't prohibit a virgin's death, it does teach that virgins go to paradise after death. Not completely satisfied with cutting short the life of the young girl before him, the official wanted to ensure that she would suffer an eternity in hell in her afterlife.

The officer turned and walked out, leaving Fatima with two of his henchmen.

"We'll take good care of her," one of them said.

Fatima fell to her knees and sobbed uncontrollably. A policeman grabbed each arm and dragged her back to the bedroom to which she had often retreated to find comfort and safety. On this cold dark evening, the room offered only a nightmare from which she couldn't escape. Now, there was only terror, and it paralyzed her so that she couldn't even open her mouth to scream.

Fatima was numb as her clothes were ripped from her body. She was thrown onto her bed. The man hovering over her stank of sweat, tobacco and garlic, which mingled with the soft, sweet fragrances from her dresser top and the pungent aroma of haleen wafting in from the kitchen.

Fatima tasted the blood from her bitten tongue and was further terrified by her frantic gasps of breath, the mewling sounds crawling up her throat with the bile and by the man's guttural grunts.

He pounded her little body and, as he punished her soft flesh with his rough hands, she felt warm blood trickling over her thighs, draining away her youth and innocence. She lied scalded by a searing pain that would never end, staring not at him but at the second man who was looking closely at her naked body. She realized she couldn't hear anything but the second man, who was laughing loudly. Then, he too took his turn with her.

Resistance was useless against the brutes, as her power and spirit were drained from Fatima's 13-year old body. She could only mumble to herself, "It's not supposed to happen this way."

Finally, when they finished taking their pleasure on her, they stood over her ruined, naked body and urinated.

"Maybe, next time, you'll remember how to wear your burka properly," one of them growled. "This is what happens when young women seduce men," he added, blaming her for her own rape.

EARLY WINTER, 1371, SOLAR HIRJI CALENDAR (1992, GREGORIAN CALENDAR)

QAZI METICULOUSLY EXAMINED HIS REFLECTION in the full length mirror. Mirrors such as his were rare in the Swat Valley of Pakistan's Northwest Frontier Province, adjacent to Afghanistan. It was a luxury the imam, or Islamic cleric, could not only afford but required. Qazi's image was a large part of who he was and, more importantly, how effective he could be.

His robes were always clean and neat, not an easy task in the desolate landscape of his homeland. His graying hair and beard were dyed a reddish color by henna, the only allowable dye in the Muslim tradition. His reddish hair, coupled with his trim shape, gave him the appearance of a much younger man.

To the commoners, it added to his mystique, reaffirmed

credibility and his faith in Allah, and his commitment to the radical interpretation of Sunni Islam, known as Deobandi.

Born **Asad Abid Rahman**, the term "Qazi" was actually a title meaning religious judge. Religious judges held considerable power in this barren part of Pakistan where Sharia law ruled. This special title was a rarity in a land that was sympathetic to the Taliban rule just across the unmarked Pakistan-Afghanistan border, over which the democratic, pro-western and often times corrupt Pakistan government had no influence and little control.

It was a dangerous part of the world, which had the increasing capability of threatening global destabilization.

This was the land Qazi called home and he was proud to be part of what he believed to be an international movement to restore the values and morals of Allah to the world. His commitment to these beliefs would be the basis for his next journey.

Sergeant Hudson finished his classified debrief and crossed the grounds of Fort Bragg, North Carolina. As one of the U.S.'s most combat ready military installations, it was home to the 82nd Airborne Division, the JFK Special Warfare School and the Army Special Forces "Green Berets."

Hudson's enlistment obligation was almost over and he was contemplating his next career move and assignment. He loved the Rangers but felt it was time to move onto the next level and challenge. Hudson was thinking Special Operations, Detachment Delta—commonly referred to as Delta Force. However, hopeful aspirants to this elite group didn't just walk in off the street. Potential future members had to be invited by a member of the Force. So while at Fort Bragg, Hudson had decided to use his time on base to put out feelers to some of his buddies and contacts.

He had hesitated in doing so following the top secret mission in Panama. His reaction following the brief fire fight at the airport scared him. He wanted to hunt and kill. But a part of him knew it was wrong. The day after returning to the United States, he had seen something about Peter O'Toole, who played 'Lawrence of Arabia'. It made him think. He understood and was tormented by a struggle with violence, loyalty, and the morality of right and wrong.

It took time, but now he was ready to put out those feelers. Then, while on his way to meet a friend he turned a corner and was immediately drawn to two sharply dressed men in dark blue.

They turned out to be L.A.P.D. Police Officers. Memories of childhood television shows such as One Adam Twelve, which represented a time when right and wrong were clearly defined, flooded the young sergeant and it hit him immediately that he belonged there. That would be his next career.

Six months later, Steve Hudson found himself standing at attention, on the infamous first day "Black Line," as a Police Recruit Officer for the LAPD.

It was a long, bumpy and dusty ride through the unmaintained roads of Pakistan's Tribal Region. Qazi was tired as he approached the remote training facility.

He had been here many times before and his status and reputation had always ensured him the best accommodations available at the camp. After all, Qazi had been quite active in the Pakistani government.

He had served as an official religious person responsible for prayer sessions and other government ceremonial formalities. He was later named to the Senate from his original Waziristan Province in the Federally Administered Tribal Areas. His time spent among the highest levels of Pakistan's government made Qazi numerous political contacts and furthered his exposure across the land. Soon his influence would spread even wider.

It also exposed Qazi to Pakistan's intelligence agency, the Inter-

Services Intelligence, commonly known as the ISI. It wouldn't take long before members recruited him into the agency, which had its troubles. The ISI was fractionalized between those loyal to a pro-Western democracy and those who preferred a more traditional Islamic Pakistan. Mistrust was common among members and Qazi saw this as yet another opportunity to gain credibility, influence, and power,

Through the ISI, Qazi received formal training in espionage, covert communications, surveillance, operational security, developing and manipulating informants, as well as other crafts of the trade.

ISI maintained regular contact with and received training from western intelligence agencies, including the American Central Intelligence Agency. As a result, Qazi received hands-on training from some of the best intelligence agencies in the world. He then visited camps like the one he was approaching to pass on what he had learned.

As Qazi neared the camp, he came on a guard shack at the outer perimeter. Two teenage boys holding assault rifles appeared from behind the structure and challenged the approaching vehicle.

"Assalamu Alaikum." The lead guard called out the common greeting used by Muslims worldwide, meaning "peace be to you."

The second guard stood back on the opposite side of the road with his weapon at low ready as he suspiciously watched the visitor.

"Wa alaikum assalam wa rahmatu Allah," Qazi replied, wishing peace onto the young guard along with the mercy of Allah.

The expression on the boy's face suddenly changed. There was no doubt he recognized Qazi Asad Abid Rahman. In his surprise the young guard began to say something but stumbled for words, while he waved Qazi through the checkpoint.

As Qazi drove into the training facility, he was greeted by dozens of cheering men in military training fatigues. The presence of Qazi in their midst was an honor and seen as a sign from Allah himself.

As **Jennifer Wade** walked into the room, she saw that they were all dressed in dark clothing: Sweatshirts, ski masks or black bandanas, gloves, pants, and dark colored back packs. Her adrenaline was pumping. She'd been involved in other forms of direct action but she knew that tonight's mission would be different.

She had managed to get involved with a radical splinter group of the Animal Liberation Front, more commonly known as ALF. This subgroup was a spin-off of the main public group and their actions were never sanctioned, at least publicly, by the ALF.

The subgroup justified its actions as necessary to influence public policy and prevent widespread abuse of animals for testing, food and luxury clothing. Many of the members viewed the rights of animals over the rights of people. Jennifer knew that tensions were getting high among several members and she had been anticipating tonight's phone call for the past several days.

She had already been involved in such action as vandalism, threats and animal releases. Animal releases could include the freeing of animals in captivity at any number of testing facilities or in the release of hundreds of mice on the grounds of an elementary school or other institution.

The group had also targeted local chain department stores selling fur coats and disrupted and intimidated businesses and customers with protests and sit-ins, which included chaining themselves together.

These were more nuisance types of activities and while they could be unnerving and costly to the victims, they never reached the level of aggravated personal violence that Jennifer was anticipating from tonight's mission.

Earlier in the evening, as Jennifer drove to meet the rest of the group, she had remembered the last late night mission in which she participated.

A local university was involved in animal testing for medical research. Security at the testing lab and medical center was high, which made it impossible to target. Instead, they relied on finding soft targets associated with the lab. They wanted to frighten people connected with the testing facility but unrelated to the animal issues, as they believed they could persuade them to cease their business activities with the lab facility and force the lab to close.

In this case, they had identified the lab's bank. They figured the bank's president would have a lot of security, so they went one step further and identified the retired parents of the president and decided trough them they would get to the bank president, and thus the bank, and finally the lab, their ultimate target. In their fevered minds, this made perfect sense.

They had gone to the retired couple's' house in an upscale West Los Angeles neighborhood which was quiet at that time in the early morning. They had forced open a side window and unwound a garden hose and inserted it into the dining room. They were pleasantly surprised to find that the couple had just remodeled the entire first floor and installed new hardwood floors. They had turned the hose on and let it run all night and into the morning. The group imagined that it would have run for several hours before the homeowners awoke and that the damage would well exceed several thousand dollars.

The participants laughed among themselves for days over the incident. Jennifer had kept meticulous mental notes during and after. Similar to the previous night, tonight's call had come late, unannounced, and with little time to meet up with the group, giving her no opportunity to make a phone call before leaving her apartment.

She had arrived at the apartment of one of the members and

walked in to see four people there. She was the fifth and final person and the second woman.

Jennifer stood only 5'02" and weighed 105 pounds. Her blonde shoulder length hair fell over her firm and trim frame. She was attractive by any standards. As she greeted everyone in the room, her eyes lingered until making contact with Jimmy, one of the men who she knew from a previous mission.

Jimmy always wore baggy and layered clothing but Jennifer could tell he had a solid muscular frame, even if he didn't advertise it. He was the typical strong but silent type and Jennifer could not remember ever having a full conversation with him. She felt an odd attraction to him but knew that any romantic relationships was off limits for an undercover officer.

The leader of the group was an animated and angry young man named Phil. He was definitely the most violent in the group, and it was clear to Jennifer that many in the group followed him out of fear.

He was rambling on with his usual rhetoric, justifying the violence of their actions. "The bottles are filled with gasoline" he said.

Phil had worked himself into a fury because the last mission hadn't produced the intended results. He had become obsessed with the elderly couple and the fact that they were an easy target.

"Jimmy, you and I'll sneak up to the house and douse the exterior with gasoline. As we run away, we'll throw some Molotov cocktails and burn that damn house down. Those old people can burn inside, just like the animals they help kill every day."

There was silence. Jennifer made eye contact with Jimmy and he nodded. This was it. They were about to escalate to arson and possibly murder in the furtherance of the animal rights cause.

"Jennifer, I want you to drive the car with me and Jimmy."

"You got it," she responded with feigned enthusiasm.

She couldn't believe it had gotten this far and was trying to figure out how to handle the situation from this point on. Her head began to swim with possible solutions as Phil continued revealing the rest of the night's plan.

She was alone with a group set on murder. If her true identity were revealed, her own safety would be jeopardized. To this point, she had managed to infiltrate this group of radical environmental and animal rights extremists and monitor their activities. She had determined the seriousness of their intentions, which were quite clear now. This group was considering and planning for murder.

Deep undercover work was tricky. She was given a new identity, removed from the Department records, prohibited from all Department facilities and functions and isolated from all of her current friends and family.

The official Department term was "650'd," a term derived from Room Number 650 of the old LAPD headquarters building, Parker Center. It was the room where undercover officers and detectives would go to have themselves officially removed from the Department files.

Jennifer decided she'd try to send a text message to her handler before leaving the apartment. She knew he wouldn't sleep until he heard from her.

She was typically unarmed but lately she kept a 5-shot, 3 inch, snub nose revolver in a concealed cut out on the left side of her driver's seat.

As the group gathered the necessary items, Jennifer went to use the bathroom. She couldn't risk being overheard on the phone so she sent a quick text message. So many things could go wrong. She prayed the text would go through and that her handler could react in time.

Probationary "Boot" Officer Hudson was just three weeks out of the Academy. His time spent in the Rangers had served him well and prepared him for the physical aspects of Academy life. However, the physical regimen of the Old Elysian Park Academy was demanding and required not only physical endurance to complete the training but mental toughness, as well.

Runs nicknamed "cardiac," an entirely uphill winding switch back and "stairway to heaven," a long uphill staircase, required heart and spirit to complete and struck fear and dread into many of his Academy classmates during the grueling seven month training program.

Hudson was now patrolling the North Hollywood area of the San Fernando Valley with his senior field training officer, **Franco Garcia**. Garcia was a crusty older officer with his younger, more vibrant days behind him.

Nonetheless, Garcia was always ready for anything, having worked the majority of his career as a CRASH officer in the busier part of East Los Angeles, known as Hollenback Division. Community Resources Against Street Hoodlums, or CRASH, was LAPD's aggressive anti-gang unit created to combat the growing effects of street violence.

Garcia referred to Hudson as "young gun" while Hudson referred to his training officer as "Sir" or "Officer Garcia."

The training officer and his rookie partner were halfway through their shift when they received a radio call about a man with a gun. When the comments to the call stated to see an earlier incident, the senior officer knew right away there was more to this call than was first indicated.

As the officers rolled Code-2 High, uninterrupted priority call without lights and sirens, to back the primary unit, Hudson read the comments, which were displayed on the in-car computer system known as the Mobile Data Terminal or MDT. "SEE PR STATED NEIGHBOR IN APT 215, M/W, 35-40 YRS, POSS 5150, WAVING GUN FROM BALCONY AND THREATENING PASSERSBY."

Just then, the radio crackled again, "All units responding to the man with the gun call, Code Alpha..." a meet-up location to devise a strategy to brief on the upcoming tactical event. When they arrived, they learned that officers had responded to the same call, earlier in the day. A search of the area revealed that the suspect had left.

Apparently, he had returned. The suspect's apartment was located on the second story, with a balcony overlooking an outdoor walkway through the apartment complex and between buildings. An access stairwell was next to the suspect's apartment.

The balcony afforded him a high ground tactical advantage. The officers devised a plan to approach, wearing their ballistic black helmets and proceed in a "stick" tactical formation.

As they reached a staircase, they'd split into two teams. The Arrest Team would climb the stairs to the second floor, knock on the suspect's door and take him into custody. This team consisted of a supervisor, two arresting officers, two cover officers, and one officer with a taser to offer a less-than-lethal force option.

The Rear or Perimeter would consist of the other two officers, whose responsibilities would be to take positions of cover and watch the back balcony to prevent any escape, as well as to keep citizens from interfering with or accidentally walking into the arrest team's operation.

The officers were armed with their 9 mm Baretta handguns, drawn at the low ready. They were approaching the stairway entrance and there didn't appear to be any activity in the apartment. They continued forward, with the balcony in full view.

When the team was a few feet from the stairwell door and ready to split, around the building corner, straight ahead of them, came the suspect.

He carried an assault rifle and began firing even before he had raised the rifle in the officers' direction. The officers scrambled backwards, almost tripping over each other as they tried to return fire without getting in each other's way.

Rounds were flying everywhere when Hudson heard the only female officer cry out.

"Jesus Christ! I've been hit," she screamed.

He glanced over to see that a large chunk of her right shoulder was missing.

The suspect raised his weapon toward her again, to finish her off. Hudson instinctively stepped in front of the downed officer and engaged the suspect. His aggressive actions caused the suspect to flinch long enough for the other officers dragged their downed partner to safety.

Hudson couldn't believe it when he saw his shots, perfect center mass hits, bounce off of the suspect's chest. His 9 mm rounds didn't have enough power to penetrate the suspect's body armor. Now, the suspect had the new rookie officer in his sights.

"Get Down, Hudson!" he heard.

Hudson sprang into the stairwell and out of the line of fire. His partners had pulled the downed officer backwards in the other direction. Hudson could feel the high powered rounds slam into the wall and door behind him. He was alone and faced with stairs up and stairs down.

He knew he couldn't stay put and had to move. He chose down, which led to a parking garage. As he moved, he heard the suspect enter the staircase behind him.

Hudson was now the hunted. Alone, outgunned, trapped in the parking garage and with a suspect wearing heavy body armor, he knew he didn't have much room for error.

He hid between some parked cars against the far wall. He could hear the suspect's footsteps as he approached. Hudson crawled around the front end of the car that was parked between them.

As the suspect passed his hiding spot, Hudson carefully came around the other side of the car and moved in quietly behind the suspect. He leveled his front sights on the suspect and obtained a good sight picture.

Although the suspect was wearing body armor, he didn't have any protection on his head. "Stop there and drop your gun!" Hudson demanded.

The suspect had no intention of doing so, he turned fast while raising his gun to fire.

Hudson was in position and ready. "Doom on you," Hudson thought as he gently squeezed the trigger and dropped the suspect to the pavement. It felt good.

Hudson would later be awarded the Medal of Valor, the Department's highest honor, for his life-saving actions.

After a particularly rough Chicago winter, **Ismail Ibn Marzook** was grateful for the break of spring and mildly pleasant weather before having to endure the oppressive Midwest humidity of the late summer months. Originally from Afghanistan, Ismail was accustomed to adverse climates, and he always marveled at the human ability to acclimate to varying weather conditions.

Ismail arrived early to work every day, following after his daily ritual of attending the Muslim early morning prayer known as Salutu-l-FDanr. After prayers, he would often remain in the mosque and discuss issues of the day. He would listen as **Mohammed Chehade** and **Rabin Haddad** led discussions about worldwide Muslim suffering and immoral western decadence.

When Mohammed and Rabin opened a new office in the quiet Chicago suburb of Palos Altos, The Foundation of Secours Mondail, otherwise known as Global Relief Foundation, they offered Ismail the job of office manager.

Rabin was a dynamic and charismatic Pakistani and had a way of influencing those around him. It was rumored throughout the Islamic center that Mohammed was heavily connected to radicals overseas. But that was only rumor.

Ismail's thoughts were interrupted by the ringing of the office telephone.

"Hello."

It was a call that would forever change the way Ismail identified himself.

Several hours later, in a small, well-lit delivery room of Palos Community Hospital, Ismail became **Ismail Abu Fahim**, or Ismail, the father of **Fahim**, as he proudly looked over his newborn first male child, **Fahim Marzook**.

Over seven thousand miles away, another proud father was looking down on a newly born child, the second of his two daughters. **Husayn Helmandi's** eyes gleamed through his hardened features.

Husayn was a wealthy landowner and well respected warrior and leader who had earned a fierce reputation as a Mujahideen during the Soviet invasion. He had seen years of conflict, from the Afghan Civil War and the Soviet invasion to the collapse of the Democratic Republic of Afghanistan, due to Mujahideen resistance.

The rise of the new, Mujahideen Taliban government, he believed, would create stability.

He had made plenty of political connections but in doing so had also made his fair share of enemies, some for no other reason than greed and jealousy of the location of his land.

He decided that his native country might not be the best place to raise his children and he didn't doubt that he could find a way to manage his farms and crops from afar. The money brought in from the world's most lucrative region for opium crops would enable him to buy the trust of other familial clans to manage his lands.

He would also be in a better position to oversee the importation of his goods to a country with a healthy appetite for his product and provide him a lifestyle of luxury at the same time.

On Husyan's U.S. Immigration Application File, known as the A-File, he proudly listed his affiliation as an anti-Soviet Afghani Mujahideen Freedom Fighter.

Jennifer Wade had been handcuffed and transported to the Van Nuys Jail Division. All five members of the subversive group were in various stages of the booking process.

They were kept separate but could see each other from various vantage points. After Jennifer had been processed, photographed and fingerprinted, she was led away from her booking cage by two serious looking detectives in suits and ties.

It was 4:30 a.m. and she looked every bit as exhausted as she was. It was necessary to protect Jennifer's identity as long as possible. The fact that the group had been infiltrated by law enforcement would be revealed to the remaining defendants shortly after the arraignment. For the time being, it would benefit investigators during any interrogations and lock in any statements made. Detectives were expecting everyone to "lawyer up" and not speak to investigators. There was always an abundance of legal rights activists who provided free legal advice and seminars to the environmental and animal rights crowd.

They made sure the activists were well versed in how not to cooperate with law enforcement and were always ready to file civil suits against any government entity they could in hopes of an easy settlement.

The City of Los Angeles was famous for deep pockets and easy settlements. That was mildly interesting to the detectives at this point. They were concerned with doing everything by the book and protecting their undercover's identity as long as they could, including the potential of running what is known as a "Perkins Operation." During these additional undercover investigations, a confidential informant is placed in a cell with an arrestee to obtain a statement or confession which can be used to bolster a criminal prosecution.

The takedown had gone perfectly, from Jennifer's standpoint. Phil and Jimmy had just finished pouring gasoline around the perimeter of the house as the elderly couple slept inside, oblivious as to what was about to happen. Simultaneously, and out of nowhere, a police helicopter swooped in and illuminated the entire yard with its spotlight.

Police motorcycles and black and whites came tearing down the street on top of the group. Everyone, including Jennifer Wade, was stunned at the effectiveness of the takedown.

Undercover officers were able to detain the two lookout vehicles before the activists knew what hit them. Everyone was in custody and evidence had been obtained. Officers felt they had quickly sealed a prosecutable case.

Now, Jennifer was led upstairs to the Van Nuys Detectives Squad Bay, where they had utilized a conference room for a mandatory debriefing. A radical group had been disrupted and a great case could be presented to the District Attorney. Once Jennifer completed her debriefing, her undercover role would be over and she could go back to her normal life.

Jennifer would later meet with Department psychiatrists to ensure a safe and healthy transition from her undercover role. In the meantime, she was debriefed by other officers and detectives from LAPD's Anti Terrorist Division who were cheering her success and safe operational conclusion.

There was food and fresh coffee waiting for her. She had been there for about an hour and was unwinding when unexpectedly, "Jimmy" walked into the room smiling and unrestrained.

Jennifer was shocked and remained so when she learned that "Jimmy" was, in fact, Detective James Butler, another undercover officer and, unbeknownst to Jennifer, her back-up officer throughout the assignment.

It was decided. Qazi Asad Abid Rahman was needed to do Allah's work in the land of his enemy. The council that made the decision had consisted of other like-minded Muslim Islamists of similar influence and power.

Once outside the security of the remote training camp, Qazi knew that it might be a very long time, if ever, before he saw some of his brothers again face-to-face. For operational security, direct communication among the members of this group was prohibited. They all knew and understood this and would not violate the procedure at any cost.

They were bound together by a lifelong calling to spread Islam throughout the world. They were not afraid, even quite willing, to use violence when they felt that the timing was right and necessary.

Their cause was gaining global momentum and the Western powers were becoming weak. They were not fools. The council knew Western military technology remained unmatched on the battle field, particularly American, but they also knew the people and culture had grown soft.

They saw liberal social policies were weakening the social fabric throughout all of Europe and America. All through history, Islam had taken advantage of similar social conditions by claiming tolerance and diversity until a solid foothold was established.

Qazi could set up operations easily in America and claim discrimination and religious legal protections, making it easy for him to operate in the land of his enemy. Lax American immigration policies would allow him and his family a smooth transition process.

The council had long studied the policies, practices, and history of the United States to the point that they knew more about America than most Americans themselves.

"It is time. Begin to ready yourselves. Pack your things. I will be leaving quickly. And you will follow." Qazi had returned to his home village to give his family the news of their upcoming departure. There was a clear mix of excitement and nervousness on his children's faces.

"Qazi! Qazi! Qazi!" the crowd swelled to an uncommon roar. It was the end of a three-day celebration to honor the esteemed religious figure and to bless him in his important journey.

After the celebration, Qazi was chauffeured to Islamabad, the Pakistani capital, where he met with other like-minded government contacts. All of his immigration papers and travel documents were provided.

There, Qazi was again celebrated, and a week of late night dinners, alcohol, and pleasure girls ensued. Despite his religious titles and reputation, he viewed these pleasures and simple vices as entitlements.

In a blink of an eye, it was time for Qazi to go. He flew from Islamabad to Germany and then, eventually, to the United States. There he would decide on the targets and set his new plans in motion.

Spring, 1993

"To love the prophet Muhammad is to hate those who hate him."

Qazi was in the middle of the Friday afternoon Jumma services at the Jamestown, West Virginia mosque, where he had been staying since he arrived in the United States.

"The enemies of Islam are those who do not practice it in the strictest forms," Qazi continued.

This brought mumblings from several members of the mostly moderate congregation. But Qazi was an accomplished speaker who wasn't about to let some grumbling interfere with his sermon. He had anticipated some resistance and planned the transition of his tones accordingly.

"The only way to defeat the Jew is by jihad." Qazi was in a controlled rage as he carried on with his anti-semitic rhetoric. As he raged on, Qazi was also scanning the crowd, trying to identify what portion of the crowd was sympathetic to the radical views he was espousing. In particular, he wanted younger members of the audience. It was these members he knew he could mold and who would become instrumental to Qazi's long term plan.

After the sermon, Qazi met with a young university student who had been leading prayer services. The student was honored to receive such attention for Qazi.

"Do you enjoy the congregation listening to the words of Prophet Mohammad as they come through you?"

"Yes Qazi."

"Do you give yourself and all that you are to the Prophet?"

"Yes Qazi."

"I was thinking I would take you under the warmth of my wing and teach you the things that will make you powerful in the eyes of the Prophet. Would you like that?"

"Yes Qazi. Very much. It would be an honor for me and my family."

The mosque was too small to have its own full time imam and this young student would fill the void of leading prayer services and delivering sermons, between his university studies. Qazi began to ensure that this young student received the proper training in accordance with the strictest interpretations of Islam, while building a trust he could use later. Just as importantly, he made sure the congregation treated him with the highest level of praise, so the student began to feel importance grow.

Qazi ensured that his young apprentice received sermons from Saudi-based resources that provided subject matter material for people without the proper religious training. All of the material was entrenched with the radical Saudi Wahhabi interpretations of Islam.

HOMEGROWN

It took several months, but the student finally had Qazi control of the Jamestown mosque, through which Qazi had established an environment where extremism could grow and then thrive. Qazi then put in place several other policy changes. Women were no longer permitted to worship in the same room as men. They were instead secreted behind curtains in the back of the room.

Women were also required to use head coverings on the mosque grounds and were encouraged to wear the complete traditional coverings of the burkha. Men were encouraged to grow beards and those who didn't were not allowed to sit near the front during prayer services. Men were also required to roll up their pants over their ankles when on the mosque grounds. Discussion around the mosque now included a fusion of politics and religion.

PART II : FOUR FOOTED

17 Years Later – Post 9/11 America

Frank was on top of the world. He was a senior at Taft High School, a public school located right on Ventura Boulevard in Woodland Hills, an upper middle class neighborhood in the western part of the San Fernando Valley. He just turned eighteen and was a star wide receiver on the varsity football team.

The season was off to a great start and there was early talk of a state championship. Frank was popular and well liked among his classmates as well as with many of his teachers. His best friend, **Cody**, was the star quarterback. They made an impressive team on the football field and they were inseparable off of the field.

Already six feet tall, both were tall and wiry. Frank had dark hair and eyes, while Cody was fair in all his aspects. The success of the varsity team created a campus excitement that was contagious and everyone saw these friends as the reason for the school's success. They were more popular than ever. It was a Saturday, late afternoon, after another blowout win the night before and they were at Cody's house hanging out, when the phone rang.

"Hello." Cody picked up on speaker.

"Hey, Cody, it's me, Cindy."

Cindy Lopez had taken a sudden and aggressive interest in the football team's star quarterback.

"Are you guys going to that house party tonight? I'd really like to see you there."

"I'd really like to see you there," Frank mocked, poking fun and imitating the flirting girl as he skipped around the room.

Frank had always been a laid back and fun loving person who enjoyed a lot of friends and popularity. He was a charismatic leader both on and off the football field.

"Maybe we'll stop by later on. Let me see what's going on." Cody hung up. He always tried to play it cool with the ladies.

55

"Dude, Cindy is the ugliest kid ever in the creation of children."
Frank laughed.

"You're stupid."

They both knew how hot Cindy was, short, pretty, long dark hair, and deep brown eyes. They also knew Cindy's reputation, which was on the wild side. She liked the bad boys, which was no secret. But like any other single, 18 year old boy, these two really wondered if she was "on the go team," meaning would she be an easy lay.

"You just wish she wanted you as bad as she wants me." Cody and Frank loved giving each other shit.

"Can't you see she's just using you to get to me. Hey, maybe she wants both of us!" said Frank.

"Ya, maybe I'll ask her what her dirtiest fantasy is and see where it goes," Cody continued as the two friends continued to both banter and fantasize.

Cindy's next call was to **"Lil Rey."** "Lil Rey" wasn't his real name, but his gang or street name.

"Mondo, it's me," Cindy said to her ex-boyfriend.

They had been on and off for the past few years. "Mondo" was Cindy's name for **Reymundo Lopez** and he was her first true love. He treated her like crap and cheated on her on a regular basis. But she hadn't yet realized this.

"Lil Rey" was an active member of the Canoga Park Alabama street gang and immersed in the violence and criminal activities of the gang. He had been kicked in and out of the neighboring Canoga Park High School and other continuation schools, for fighting and other antisocial behavior.

"I've missed you, babe," he said. "It's been a while. When can I see you again?"

"Well, if you want me, you can come and get me. I'm going to that house party tonight over in the Hills."

"Where is it? Maybe I'll come by later on."

Cindy knew well his short temper, potential for violence and jealousy. She'd been on the receiving end of his rage on more than one occasion. She just didn't care.

"I don't' know but I'll text you the address when we get there."

Cindy was intent on winning her boyfriend back and Cody, the football star, was unknowingly an instrumental piece in her plan. She would make sure that "Lil Rey" would notice her new romantic interest. And she believed he would get jealous and then want her back.

Cindy, like so many other naïve young women attracted to the "bad boy" persona, was convinced that she could change Lil Rey, tame him and make him hers. She was young, cute, popular with the boys, and she allowed him to do whatever he wanted to her, no matter how abusive. She believed that it was a sign of love and a compliment to her sexual prowess and what the boys wanted. It took most girls in similar situations sometimes twenty years to start realizing the mistakes of their youth. Cindy was on her way to being no different from the thousands of women who would take buses or borrow cars to visit their baby's daddies, children in tow, to the visitation rooms of jails and prisons throughout the country.

Frank was handed a beer from the keg at the house party. He was on his way to the backyard, where he was hanging out, when he made eye contact with Cody, who was dancing provocatively in the main room with Cindy. Always a flirt, Cindy gave Frank a clear, inviting, and what Frank saw as a dirty look. They shared a smile. As Frank walked back outside, he overheard other girls at the party gossiping about Cindy. They didn't like the attention she was getting from the two friends.

He couldn't have been outside for more than ten minutes when he heard some confusion and yelling from inside. While it wasn't unusual to hear arguments and fights break out at house parties, this crowd didn't appear to have any trouble makers in it.

Something instinctually told Frank that something was wrong

inside the house and he started moving towards the sliding glass door when...

POP!....POP! POP!

"This is all a bad dream," Frank told himself. He couldn't believe what had happened and he felt like he was in a trance. It was close to six in the morning and he was at the police station. He had been up all night, for what was one of the longest nights of his life, giving his account of what had happened to the investigating homicide detectives. He had explained everything he knew over and over again.

The voices in his head wouldn't stop asking, "How could this happen? How could she do such a thing? How would he explain this to Cody's family?" He didn't have the answers. He had never experienced such a reckless disregard for human life and selfishness before. He was in a state of shock. One thing he did already understand was that he would never be the same. The events of the past night would change his life forever.

An officer escorted Frank out of the station. His father, clearly concerned and worried, was waiting in the police station lobby. Frank had maintained his composure throughout the night. However, when face-to-face with a supporting loved one, he finally broke down and sobbed in the emotional safety of his father's embrace.

The sun was coming up as they drove home. **Ismail Ibn Marzook** called to his son, **"Fahim."** Although he understood the reasons for his son's adopted name, he refused to address him by this nickname.

"We need to talk about some things." The two drove to a nearby Denny's for breakfast. Although Frank, or Fahim, was physically and emotionally drained, he knew not to question his father's intentions and the seriousness of his tone.

"Fahim, the American way is no good," his father began. "I am sorry you had to learn this lesson in this way. The way of the West is filled with hatred and evil."

Fahim sat and listened as he took it all in.

"I am sorry for the loss of your friend. Now, it is time you learned the true way, the way of Allah. You see, this is all in Allah's great plan. Your friend died to save you and show you the true meaning of life and redemption."

He went on to say that it was meant to be this way. He must go and find the way.

"I will send you to study with a great man. He is close by. No one knows his true name. He is known as Qazi. You will learn what is truly important in life from him."

"I need to see your license, sir," the undercover vice officer said. Vice cops had entered the filming location and seen enough before asking who was in charge.

"Okay, Officer, but I really would appreciate it if you'd cut us a break" answered **Antonio "Tony" Marino.**

"Where's a cop when you need one?" Tony asked himself. Just last night, he was shaken down for protection money by the local chapter of an outlaw motorcycle gang at the second class topless strip club. He didn't mention to them that he was part owner of the place.

The bikers hung out there regularly and provided narcotics, mostly crystal meth, to the girl dancers. The bikers claimed the club as their turf without actually owning it. They also ran a small-time prostitution ring out of the club, which catered mostly to the Hispanic day laborer population living in the area off Sepulveda Boulevard in the Valley, north of Los Angeles.

While the regular biker presence intimidated Tony, it also kept a host of other criminals from causing unexpected problems at the club. Tony made his money from beer sales, cover charges, stage fees and taking a percentage of the private lap dance fees earned by the dancers.

The bikers made money from narcotics, prostitution and the protection racket.

"You guys don't have any filming permits on file with the city," the vice cop said.

"Yeah, I know, but we weren't expecting such a nice day. It all kind of came together at the last minute."

It was the first nice spring day after a long, only by Los Angeles standards, cold winter. Tony decided to take advantage of the weather to jump start the summer film productions.

The San Fernando Valley of Los Angeles was well known as the adult filming capital of the world. It was relatively easy to find any number of the numerous multimillion dollar estates willing to rent out their lavish properties for a hefty sum. And there was big money in the pornography business.

"I understand you're just trying to make a few bucks and take advantage of the day," the officer said. "But the neighbors have some legitimate complaints."

He pointed next door while trying to remain aware of the position of the girl performing her job as fluffer and her male flufee, who were meandering about.

"No problem, officer. I know what I need to do." He was thankful that the officers didn't spend so much time looking around that they found the wide array of drugs scattered about in what felt like plain sight.

It wasn't too difficult to find attractive young women to perform in front of the camera but all too often they came with baggage in the form of drug and alcohol abuse.

"Not my concern," Tony told himself, "as long as they show up when they're supposed to."

Tony Marino had been born into a Roman Catholic, Italian, blue collar family in the Dyker Heights neighborhood of Brooklyn, New York. He was the son of a low level foot soldier for one of the New York Five Families. Due to complications during his birth, his mother was unable to have any more children.

Tony was an average kid growing up. He had several childhood friends but wasn't considered popular by any stretch. He didn't excel at sports or in class and he considered himself lucky to graduate high school.

Tony didn't get involved with any friends who gravitated towards criminal activity in search of easy money. Nor did he follow in his father's criminal enterprises. Tony's relationship with his father had always been distant.

However, Tony did possess a good amount of common sense and he managed to avoid significant trouble growing up. He had always been quiet and reserved. His religious faith and belief in the Roman Catholic Church had been shattered early on in his life due to an isolated incident with a priest while he was serving as an altar boy. Tony never went back to alter boy duties.

After high school, Tony moved to Los Angeles with a friend to pursue the warm climate and Hollywood dream. He got the weather for sure, and at least a taste of his dream.

It had been a decade and a half after the arrest and dismantling of the extremist animal rights group of extremist. Jennifer Wade had long been since promoted to Captain. At the conclusion of her undercover investigation, Jennifer had begun dating and eventually married Detective James Butler, who had also been promoted to Captain. Although that too had long since ended.

Wade had over seen some of the best detectives in the department and some of the most complex investigations in the city. She was well respected by the officers and detectives who worked for her.

She always led from the font and by example, and that always went over well in any police department.

She had been there and done that as an officer and a detective and as a result she earned her promotions from substance and experience, which was reflected in her leadership philosophies. She truly loved and respected the people in her command and she put their best interest first and foremost.

She was now the Commanding Officer of the Anti – Terrorist Division. She never forgot what it was like to have her rear end on the line. And understood through experience that making it home safe depended heavily on the quality of her fellow officers. So, she made it a point to sit in on every interview and oral board for officers and detectives applying for an assignment in the Division.

As usual, this morning Captain Wade was assisting with interviews.

"Good Morning, I'm Captain Wade, Commanding Officer of Anti-Terrorist Division. Thank you for coming to interview with us today." Captain Wade was immediately impressed with the Medal of Valor recipient and now veteran officer and detective who sat before her.

"Thank you, ma'am. Nice to meet you," responded Detective Steve Hudson.

Farooq feared that Allah would be displeased with his evening prayer but he couldn't keep the resentment and disappointment from dominating his thoughts.

Earlier in the day, as he was hauling decaying, putrid plants to the curb, he'd been humiliated to be seen at such menial work by an emissary from his Islamic group. But, the messenger paid no attention to the work, he just stated the message as told to do: the mansion was now one of numerous targets, which would work together for destruction in harmony. And with the rise in the size of the mission, they would now be sending someone else to lead the mansion's part of the plan.

Farooq was furious, but did not reveal any of his anger to the messenger. He simply said, "Understood."

He felt he was being disrespected. He cursed his infidel of a mother and swore that, one way or another, he would be the true servant and martyr of Allah.

"There he is."

"You got him?"

"X marks the spot."

"Bing. Bing. Bing" The sound of the digital camera cycled through one after the other as the trooper took picture after picture of the target.

"You really should mute that camera, rookie." The two troopers, like any other close team, always gave each other shit.

The two South Carolina State Troopers were assigned to Internal Affairs. They were on a special assignment, at the request of a county sheriff, to investigate one of his deputies. The sheriff's department was too small to investigate their own, so it was not uncommon to call on the resources of the State Police for investigations involving criminal or other serious misconduct by local officers.

"If I wasn't seeing this myself, I wouldn't believe it."

"This guy is a traitor and he ought to be hung." The trooper in the driver's seat took a pull from his coffee mug.

"Come to Daddy," he said, as he continued to snap away. "You rolling video on this, partner?"

"YouTube ready, baby!"

Both troopers knew full well that this video would never reach public domain. Sadly, with all the bureaucracy, they knew that public exposure may be the best way to actually bring these guys down. But, of course, the consequences would be too great for everyone involved.

"How could this guy have passed a background investigation?"

"Who knows what these locals do. Not sure if they actually give a shit. Actually, I know they don't."

The troopers weren't any different than the rest of their force. They believed they were smarter and better trained than the officers on the county, town, and municipal levels. Of course, the other side saw them as arrogant and elitist, and were always insulted by the way they carried themselves. Both sides knew how the other felt and really didn't care. At it's best it brought out some good jokes and upped each other's game. At its worst, it brought out fist fights that would never get reported.

The target of this surveillance was a sheriff's deputy. The original and official allegation from another member of his team was that he was working off duty without an approved work permit. Law enforcement officers were typically required to obtain a work permit, issued by their employing agency, to ensure that there were no conflicts of interest or other activity that might bring embarrassment to their oath of office and agency.

Hussein Nazari was an eight year veteran of the sheriff's department. For the past three years, he had been a member of the county's regional SWAT team, where he had a good reputation.

Hussein Nazari was also a devoted Muslim. He was allegedly teaching sensitive law enforcement SWAT tactics to a private group of non-law enforcement personnel.

Today, the two state troopers were watching him teach advanced shooting drills and tactical movements at a shooting range just outside of his jurisdiction.

He was definitely violating his department policy by disclosing sensitive police tactics. But he was also violating the trust of his brother officers. And this team now believed he was also selling out his fellow American citizens, because every part of their training told them these students were a group of Muslim religious extremists.

And they were right. Unknown to the two undercover investigators, this group was affiliated with the radical Islamic organization known as **Jamaat-ul-Fuqra.**

The Jamaat-ul-Fuqra was a terrorist organization with origins inside Pakistan. The organization operates worldwide, including throughout North America. Members of the Jamaat-ul-Fuqra are known for their extreme hatred towards westerners, and the goal of the organization was the spread and purification of Islam through violence. Its leaders had been linked to Al-Qaeda and Osama Bin Laden.

"If it looks like a duck, talks like a duck, and walks like a duck..."

"It's a duck!" The two laughed out loud.

It didn't take a national security clearance for the troopers to know that this group being trained was involved in some pretty serious and heavy stuff.

They also saw how their counterpart acted among this group and they didn't like what they saw. They were too far away to record sounds. It wouldn't have mattered because they were all talking in Urdu, one of the two official languages of Pakistan and the one identified with Muslims.

"This stuff is going all the way to the colonel himself and the local sheriff will be all over this too."

"That's just the start. Feds and FBI too."

"FBI. Fucking Bunch of Idiots couldn't investigate a god damned thing."

They both laughed at the incompetence of their federal counterparts. They had been around long enough to hear endless stories of investigative blunders made by the Bureau. And like all their comrades believed they were only good for taking credit for all the good old fashion police work done by real street cops.

Despite the 9-11 Commission Report and vows and pledges of shared cooperation, everyone in the law enforcement community knew that nothing had actually changed. Agents from the FBI never shared any information with anyone.

And they rarely did any field work, either. And when they did, their tactics were awful. The running joke in the department was that if you wanted to find an FBI agent, you'd have to get him Monday through Friday, between 8:00 am and 4:00 pm, and he would be at his desk behind a computer.

Like any other profession, it is one thing to be arrogant and good but arrogant and incompetent was another thing entirely. But in this sort of work, being right and wrong often meant being dead or alive, so experienced street cops have very little patience and absolutely no respect for such a combination. Other special agents from all the other federal agencies were generally a good match with local and state officers. But the FBI didn't play well in the sandbox with anyone, even other feds, who felt the same way towards the Bureau.

The two state troopers remained in their surveillance van, which was parked and turned off despite the rising heat and humidity. It wasn't quite noon and it was clear it was going to be a brutal one. They were already dripping in sweat, and they had removed their t-shirts and were wearing only shorts and running shoes. Their duty guns were always within reach in the cramped quarters of the van. And they were dug in, surrounded by all their cameras, radios, cell phones, equipment, surveillance target paperwork, food, and tons of water.

They wouldn't even leave the van to use the bathroom. They brought empty gallon containers to relieve themselves in. Police surveillance always sounded and looked sexy on tv or in movies, but there was rarely anything glamorous about it. They remained inside of the van while Hussein Nazari and his group broke for lunch. They weren't in a position to see Nazari take a phone call or hear the conversation.

"Hello, Brother!"

"How is your training going?"

"Have you been assigned your duty station yet?"

"Ah, Islamabad, very fitting indeed. We will have to talk more in person."

"Yes, I will see you at your graduation."

"Asa Lama Lakum, my brother. I will see you soon."

Tony had a working relationship with some of the outlaw bikers who came into his second class strip club. However, Tony was intimidated by them and was smart enough to keep them at a distance. They were unpredictable, often under the influence of a variety of drugs and alcohol and prone to violence.

His club was primarily a cash operation and at the end of any given night, there were typically several thousand dollars on hand. It was the primary reason Tony maintained current state required security guard licenses. He could carry a concealed firearm at his business or while acting as an armed guard.

Security work was not something Tony was particularly thrilled about but there was consistent money to be made in the industry.

Tony's club had been receiving an increasing amount of negative publicity, thanks to a city councilmen was waging a very public battle over the club. Tony and his partner had managed to hang on, but it was only a matter of time before they'd have to close shop.

Ever since he was a kid, Tony had felt like he was moving through life without any real direction or passion. His cousin owned a private security company and was always offering him side jobs. Tony decided that he'd call his cousin in the morning.

"Nice to know you," said **Abu Mulaika.** Mulaika was a Pakistani immigrant who had only been in the United States a few years. Today, he was ordered to take the Boss' cousin, a guy named Tony, on his security detail.

Security guard companies often mimicked local police agency uniforms to give the appearance of actually being police officers and to enhance the image of the security guards. Abu Mulaika was dressed in a dark blue shirt and pants. The uniform shirt had arm patches with the words "Gold Star Security Services" and Abu wore a star shaped gold badge on his left breast.

The uniform was a combination of blue uniforms worn by municipal police departments and the badge and patches similar to those worn by the California Highway Patrol. Abu Mulaika wore a utility belt which contained handcuffs, a baton, and a can of pepper spray. He was otherwise unarmed.

"Ya, good to meet you, too, Abu," Tony said. "What's this place all about?"

"It's a hookah lounge. People come here to smoke flavored tobacco in large water pipes."

Hookah lounges were an extension of Middle Eastern cultures and were becoming increasingly popular in the United States, Canada, and Europe. The smoking lounge reflected an open air outdoor café, which served a variety of Middle Eastern pastries and snack food such as humus and kebabs.

There was a large tent which contained tables and two flat screen televisions as well as outdoor tables and futons for people to lounge on. They didn't serve any alcohol and as a result, the hours of operation were not restricted.

The crowd was a mixture of people of all ages, ethnicities, and religions. Once the bars closed down, many partygoers liked to continue their evening by going to this popular smoking lounge. The large number of already intoxicated late night parties made it a good practice to hire regular security guards.

Tony was dressed in on open collar shirt exposing several gold chains on his chest and a sports jacket to conceal his firearm. Gold Star Security had just accepted a contract from the hookah lounge to provide uniformed security services and traffic control in the parking lot of the lounge.

Inside security services were contracted by a company strictly employing off duty police officers. These officers were always armed, and better trained in conflict resolution and de-escalating confrontational situations. They were also more experienced in taking quick and decisive action, if necessary.

Tony was on hand as an executive assistant to his cousin for quality service purposes. This was a new contract and the night needed to go smoothly. Although it was his first night out, Tony's job was to monitor Gold Star's security officers, coordinate with the off-duty officers and make sure the manager and employees of the hookah lounge were happy. With that said, he spent most of the night watching and learning and trying to get some good buddy time in with the guys.

Through the course of the night, he learned quite a bit. He had never paid so much attention to all of these people and cultures around him. He enjoyed sampling the flavored tobacco with the lounge manager and the buzz that it gave him. He enjoyed the many beautiful, classy and nicely dressed women who visited the location. They were unlike the women he was used to being around.

He hit it off with one of the off-duty officers who had access to more armed security details than he could handle. The best part of Tony's night however, was his new Muslim Pakistani friend, Abu. Tony was impressed by Abu's work ethic, quiet confidence and religious devotion. There was something about Abu's calmness and larger faith that intrigued Tony.

Dawud Ali Nazari was already seven months into a nine month tour in Pakistan. At twenty seven years old, he was fresh out of the

Quantico FBI Academy when he was chosen for this overseas tour due to his language and cultural skills, but he was still learning the do's and don'ts of FBI life.

Dawud was a practicing Muslim. His father was Egyptian and his mother was from Jordan. Dawud himself was born in Egypt but immigrated to the United States with his family when he was twelve years old. They settled on the southeast seaboard.

Dawud cousin, **Hussein**, had lived with them since he was a young boy. Hussein's father had been in the Egyptian military. He was killed in a training accident in a helicopter crash that killed his entire unit. Although technically cousins, Hussein and Dawud had lived as brothers ever since.

Dawud was able to access the internet through his FBI office in Islamabad. He liked to read stories from his home town. Today, The Carolina Star newspaper was reporting that a South Carolina police officer had been charged with statutory rape after signing a marriage contract with the family of a 14-year old girl. An audible sound came out of his mouth.

"Hussein Nazari, 31, an eight year police veteran, had signed a contract and paid a dowry to the girl's father before a Muslim ceremony was held last month," police told the Carolina Star.

Because the girl was a minor, under South Carolina law Nazari could not legally marry the girl without a judge's order. According to the article, police said that relatives of the girl who opposed the marriage had taken the girl to live with them and then alerted police to protect her from further alleged sexual abuse by Nazari.

Dawud read on, "Three days after Nazari allegedly threatened the relatives, someone fired five shots into the home of the girl's uncle. No one was hurt."

Nazari was arraigned on one count of statutory rape and ordered held on $100,000 cash only bail. But despite all of that news, the line that Dawud found the most unsettling was the article's last, "Police investigators revealed that Nazari had been the subject of an Internal Affairs investigation, but that additional details were not available."

Dawud could only hope that the connection between him and his Hussein would go unnoticed by the Bureau. Although a violation of Bureau policies, he wouldn't disclose the information to his superiors.

He was in a third world country and scheduled to transfer back to the States in a couple of months. He had been a riding star moving quickly through the ranks. He wanted to stay off of everybody's radar at this point. And, despite Hussein's troubles, Dawud was looking forward to returning home to meet this new bride. Dawud's family had already made all of the arrangements.

"Front Sight. Front Sight. Front Si....BANG!"

A perfect surprise break, Hudson told himself as he ejected the magazine from his Glock .40 caliber handgun. He'd been around firearms a long time and as a former Army Ranger, he had the best training available. He was an expert marksman.

Others often told him he was a natural shot. He always replied to such comments with a humble smile. But he knew how good he was. And in Hudson's opinion, there was nothing natural about shooting. Being responsible for causing and controlling an explosion inches from your face was a completely unnatural instinct.

Hudson found that shooting and expert marksmanship was an acquired skill that took constant discipline and practice. He practiced frequently and maintained membership at a local indoor firing range where he practiced basic marksmanship skills and weapon malfunction drills. He also practiced at the LAPD ranges and regularly shot the Department's Combat and Bonus shooting courses.

All members of the LAPD were required to qualify on the Combat Course every other month. The qualification course consisted of shooting thirty rounds alternating between two targets at various distances under time requirements. It also included a "Failure Drill" in which officers were trained to take head shots. The reason was that if two shots to the body failed to stop a suspect during a deadly force encounter, officers had to assume the suspect was wearing body armor. If such a threat were present, as in the famous LAPD North Hollywood Bank of America shoot out, officers would need to take a head shot and shut down the computer, so to speak, to stop a suspect's violent actions.

Contrary to popular belief, civilian police forces in the United States don't train to shoot-to-kill. Rather, they train to "shoot-to-stop." Stop the threat with the necessary reasonable force required and then effect an arrest. This is why police handcuff a suspect after a shooting incident.

The Bonus Course of fire was a more demanding and faster forty round practice course. Higher stress levels were created by faster firing sequences in shorter times. Stress was also created by an internal competitive quality found in most police officers.

One of the basic principles of marksmanship was to concentrate on your sight picture and alignment, not on the holes in the paper target. This was easier said than done and impossible when standing on the firing line with other officers, as everyone wants to show they have the cleanest target. The temptation to compare your shots with the person on either side of you had a tendency to amp up anxiety levels, making it difficult to focus on the basic marksmanship principles.

It was one of the reasons Hudson liked to practice the basics at his favorite local range where his membership remained at seventy five dollars a year, because he worked in law enforcement. He was always thankful for the way local businesses treated members of the LAPD and other agencies for that matter. And this place was always well kept and always had an abundance of ammunition and targets available onsite for purchase.

Hudson reloaded his magazine with a handful of rounds. During slow fire, he always reloaded an unknown number of rounds as not to develop subconscious habits of always loading the same amount. It would also ensure that he focused on each round as opposed to what he had left in his magazine.

He acquired a good pistol grip and he pressed both palms together as he raised the pistol to his eye level, never lowering his head to the weapon and upsetting his shooting platform. He closed his left eye and focused his vision on the front sight or post at the tip of the barrel. He ensured that the front post was centered evenly between the two rear sight posts and he observed the familiar blur of the blackened silhouette target down range.

Keeping his focus on the front sight, he began to control his breathing into a slow and steady pattern and to slide his right index finger from the frame of the Glock and onto the trigger. Before beginning his trigger press, Hudson always started repeating out loud: "Front Sight. Front Sight," waiting for that surprise break, "Front Sight. Front Si…" BANG!

Qazi sat out by the pool of his house. It had been a searing hot day in the San Fernando Valley. Los Angeles summer heat extended well into October and Qazi welcomed the coolness as the evening sky set in. His loosely flowing white robes kept him comfortable and countered the effect of his long, thick beard.

He enjoyed this time of the day and regularly found calmness as his eyes gazed over the garden where his family grew fruits and vegetables.

His eyes eventually rested on the building behind the house. The Woodland Hills Islamic Center consisted of a large domed building which contained the mosque itself, a small school, several offices and a banquet hall. The Woodland Hills Islamic Center property also included the residence where the Imam—Qazi—lived with his family.

After spending time in West Virginia, Qazi had decided to move on. He couldn't stay in Morgantown forever and he needed to expand his operations. Qazi knew that there were several communities outside of Sacramento and San Francisco with large Pakistani and Afghani communities.

He had spent several weeks in the Lodi area of Northern California. As he sat lost in thought, he remembered his friend, **Umar Hayat**, and his son, **Hamid**, who he had stayed within the quiet community between Sacramento and Stockton. Qazi considered both father and son to be honorable but knew that they talked too much. They had let the American lifestyle make them lazy and careless and, as a result, they made several mistakes which led to their arrest by the F.B.I. for supporting their brothers in the furtherance of their cause.

Qazi was smarter and told himself to learn from their mistakes. He would be more disciplined and always mindful of security and secrecy. He gave Hamid credit for not speaking to agents of the federal government. Qazi had been concerned that Hamid would break under interrogation tactics and reveal information on several of the camps he had arranged for Hamid to attend.

Throughout his prosecution, Hamid had stayed loyal to the cause, which Qazi believed was spreading like a wild fire across the globe. He believed this to be a sign from Allah that the world was again returning to the glory of Islam.

Qazi was convinced that he would do his part to accelerate that return and to purge and cleanse the world of the evil influences of the West.

He would continue his life's destiny in the very shadow of his enemy and… His thoughts were interrupted…

"Qazi, there you are. It is done," said Fahim, who had risen to one of his most senior and respected students. Qazi was thankful for Fahim's father who always stayed to true to Allah and faithful to Qazi.

"Tell me."

"We waited for them in the parking lot. When they returned to their car, they were told it was Allah's will. I convinced them physically, enough to scare them, but not seriously hurt them."

"And then…"

Qazi wanted all of the details.

"The police came. Someone must have called them but they didn't do anything. They only made a paper report for assault and battery."

"No arrests?"

"No. Nothing. The police never do anything in this country. Criminals run free. There's no order or respect for life. It is why we must act now and do Allah's work to restore human decency. It is Allah's will. Is it not, teacher?"

"Yes, it is. He has told me this. But we must be patient. Learn and practice patience."

Qazi was always taking the opportunity for a teaching moment to mentor and give direction to his students.

"Where are the others?" Qazi asked of the remaining eleven students.

"We are all ready, waiting for your arrival."

"Very well, **Fahim**. Let them know I will be there shortly. I have a very important function to attend later tonight after prayer."

Most of his students had now entered the second stage of the radicalization process: Self-Identification. They had passed through stage one: pre-radicalization. They were progressing toward a belief in Salafi Islam—to becoming part of the extremist Sunnis who believed themselves the only correct interpreters of the Koran. And they would come to believe most moderate or mainstream Muslims to be the worst of the infidels and non-believers. Tolerance was not in their view of the world. His students at this stage of his teachings had given up drinking, smoking, gambling, drugs, and urban clothing and music. Some were growing beards and they were wearing the traditional Islamic clothing. Soon, he –Qazi – would bestow a Muslim name on each of them.

After finishing the evening's classes, Qazi attended a house warming party for one of his close associates.

Husayn Helmandi and his immediate family had recently moved into their new residence. Although Helmandi had owned the property and large home for several years, he had rented it out as a fraternity house to students from nearby California State University Northridge.

The house was located in a quiet, upscale neighborhood filled with large, older homes. After several years of ongoing nuisance complaints from a neighborhood that had grown tired of the fraternity's loud and late night rowdy behavior, the city attorney's office had finally started to take action.

Nuisance abatement proceedings had been initiated and Husayn's attorney advised him to terminate his renter's lease agreement or face costly fines and fees which promised to be a lengthy process, which he was sure to lose.

"Welcome, Qazi," Husayn said as he greeted his newly arriving guest. He guided Qazi through a maze of guests toward the food. These guests were mostly business associates, friends and extended family.

"Thank you, old friend, you continue to be quite the socialite."

"Yes, it is important to maintain my image as a successful businessman who has assimilated to the culture and achieved the American dream."

Husayn had indeed proven to be a smart and cunning business-man with many ventures and investments. He'd initially made a lot of fast money on his arrival in the country through the sale of heroin from his homeland.

He had quickly connected to an Afghani narcotics smuggling ring stretching from New York to Los Angeles. When he first arrived, American law enforcement was overwhelmed with Colombian cocaine and nearly all of their resources were allocated to the Gulf of Mexico and Florida.

No one was paying any attention to a large group of Middle Eastern immigrants who were growing a heroin industry unchecked. There was a chain of mom and pop shops in New York which, in addition to making New York style pizza, were fronts for the international Afghani heroin trade.

Helmandi had tapped into this network and expanded into Los Angeles. He had been smart with his money and had invested all of his profits in legitimate businesses and real estate. He remained disciplined and wouldn't allow himself to get addicted to the drug or the quick and easy money.

Qazi admired this quality in his friend because it showed his self-control and intelligence. Helmandi had purchased numerous apartment complexes in lower income, mostly Hispanic, immigrant communities. He'd also invested money in several companies for which he did nothing but put up the initial money as an investment.

Some had failed but others had done well, and he had already made plenty, so he could remove himself directly from the drug trade. He knew that it would only be a matter of time before it would be exposed, on one level or the other, directly as being involved in narcotics activity.

He would however, remain involved, although removed several layers, to an international network funneling the drug into Europe and Russia, the land of his old enemies. He knew that by living in California, he'd never be tied to a Middle Eastern drug network. Government resources would never be that efficient, at least not for any conviction of a respected business man and United States citizen, in any criminal court.

"Yes, I understand fully," Qazi said.

"How did your classes go tonight?"

"They went well. **Muhammad** and **Mustafa** are almost ready to go on to the next phase. We will have openings for two new students in the future."

"Very well. The party will be over soon. Relax and make yourself comfortable in the back. We will start our meeting then."

"Thank you, I will."

It took Helmandi less than an hour to say goodbye to all of his guests. The women automatically started the cleanup process. There were five men who stayed behind. They met in a large office-lounge in the back of the house. They'd remain undisturbed. The women understood not to interfere in the affairs of men.

Qazi knew everyone present. **Habib Khan** ran a mosque and small Islamic school in nearby Ventura County. **Ziya Gokalp** was an accountant who also maintained several web sites. One of those sites had been identified as an Al Qaeda web site by the Indian government and subsequently it was shut down. **Mahmood Erdogan** recently opened a Middle Eastern market and catering service after experiencing trouble with a small high end car dealership.

This group of five referred to themselves as "The Council." They were the only officially sanctioned representatives of the Taliban in Southern California, and they had no love for their newly adopted homeland.

"Let The Council convene," Qazi stated.

Qazi had remained in a quiet state of meditation while the others arrived in the room. Qazi only spoke when he felt he needed to discuss matters of importance. It was part of the image that he created for himself as a holy man of special significance

To challenge or disagree with Qazi was to disagree with the Prophet himself. It gave the holy man a great deal of influence and demanded respect even from this group of men, who had already earned reputations as established and successful jihadists in their own rights.

They themselves were in awe at the ease in which Qazi's young students took to his preachings. His use of imagery and way with words progressed the minds of the students quickly, so they believed in Allah's will, and then the cause in record time. Amongst themselves, they even made use of the word brainwashing. And they were fine with it.

Qazi believed, or at least wanted everyone else to believe, that he may be the 12th Imam. A mystical and supernatural being, the prophecy of the 12th Imam is the belief in an individual who emerges out of humanity to bring glory to Islam and make Islam victorious around the world. At the end of days, civil war, chaos, bloodshed and mass deaths would rule the earth. And then "The Guided One," or the 12th Imam, would emerge and with Allah's command bring peace and justice to the earth, by establishing Islam throughout the world.

Many Islamists believe that they could accelerate the reemergence of Islamic glory and law to the earth by helping bring about the end of current world orders. This was the belief of everyone sitting at The Council.

Although no one at the table actually believed that Qazi was the 12th Imam, they wouldn't challenge him and they knew and understood the importance and impact of his subtle suggestions and hints to such status, especially to the group of Qazi's twelve students.

"What of **Naim Ibrahimi?**" Ziya Gokalp asked about the former Imam and head of the Woodland Hills Islamic Center.

"It has been taken care of," Qazi replied.

"By who?" Mahmood Erdogan asked. "Which of your students handled it? Do you trust that they completed the job or should I..."

"No," Qazi replied, cutting off Mahmood.

Qazi knew that Mahmood would have liked to take care of the

former Imam himself but feared overkill in his response. Mahmood thrived and yearned for the opportunity to inflict pain and suffering on his enemies. The look on Mahmood's face warranted additional explanation.

"Fahim and several of the other more senior students scared him. That will be enough to make him go away for good."

Qazi didn't want the Imam to be hurt, just scared enough to no longer interfere or offer any resistance to their takeover of the Islamic Center. Qazi also didn't want any unnecessary negative contacts with American law enforcement. He would need to start manipulating them soon enough.

Seeing the need to move forward, Helmandi stated, "Then, I would like to welcome and congratulate the new Board of Directors of the Woodland Hills Islamic Center."

The takeover had come quickly enough and was easier than one would have expected. The former Imam was naive and weak. Qazi had arrived with impressive credentials and charisma.

It didn't take long for loud accusations of embezzlement to be leveled against Imam Siddiqui. They were false, but once the seed was planted Qazi's subtle but convincing words sealed the Imam's fate. Quazi promised honesty, openness and financial funding opportunities. He then acted quickly on peoples' emotions and outrage.

His first official act as the Center's Imam was to fire the previous Board of Directors and replace them with his trusted associates. Once they had control of the institution, they could easily increase their power and control over the local community and resources.

Control over the institution meant ideological control of the message delivered to its members. Local businesses who relied on the support of the Mosque community would not go against the new board for fear of being isolated from a community on which their livelihood depended.

The takeover of the Woodland Hills Islamic Center had occurred without breaking any laws. The police would not be involved.

American law enforcement would view any complaints by the former administration to be a civil matter. It was not the job of the American government to police ideological perspectives. And the American public was too focused on political correctness to understand the tactics and strategies employed successfully by these men, or any extremist groups around the world. These men knew that if nothing changed, extremist groups operating in the United States would continue to expand their spheres of influence by seizing control of Islamic facilities from more moderate Muslims. Extremist doctrines would flourish, radicalization would multiply and new threats to America's war on terrorism would spider web out indefinitely.

There would be no stopping the emergence of the new age of Islam.

MAHMOOD ERDOGAN, MALE, MIDDLE EASTERN, 35 YEARS OLD, CRIMINAL RAP SHEET FOR BATTERY AND CRIMINAL THREATS. Detective Hudson was doing computer work-ups on a lead which came in through the Anti-Terrorist Division's Tip Line.

Mahmood Erdogan had owned a small car dealership in the neighboring city of Burbank, which specialized in Mercedes Benz and other high end used vehicles. Several of the employees had called the Tip Line, giving information on their former employer who had failed to give them current or back pay.

They claimed to have been too intimidated by him to have called the authorities sooner, because Mahmood had shown them photos of him training as a Mujahadeen in Afghanistan, where he said he was known as "Mad Max, the Terrorist."

Detective Hudson was trying to get as much information

on Mahmood Erdogan as he could. He didn't have any vehicles registered to him and it was likely that he was driving a variety of cars, on temporary dealer plates, which were all listed to Green Star Auto Sales.

There was no sign of Mahmood Erdogan when Hudson visited the abandoned office and garage. However, he was able to find two possible residences associated with Mahmood. Both were high end houses located in exclusive areas. It would take a little more planning for the undercover detective to go unnoticed in these neighborhoods, where he could expect a greater degree of video surveillance, roving private security patrols, and watchful neighbors, all of whom may or may not talk about suspicious activity.

Hudson couldn't count on obtaining any information for interviews at this point. He'd have to do some more homework and tread lightly during any checks of the locations.

There was no way for Hudson to know that Mahmood was now renting a large storage facility with a couple of old friends under the name Nassim al Waqqas. And he had a feeling that he wouldn't be closing out this lead anytime soon, when the phone rang.

"Hey Boss, what's going on?"

"Hey, Steve, are you in the Valley?" The caller was JC, the nickname everyone in the office used for John Carter, who was one of the senior detective supervisors.

"Yeah, JC, I'm running down the 'Max the Terrorist' lead. Do you need me to handle something?"

"Can you call this guy?" JC asked. "He goes by the name 'Vick.' He's a Pakistani guy. He says he has some information for us that we might be interested in. Could be a good chance for some source development."

"Sources" were people who were involved in a community and provided information of interest to law enforcement regarding possible criminal or terrorist activity. Sources were hard to come by in the Muslim community and it would take several years for law enforcement to develop a trust and working relationship with these communities.

"Anything else I need to know?"

"No, not yet. Just give him a call and let me know if you need anything. His phone is 818…"

"No problem. I'll meet him and give you a call when I'm done."

"OK. Thanks, Steve."

Hudson wasn't much for small talk and liked to get down to the business at hand. However, he knew that developing sources took time and patience to build relationships and develop trust. He also knew that it was easier to work with sources rather than informants.

Informants provided information but handling informants required a ton of administrative paperwork and posed risks to an officer's safety. Informants were typically criminals who were working with law enforcement to reduce or eliminate current criminal charges. Cops and prosecutors referred to this type of arrangement as "working off a charge." But sometimes, law enforcement would pay an informant for his information. Informants had other reasons for their actions, such as revenge and greed.

The whole idea of honor among thieves was a myth for Hollywood movies or urban legends. Most criminals were self-serving and, at the end of the day, would do what was in their best interest.

The benefits of running informants was that they could be directed on behalf of law enforcement. Developing sources took endless hours of relationship building. And the detective needs skills in breaking down a variety of cultural, language and background barriers. It inevitably became personal, as he or she needed to take real interest in all parts of a source's life, including his or her family, employment, culture and homelands.

It was a chess game that always meant thinking ahead and asking hard questions with yourself— "Where can I place this guy?" and "How can I use this person?" and "How far can he or she be trusted?" "Is the information reliable and credible?" and "How can I verify anything this person tells me?"

The handling officer also had to put the source's safety and security above other interests and be able to see the bigger picture. The best arrangement for a cop was a voluntary non-criminal source who would eventually agree to become an informant.

This was Hudson's goal. However, if the source didn't like the officer from the beginning, there would never be a second meeting. A source had to feel comfortable, trusting and had to like his new partner.

Hudson had arrived at the agreed upon Starbucks early, allowing him time to get a table in a corner of the outside patio where they could talk with some privacy. Arriving early enabled him to sit in a position where he could monitor who was coming and going and all the patrons sitting around them.

He was wondering about this new source and what he might have to offer, when he noticed a casually well dressed and slightly overweight, middle aged Pakistani man walking towards the coffee house. The man was looking around as if looking for someone but not quite sure who that someone was.

Hudson continued watching the man as he walked nearer, looking for any bulges under his clothing indicating a weapon or any indication that the man hadn't come alone.

Once satisfied with his cursory check, Steve got up and nodded as he made eye contact with the wandering man.

"Hi, Vick, I'm Steve. I think you're probably looking for me."

They shook hands and sat down and ordered a cafe latte. Hudson ordered a black coffee no sugar. Hudson tried to be relaxed and amiable as they stumbled through the small talk that Steve despised. He feared he was losing the struggle when Vick said, abruptly, "Please pardon me a moment."

Hudson tensed as Vick half rose from his seat and leaned over to pick up a folded newspaper from the next table—a paper folded in such a way that it could conceal a small pistol. Hudson's hand moved slowly toward his own pistol as Vick sat back down.

Vick opened the paper. There was nothing concealed. Their drinks arrived. Hudson relaxed and and drank his coffee while Vick turned to the sports section.

"Do you follow football?" Vick said. "Professional football, the Rams."

"Well, yes, I do. Though the Rams have had better teams."

"Indeed, they have." He put down the paper. "I see in the paper that they failed to make a trade for the tackle they need, now, they've let the trade deadline pass."

Hudson relaxed further. He felt he was home free. Pro football was small talk that he could enjoy. And, to its more devoted fans—and Vick was obviously one of them—it wasn't small talk at all.

Farooq was seething with anger as he got off the bus and walked toward the Playboy Mansion. He had gone all the way to the man's home and they wouldn't even admit him to some secret meeting taking place in the back.

He had to deal with some young disciple of Qazi's, an arrogant Pakistani who told him that, in good time, he would be informed of his duties. He did get the news he was anxiously waiting to hear, that the great day was getting quite close. But to learn it from this young servient infuriated him.

His fury, which had begun to abate, flared again when he walked into his room at the mansion and found that he had a roommate.

"I'm Abu Mulaika. I'll be living here until the great day of reckoning. Qazi will speak to you through me. Do not try to contact him again."

Farooq's blood boiled but time froze while he stared at the boy. He had to say something.

"What work will you do here?"

"Security, as far as the infidels are concerned. The fools have actually hired me to coordinate protection for their upcoming decadence."

"It would help me, brother, if I know our plans."

"Help you do what? Trim the shrubbery? Your upcoming role is of some if little importance. Be patient. Now, I must go report to my employer."

Abu pivoted and walked away briskly. Farooq's first impulse was to search the bastard's belongings. No, he told himself that will come in good time, when Abu is here.

Farooq forced himself to get to work. He headed to the grounds out back and put his anger into his sharp clippers and trimming the shrubbery. He was determined that he would come out of the slaughter as a martyr and a legend to all Muslims...

"Shit!"

In his anger Farooq had clipped off far too much shrubbery. Two young women wearing what Farooq could only call "detestable" bikinis were looking at him and laughing at his mistake.

Vick sipped his coffee while waiting at different Starbucks and waited for Detective Hudson. Like the Detective, Vick also took comfort in the fact the other also enjoyed professional football. He had to trust this man. He could wait no longer. To delay would be to put his son in danger. Vick looked over the street where traffic crawled along slowly. He thought about the many complaints that his American friends and neighbors made about living in Los

Angeles. They thought it was too big, too noisy, the streets too crowded, and feared the threat of crime everywhere.

Vick shook his head and smiled gently. Until arriving in America four years earlier, he had lived in the Lyari section of Karachi, Pakistan's largest city and port.

Noise, crowds, crime... These Americans didn't know what they were talking about.

Karachi had some 21 million people, most of whom lived in slums such as Lyari. Each slum section was ruled by a local gangster, who each made allies with a different political party.

To most people in Karachi, the Taliban was just one more group of violent criminals. The sprawling seaport city was far removed, in every way, from Islamabad and from Qazi's idealized Pakistani Taliban world.

Vick had managed to lead a quiet enough life in Karachi, primarily because of family connections to Ibn Baroumi, the leader of one of the city's most ruthless and effective gangs.

He had run a small laundromat that would have gone under if he hadn't had the foresight and courage to expand into the linen laundering business and landed a couple of accounts with large restaurants.

Vick often took advice from Baroumi, who pushed him to leave Karachi and move to America, particularly Los Angeles. Once he arrived, he couldn't believe the combination of climate, open space and tranquility of Los Angeles. Within a year, he had opened an upscale dry cleaning business and a linen laundering service that landed a prime account—the dining and catering facilities of the Getty Center, one of the richest museums in the world. Vick knew its location, hanging over the 405 pass and West L.A, and its breathtaking design equaled the impressiveness of its collection.

He was gearing up for the museum's annual fund-raising ball. But there was an evil lurking behind the event and an unexpected fear was growing inside him. With the event imminent, Vick decided to take a huge leap and disclose all that he knew to this Detective Hudson.

Qazi dismissed his young acolytes and retired to his study to drink tea and enjoy the solitude. Everything was coming together as Allah willed and now that he had a confirmed entree to the museum gala, his spirits soared.

Young Karim was the most promising of the teenage boys who had just professed their great love and devotion to Allah. And to Qazi, the Imam, God's surrogate on earth. Karim was impressively bitter and derisive of the Western society in which he was told to live. He was eager to give his loyalty, his very life, for the great cause, headed by Qazi. Karim would do anything Qazi instructed.

Qazi had, so far, been correct in all his recruiting and knew that he had developed an instinct for picking the right acolytes. As he drank tea, he assured himself that Karim was no exception.

Qazi would have been stunned, enraged, if it were even suggested to him that, while he might have a great grasp on the mentality of a certain kind of young Muslim boy, he was seriously naive about the feelings, beliefs and postures of the average American teenager. But he was. And Karim, in only four years, had become quite typical.

When Karim ranted about his miserable life in Los Angeles, the genesis wasn't due to the 'evil' ways of Western society, but something much simpler. He had just been dumped by a girl he thought he would love forever. And he just failed algebra.

He spewed hatred of his life and a healthy disgust for what Qazi understood as the entire female species. In Qazi's brand of extreme Islam, there was a wide, deep streak of misogamy. Qazi took Karim's feelings for something much deeper than they were and he believed his teachings were taking wonderfully.

Qazi was overly confident. Once he widened his recruitment

efforts beyond those who already venerated the Imam, he didn't see how he was venturing into an area he urgently needed to avoid.

Brilliant while isolated in the wasteland training camps of Pakistan, revered in important circles in Islamabad, eagerly embraced in a West Virginia mosque, Qazi had never lived in the real world. And he had certainly never had any experience with American teenagers, particularly those in Los Angeles.

Qazi should have remained the strategist of this grand plan, isolated in the mosque among his adoring Muslims. He should have left the tactical aspects of the plan to people who had experience working in America, such as Fahim. For example, Qazi had sent the same two Muslim men back to the zoo, to take pictures and sketch drawings. Of course, Fahim would know not to do this.

Karim had attended the mosque faithfully for a long time. Confident in his strategy, Qazi picked a private moment where he believed he would empower Karim as needed and he shared his plan to target the Getty Center. But the revelation simply scared Karim. Frightened, Karim went straight home and betrayed Qazi by telling his father everything.

Now, armed with what his son told him, Vick sat sipping a second coffee and spilling all he knew to Detective Hudson. This time there was no small talk about pro football.

Although relieved to share the information, Vick was disturbed by Hudson's insistence that Karim continue to attend the mosque and feign continued loyalty to Qazi.

Hudson walked away from the meeting with Vick in a particularly good frame of mind. At JC's suggestion, he had found a solid source of information. He knew that Vick was upset about what he wanted his son to do, but so be it.

Hudson's walk took him past a greengrocer, where he bought a half pound of seedless green grapes, which he ate as he walked. Hudson loved fresh fruit of any kind and considered its year-round availability one of the perks of living in Los Angeles.

During his peripatetic childhood as an army brat, he was often forced to live in places where nothing was fresh for much of the year and, during the winter, there were no leaves or flowers of any kind.

He suddenly smelled lilac, as a beautiful 'California' blonde walked by. It occurred to Hudson that he had actually never seen lilac, though he loved the fragrance. Jennifer Wade always smelled of lilac and always fresh, clean and invigorating. It wasn't her smell alone, but it may have started there—Jennifer seemed to be everything he had ever wanted in a woman.

When the City finally closed down his second-rate strip club, Tony was surprised at how relieved he felt. He had grown tired of his partner and more than tired of the motorcycle gang, which was getting more avaricious and difficult to satisfy.

Tony would have felt like he'd taken a long, hot shower that cleansed him of something foul and unclean, but that night he wound up in bed—for absolutely the last time, he vowed—with Candy, a dancer at the now former club.

Candy was supple and game for anything but up close and personal her face and body revealed the mileage she'd put them through, including track marks from her long addiction to heroin. When Tony finally got her out of his place, he literally spent 40 minutes in a hot shower.

He was due to join Abu for work at a hookah parlor and he feared he'd be late. He dressed quickly, strapped on his holster and gun, and hurried out, only to be stopped in the street by a short, rat-faced, wiry man who showed more mileage than Candy.

"The lady works for me now. Fork over some dough. She don't work cheap, pal."

Christ, Candy had a pimp, one who must have the worst breath in creation.

"Forget it...pal."

Rat-face blocked his path. "I'm ain't screwing around. Gonna cost you two bills to walk away in one piece."

Tony shoved Rat-face, who shoved back and revealed a pair of brass knuckles. Tony looked long enough to see both hands had E-V-I-L tattooed across the top of his fingers.

"Shit. Get out of my way."

"Don't think I won't use these. Just ask the little bitch here."

Rat-face moved the knuckles toward Tony's face but Tony blocked the move with an elbow. He pulled out his pistol and smashed it into Rat-face's head, then pistol-whipped him about the body. He crumpled to the sidewalk, making little mewling sounds and rocking back and forth.

"Good, you shit-sucking scum," Candy said. She kicked him in the stomach, bent down and extracted a fat wad of bills from his front pocket.

"Guess you want some of this, Tony."

"No, no, just get the fuck out of here, Candy."

She didn't have to be told twice. Tony also fled the scene, feeling grosser than ever. He has an ominous feeling this would come back to haunt him.

When he reached the hookah parlor and talked to Abu, he felt as though he was covered with filth. Abu was a truly good man who never talked about his faith, he had even had Tony to dinner at his home. Now, in an odd way, Tony felt unworthy of being Abu's friend.

"You're troubled, my friend," Abu said. "You seem a man without direction or purpose in life."

Tony merely nodded. He knew Abu was right. Tony was

wallowing in its muck and misery. He knew he had to pull his shit together.

Abu was a man who, obviously, had direction and purpose. He was also a man who believed strongly in a god Tony knew nothing about. But there was a confidence and clarity in Abu's face that intrigued Tony.

Tony knew he needed to change, to save himself. And right there he gave in. He turned to Abu, "Please tell me about your God."

"Allah, be praised," Fahim muttered aloud as he watched Jennifer Wade stand, in full dress uniform, at the monthly community meeting held between the police department and the Muslim community. "She's a cop. And a captain."

Fahim didn't know how this knowledge might help him in the great venture he was heading, but he felt certain that it would be invaluable. He knew also that Qazi would be pleased, but Fahim decided that he would wait until he had a better understanding of how the police captain could be used. He also knew for sure that he would never tell Qazi about his lust for this American cop, who he could see as nothing but a whore. Fahim didn't really feel any guilt about that.

Steve Hudson emptied the entire magazine without satisfaction. "God damn," he grumbled while he reloaded.

He wasn't enjoying his time on the shooting range. He was too distracted to concentrate properly or to take satisfaction at his accuracy with a pistol. He emptied the gun again, checked for safety, and packed up.

He drove to Balboa Lake Park and took a long walk, something to which he rarely treated himself to. It was a mild day with moderate breeze. He walked along the path around the lake as he tried to collect his thoughts.

Vick was turning out to be an incredibly valuable source, but combining Vick's information with the other intelligence being gathered about these Muslim extremists was creating a vast and much too amorphous picture of a variety of extremist threats to Los Angeles.

Later that day, Hudson was meeting with JC and Jennifer Wade for a case update. He wasn't sure what he'd tell them. So far, the police only had a lot of vague information on already known, and some unknown, targets but nothing concrete. Hudson believed Vick to be truthful and his information to be real. Vick believed a terrorist threat was imminent. Hudson was listening. He knew he and his team needed to move fast.

JC's role as a supervisor meant he was responsible for a team of specialized detectives investigating international terrorism. There were six other detectives in JC's squad. Each detective handled his or her own case load which included leads or full blown investigations.

The detectives all worked together to assist each other with simple things like partnering for an investigative lead or for complex investigations where the entire squad worked together for operations such as a moving surveillance.

JC managed coordinating resources, team building, the assigning of leads and investigative cases, as well as preliminary analysis to link the various cases handled by his squad.

He was also responsible for attending monthly case briefings from other squads within Anti-Terrorist Division, as well as attending meetings with other local, state, and federal agencies, in attempts to connect the dots, link other ongoing investigations, and coordinate interagency responses and resources.

JC had been in the Anti-Terrorist Division for twenty years and was widely considered the department's expert on international and domestic terrorism. In addition to being the department expert, he was known as a great supervisor and overall good guy. It was a rare trait to find all three. People that worked underneath him loved working for him.

The first thing that Hudson noticed about Jennifer Wade was that she had lost weight. She seemed drawn and nervous. For the most part he attributed this to her apparently bitter divorce from Jimmy Butler a few months earlier. But he had a feeling there might be something more behind her current state.

In addition to John Carter, two additional squad members were present – Ryan Riley, part of a long line of Rileys, a storied family of Irish cops in New York, and Pedro Gonzales, a Los Angeles native. One member of the squad was out on sick leave and two were on assignments.

Riley reported first, "Basically Cap', the nuts and bolts of it is that the zoo staff has reportedly seen suspicious Muslim visitors in the park this week."

"What in hell is that supposed to mean?" Wade asked. "More and more these days, any Muslim activity is likely to be reported as suspicious."

"This weighs down the team as we do have to investigate every lead," Carter said.

"Yep. I've sent a detective to check it out," Riley said. "Just what in hell do we actually know about any real threat from extremists?"

"Well, we know they're targeting The Getty on the night of its gala," JC said. "But, the zoo? I'm all for having it checked out but, really, the zoo?"

"Except for the museum, we don't have much," Riley said. "It's all so damned nebulous."

"It's all pretty much Jack shit," Wade said. "What about the imam at that mosque. The new guy seems to carry some real weight. He is preaching some serious hatred towards the red, white, and blue."

"Qazi," Hudson said. "We know he's recruiting gullible young Muslims for…whatever's planned."

"He's not recruiting all those young men for nothing," Gonzalez said. "And there are reports that the young men are being trained on the grounds of the Islamic Center but there are guards everywhere and we can't confirm anything."

"Why don't we try this?" Hudson said. "We know when the museum gala is taking place. Let's check and see what else of significance is scheduled for that Saturday night."

Everyone agreed that this was a promising course of action.

When the others left the meeting, Jennifer asked Hudson to stay for a minute longer.

In Karachi, while living with a cousin, Fatima met **Khaled Daman**, an older man who owned his own taxi. His wife had died of what Khaled would only describe as the appalling hospital situation in Kabul.

Nothing needed to be explained to Fatima about Kabul hospitals. Since the Taliban took power, only men were given adequate medical treatment and admitted to Kabul's regular hospitals. Her own mother, pregnant and about to deliver, was denied entrance to her local hospital. She—along with all women of Kabul—could only gain entrance to a wreck of a facility, old and dilapidated, with only a couple of women doctors and few nurses. The facility lacked cleaning supplies, safe water, surgical instruments, pain killers, medications, electricity and oxygen. There were few beds. The waiting room was a nightmare of a place, so overcrowded that even women about to deliver had to fight for a place to sit. It reeked of their water, blood, sweat, urine, cigarette smoke, stale tobacco, unwashed flesh. The wailing, gasping, crying, grunting and screeching created a never ending cacophony of suffering.

Fatima's mother died in agony on her second day in the place and her father soon after, of more grief than he could endure. Before he reached his end, though, he sold all he owned and paid one of his second cousins to get Fatima out of Afghanistan and to look after her in Karachi.

He spoke of his love for Fatima and she supposed that he loved her as much as he could love a daughter, but she knew full well that his main motivation was a hope that she would one day give him male grandsons, even if he would never get to see them.

Fatima, however, had sworn that she'd kill herself rather than let a man so much as touch her. Khaled was gentle, reassuring and said that he had no need to produce more sons until Fatima finally give in, at least to the point of marrying him. She realized that she was outstaying her welcome with her cousins and her marriage was an avenue to move forward.

Khaled had family in Chicago. He sold his beloved taxi and flew to the United States. Fatima of course joined him now, though she was full of fear and apprehension.

Dazed with lack of sleep and overnight air travel, she walked through Chicago's mammoth O'Hare airport anxious to almost the point of frightened with the new world of smells, lights, and sound of American English coming every direction at wild levels. Women's hair was flying free, faces showed the effects of cosmetics, lips were painted, clothes a rainbow of festive colors. Short skirts revealed bare legs. She tried to shrink further into her burka and clung more tightly to Khaled's arm.

When she caught herself looking into a handsome blonde man's face, she gasped and lowered her eyes and, for a moment, expected the Taliban to beat her on the spot.

Khaled, who had some idea of what she was experiencing,

whispered, "You have nothing to fear, Fatima. This is what's called freedom. You'll get used to it."

Downtown Los Angeles had undergone an impressive revitalization over the past fifteen years. An artisan community had developed from the eastern downtown boundaries out of an abandoned urban wasteland. With it came a surge of new bars, restaurants, and coffee shops. A new police headquarters was built at Main Street and 1st Street, replacing the historic but poorly aged Parker Center across from City Hall. The design of the building embodied the concept of transparency which Chief Bill Bratton brought to the Department, following the Rampart corruption scandal, which destroyed any trust between the police, politicians, and the public. The entire front of the building was constructed with plate glass so anyone could literally see the activities inside headquarters, stressing a sense one with the community as opposed to the separatist and secretive ideas created by the old fortress looking building. Following Rampart, it was obvious that things needed to change and that it needed to start with perception, based on the age-old idea that perception was nine-tenths of the department's battle.

"Fahim, I have a task for you," the preacher opened as he walked with his student at the conclusion of the evening's studies.

"Yes," Fahim obediently answered awaiting further instructions.

"The infidels have created a new site to stage their oppression of Islam and attack the holy word of the Prophet. However, I have information that in their arrogance, they have made several grave errors in design."

"How ..." Fahim was immediately cut off.

"Stop!" Qazi layed on the table in front of them a map of downtown with the new police headquarters at the center.

"The police department has moved many of their specialized

undercover investigative units, including their Anti-Terrorism Division, from secret off-site locations to the new police headquarters. These officers and detectives who are now assigned to work out of the new building must park their cars over a block from the building."

Qazi pointed to the parking garage where they were parking their cars.

"They must then walk down this street... or this street, while the top command staff has reserved parking in this limited underground structure."

Qazi's finger landed on the location of the parking structure. It was on Main Street, a one-way street.

He continued, "All specialized and undercover detectives have to walk southbound from the police headquarter building and continue walking to the garage and get their undercover vehicles. They must exit the garage here and then turn right onto Main Street and head straight to the light at 2nd Street."

Fahim was new to the game of intelligence and counter intelligence. Despite this, he couldn't believe the carelessness displayed by the Department to conceal the identity of its undercover investigators.

As Chris made his rounds of the cages, he noticed that the two Muslim men were visiting the new Panda exhibit again. Many people, particularly children, were excited about the Panda that would soon arrive from China and make the Los Angeles zoo its permanent home.

But other visitors didn't take the same kind of pictures as these two men, who rarely aimed their cameras at the actual exhibit. And no vacationer or local visitor ever inquired about the safety and security arrangements on any given day at the park as these two were asking about the Panda's on the upcoming opening day ceremony.

It wasn't like a zoo would be a target for anything, but Chris knew the world was changing, and he was aware enough to know to at least follow up with his bosses.

"Hey, Rachel, you remember those animal rights freaks some years ago, the ones that wound up trying to burn some old people in their homes?"

"Yeah, I remember that. Security had gotten too good at labs and places like that so they were trying to strike at people where they lived."

"Ever hear of zoo terrorists?"

Rachel laughed. "Nah. Every once in a while we get a couple of crazies who sneak into the zoo after hours and try to release some animals. But we've upped our security against those sort of things."

"Though, I suppose if you were a fanatic about freeing animals, a zoo might be a logical target. Still…"

"Yeah, I know, it's a little far-fetched. But it strange right that those two guys keep coming back and looking around the panda exhibit?"

"People are weird! I never try to figure out what people are up to. But I will pass it along and keep an eye out myself."

"Okay. Thanks, Rachel."

Chris moved on to the next cage, but now Rachel was a little more curious than she led on. She too wondered about those guys. If she saw them here again, she'd definitely have to approach them and see what was going on.

"Steve, I know I'm in charge of the Anti-Terrorist Division but I've been concentrating on other terrorism investigations and I'm a little out of touch with this squad. I know little about the day-to-day operations of this one. Fill me in on the Woodland Hills Mosque and its Imam."

"Of course." Hudson filled her in on Qazi, explaining how

good he appeared to be at recruiting young acolytes and filling them with his quite radical views.

Jennifer was clearly disturbed, by the time he finished. It was clear that Qazi was smart and cunning and a real threat. She couldn't hide the shudder that went through her when she suddenly remembered that last community meeting she attended while undercover. The hair stood up on the back of her neck now in much the same way it did then.

"Captain, you all right? Want me to get you something?"

"No, no, it's just that...I think I'm a little run down, that's all. Go on."

Steve finished up his impromptu briefing. Although Jennifer looked surprising overwhelmed, he was relieved at the Captain's newfound commitment to his case.

Tony was flattered beyond description and nervous as a school boy when Abu took him home for dinner with his family. He was impressed beyond words when he left many hours later.

Though strange to him, the food was delicious. Tony's wife and daughter cooked and served everything, while remaining silent and dressed in burkhas with their faces completely covered.

Abu and Tony were served first, then the older son, following by the younger son, and then Tony's daughter, and finally his wife. Only the males spoke during the meal, but then only the boys briefly and only when spoken to. The wife and daughter cleared the table and then fled into the kitchen. They were seen again only when they served the two men tea in the living room.

The boys were served no tea and vanished soon afterwards. The tea was the strongest Tony had ever tasted but he was determined to sip it contently, as though he drank such tea every day.

Cautiously, Tony started asking Abu questions about his family life and about his devout and unwavering dedication to his Muslim beliefs. Abu not only answered each question with much warmth and deal, but encouraged Tony to ask all the questions he wished. The two men talked late into the night.

Tony had no idea that this was the preliminary stage of a carefully planned screening process. A more thorough vetting process with Qazi himself would soon follow. Tony over and over again found himself falling into an almost hypnotic state during their conversations, which were truly well designed, intensive lines of questioning from a highly trained intelligence officer and a powerful religious man. Tony would often watch as several of Qazi's students took turns rubbing and massaging Qazi's feet during their exhausting interrogation sessions.

Dawud Ali Nazari didn't dare visit his brother, Hussein, in the South County jail, fearing the FBI might learn of the visit and of his connection to Hussein. By accessing confidential Bureau sources, Nazari had learned that law enforcement knew that Hussein had been training Muslim fundamentalists.

Hussein had remained in jail because his family could not put up the $100,000 cash bail. They wanted him freed and acquitted but some knew if let out on bail, Hussein would flee and disappear and the money would be forfeit. Hussein would have to wait until the time was right.

Dawud felt lucky at having been hired by the FBI. He certainly didn't have the academic qualifications, military background, or law enforcement experience that many of his other Academy classmates had at Quatico. However, Dawud was a practicing Muslim and had language and cultural skills. He was able to speak, read, and write Arabic, Urdu, and Pashto fluently.

To its demise, the FBI didn't learn from the mistakes of law enforcement of the previous decade. In the late 1980's and early 1990's, major metropolitan areas across the country were plagued with inner city riots. These events served as turning points in American policing as community policing philosophies were implemented into all levels of the criminal justice system. A consistent trend in police departments was to increase the number of minority officers in each department. The idea was to better reflect the communities in which the departments serve, a noble cause. However, problems arose when major departments lowered hiring standards and ignored red flags to meet these new diversity goals. It wasn't a coincidence that due to lower standards, as the officers became veteran officers, major police departments across the country faced large corruption and misconduct scandals, including in Los Angeles with its Rampart Scandal. All of it was predictable and probably preventable if not for political correctness and expediency.

After the 9/11 attacks, the FBI followed the same pattern. To better deal with the threats posed by radical Islamic extremism, the Bureau heavily recruited Muslims with language skills. In doing so, they ignored many red flags in the background process of various candidates. Bureau background investigators relied too heavily on polygraph exams. Polygraph exams rely on guilt which triggers physiological responses in the examinee when lies are told. The problem is that guilt is a Western phenomenon and not recognized in Middle Eastern cultures. These cultures are distinctly different than Western society and are centered around tribal relationships and bringing honor to the tribe. Islam and the Quran teach that it is always acceptable to lie to protect another Muslim, especially if lying to a non-Muslim.

Dawud Ali Nazari had little difficulty passing the FBI background process and polygraph examinations. His application was streamlined. With ease, The Bureau had been infiltrated.

Special Agent Nazari was looking forward to his new assignment at the Joint Terrorism Task Force (JTTF). His wife had family in the Los Angeles area and all indications were that they would blend in just fine.

Qazi was reluctant to waste time with this Italian man but Abu had praised him so deeply that he felt obliged to at least listen to him after their daily morning prayer. Abu was one of Qazi's most trusted and effective followers and, so far, had made no mistakes in his recruiting efforts. Qazi did see the usefulness in Tony. His previous life had involved him with both criminals and police, to whom he still had access.

Some of the soldiers in Allah's army, Qazi knew, would have to be sacrificed for the great cause. The tricky part would be isolating and protecting himself in the aftermath.

At the beginning of the interview, everything about Tony disgusted Qazi. His past profession was everything that he despised. He smelled too strongly of garlic. His dark hair was too long. He often talked in an American slang that Qazi didn't understand. And the man's profanity seemed uncontrollable.

The longer they talked, however, the more Qazi began to understand and appreciate the man's sincerity and desperation. Tony surprised the Imam by the knowledge he had already acquired about Islam and how he accepted that in such a decadent Western world, "a cesspool filled with the worse kind of sin," as Tony put it, only the most extreme form of cleansing would be successful. Though Tony would always be marked as "one whose mother was a whore" and though he was older than Qazi preferred, he agreed with Abu that Tony could become a devout, unquestioning follower with far more to offer than most of his younger brothers toward the holocaust that was about to hit Los Angeles.

Mahmood's wife, Yasmine, lived a quiet life in their latest home.

Although often lonely, she never complained to her husband. She was only allowed out when Mahmood could no longer ignore her bruises and abrasions and was forced to take her to an emergency room, where she always said that she was clumsy and that her injuries had occurred from a random fall.

No matter Yasmine's condition, it was rare that Mahmood took her to the hospital. But now she was pregnant and Mahmood took better care of her because he was convinced that she would deliver him a healthy son, to match the son borne to him by his late, first wife.

After being treated, Yasmine found that Mahmood had been called away on an emergency and that she was to sit quietly in the waiting room and have no contact with anyone.

And Yasmine would have obeyed her husband's command. But a nurse offered her the chance to have an ultrasound, a kind of x-ray that would reveal whether she was carrying a boy or a girl. And her husband would never know she had it, the nurse said, if that was what Yasmine wished.

With every instinct she possessed, Yasmine felt that her fetus was female and that, when she bore Mahmood a girl, her suffering would be unbearable.

The nurse, an older Pakistani woman, spoke to her in soft, convincing words that made her feel loved and comfortable, feelings so rare that she never wanted them to end, so she finally nodded her head in agreement.

When she saw the image on the ultrasound screen, she mewled and stuck her fist into her mouth. She knew she then was a dead woman walking. Mahmood didn't believe in what he called "satanic Western devices," so he would never know the sex of the baby until the child was born.

By the time Mahmood returned for Yasmine, she was sitting quietly in a corner, praying in gasps and mumbles. Mahmood, thinking these the dutiful prayers of a pious woman, paid no attention to them.

When word filtered up to Jennifer Wade that the zoo workers' had once again seen the two suspicious men at the panda exhibit and were concerned themselves, she had a brief rush of memory: Her participation in bringing down the radical animal group headed by Phil had been the real jump-start of her rise in the police department.

Radical animal rescue groups had been relatively quiet since then and any incidents were nothing more than sparsely attended rallies against such things as wearing fur.

Still, the arrival of this new panda was stirring up unusual interest and seemed to have rallied dormant animal rights groups. Most zoos had learned how to protect themselves over the years and, with the arrival of the giant panda, zoo security would be at its height. Still, Jennifer thought, if the zoos and labs had improved security so much over the years, perhaps animal terrorists had also improved their methods. Jennifer never forgot Phil, that animal rights activist, specifically his tenacity and willingness to use deadly force. She thought the guy was a total nut.

What if those animal rights fanatics somehow allied themselves with Muslim fanatics? Jennifer shook her head at herself and smiled. She was making too great of a leap. Nonetheless, she made a note to ask JC to check on the zoo situation with a bit more regularity.

Farooq sat miserably in the back of the bar and watched some Mixed Martial Arts (MMA) match on the television. He liked MMA, or any sport that allowed violence, and the more the better. There was a time when he was a regular visitor to the very arena from which this MMA match was being televised.

But half the damned time, the tv coverage spent half the time ignoring the hard core battle and instead shilled on about some Hollywood movie about to hit theaters or being filmed in the local city of the event. This time the announcers were going on and on.

"Big fucking deal," Farooq mumbled in the American slang he had started to use.

He glanced around with some guilt, before finishing his vodka and tonic. He didn't really like vodka but knew that it was least likely to be smelled on his breath by that always snooping, Abu.

"One more time," he warned Abu as though they sat next to each other. "One more damn time, one more insult and I will destroy you—brother."

Farooq had begun to suspect that his own role in the upcoming plan for the Playboy Mansion was being marginalized, perhaps even being phased out.

His attention was drawn back to the tv, where he realized he had missed a knockout. Perhaps he'd visit that arena again soon. They had fights every Saturday night and they just announced that some of the regular MMA fans would be used as extras in the movie.

From sources on the Council, Mahmood had learned that the police were still actively trying to locate him with an effort that made it clear it was serious. There was more going on here than some disgruntled, unpaid employees. He couldn't imagine what or who had shined a light on him, but he knew he had to be doubly careful now that their plan was so near execution.

He was annoyed every time he went home because Yasmine was being almost too deferential, something beyond even being obsequious, as though she had some great secret she was trying to cover up.

But he was rarely home and refused to let it disturb him to the point of taking action.

He was about to close a huge deal that would greatly benefit his market and catering business and, along with his responsibility in the upcoming doomsday, he soon forgot Yasmine. She was now insignificant.

"But, brother, she is with child and really shouldn't…"

"No, brother, my wife is a nurse and says it's quite all right for a pregnant woman to go out, even until the eighth month. I insist."

Gerard Chaudry was too crucial to Mahmood's market and the expansion of his catering business to offend. The man seemed a devout enough Muslim, but Mahmood found his attitude toward women abominable. The man let his wife work in a hospital, where she daily touched the flesh of men, even infidels. Mahmood could not let this go.

"This is our dinner rule, Mahmood. Couples only. It is better this way. And my wife insists on it."

"You mean your sinful whore of a wife…" The words died in Mahmood's throat. This man's approval was essential, especially with the money at stake. And, why trouble himself? Yasmine didn't know a word of English. She'd sit quietly in her burkha, with her face covered, and pick at her food. But still Gerard's request was an insult to Mahmood. And he was not a man to forgive and, especially, to forget.

Gerard had rented out an upscale restaurant just off La Cienega. The six couples sat at a long table and discussed business, affairs of the world and stories of their previous lives in Afghanistan and Pakistan. Gerard's wife, though dressed in Western clothes, sat quietly and didn't say a word.

The dinner ran on and on with Gerard telling story after story, none of which Mahmood cared to hear. He continued to get more and more frustrated as they were coming up on three hours and he still had not had a chance to speak with Gerard alone. Yasmine had been sitting quietly for the entire time until she suddenly leaned over and told Mahmood that it was urgent that she go to the bathroom.

He was appalled at the thought and said, emphatically, "No, of course not."

"But, revered husband, if you don't allow it, I may…may not be able to wait."

"You will wait, you insolent little bitch…"

"I'll show her the way and stay with her."

Mahmood's gaze shot around to Gerard's wife. He's forgotten that she understood the language.

"Mind your own fucking, damned…" once again, the words died stillborn in Mahmood's throat. Gerard was looking directly at him and his whore of a wife already had Yasmine to her feet. Mahmood checked his impulse to jerk Yasmine back into her seat.

Mahmood Ergadon had no way of knowing that, the instant his wife walked from the table, it would begin a progress of events that would soon make him the most woebegone man this side of Mecca.

Fatima still wouldn't leave the tiny Chicago apartment without her husband and, even then, it was always with some reluctance. The first half dozen times she went out, she insisted on wearing a burkha and covering her face.

Finally, she was able to walk down the street with her face uncovered—though she still wore a burkha. After some little nervousness, she found she loved having her face free. It was a physical manifestation the result being that she was truly out of Afghanistan and free from the hated Taliban's rule.

She was able to spend little time with Khaled, who had taken a job driving a taxi for a company partly owned by his third cousin. He worked every shift possible, putting away money for the day he could, once again, buy his own taxi.

He made only one friend at work, an Afghani widower named **Omar Saif**.

Even though they were in the United States and free to say whatever they wanted, the two men were still careful to talk about "over there," as they always said, when they were alone and certain that no one was listening.

They came to trust each other. Omar was taken home to meet Fatima and to share the evening meal with them. He ate quickly, almost greedily, and kept praising Fatima's cooking.

After dinner, when they were relaxing with tea, Omar brought up the subject of the Taliban in the United States for the first time. It was also the first time he used the group's actual name.

After a fevered fifteen minutes, it was obvious that they all shared an abhorrence of the Taliban. Fatima was unable to admit it, even to herself, but she would come to use the word, "revenge."

Omar didn't hesitate to use the word. His wife had died in a still unexplained way in Afghanistan and it was obvious that he blamed the Taliban.

Fatima and her husband suspected that Omar was cooperating with some kind of police agency to bring down the Taliban in America... That was fine with them.

At the zoo, Hudson was referred to a young woman named Rachael, who was in charge of arrangements for the panda debut. Hudson was there at JC's request.

"Well, extra security personnel will come on duty at eight," she said. "The children get so excited when they actually see a giant panda that..."

"Pardon me. The extra security comes on at eight? I thought that debut thing was in the morning."

"Yes, it is, at ten. Saturday morning."

"But, we were certain. Someone from here called, a couple of times."

"Yes. I don't see, oh, of course. Which debut are you talking about?"

"The panda debut."

"Actually there are two debuts. One, Friday night at eight, for Chinese officials, zoo administration, people from the city, state, I don't know, the State Department. You know, the powers that be."

"So, there won't be children present Friday night?"

"I can't say that. If people want to bring their children, they can. But the rest of the weekend is especially for families."

Hudson shook his head and exhaled. "Okay, forget Saturday morning. Friday night, any extra security personnel? Any armed guards?"

"Well, sure, we'll have a couple of extra security personnel here. And we've been informed that there'll be security for the Chinese officials. I don't know anything about that."

"Neither do we," Hudson told himself.

"Do you have any armed personnel out patrolling the Panda area at night, as a matter of course?"

"I'm afraid not, Detective. Strictly rent-a-cops supplemented with the City's General Services Police Department, but I'm not sure what they are really capable of." General Services Police were a separate police agency within the City who were responsible for security of City buildings and facilities. Some officers were fully sworn police officers but most had limited police powers. They were more of an armed security guard force. If anything of significance were to happen, LAPD would have tactical command and investigative responsibility. There was currently a move by LAPD to absorb General Services Police, and their budget, into the LAPD. "There's never any violence and what would someone try to steal?" asked Rachel.

Hudson nodded. Rent-a-cops. Of course. It's only the debut

of a bear, in the name of God. Well, this has to have put any idea of terrorists having any interest at all in a bear. Plus, the State Department's Diplomatic Security Services (DSS) Special Agents would have responsibility in coordinating security with the Chinese delegation. Hudson knew that DSS was a professional organization and pretty good at providing dignitary protection. However, DSS was usually understaffed and usually out of touch with the local climate. Hudson doubted that DSS would have detected any real threat assessments from this event and may not have even bothered with checking in with local law enforcement. He made a mental note to follow up on this point.

"I did mention that something should perhaps be done," Rachael said. "But the administration, always trying to save a few pennies, wouldn't hear of it."

"So, you also saw some suspicious people here recently? More than once?"

"Quite suspicious. Saw them twice. Not only taking pictures but making detailed drawings of the area around the panda's cage."

All right, that couldn't be ignored. But just how real was what Rachael saw? Eyewitness accounts were notoriously unreliable.

"Rachael, I have to be sure that you're certain about what you actually saw and…"

"Detective, I spent three years in military intelligence, two of them near the front lines in Afghanistan. I was trained and I have on-the-ground experience in observing and reporting what I saw. Accurately."

"Ok. Convince me, Rachael. Why do you think those men were here, making maps and taking pictures? And they were definitely Afghanis and not…"

"They were absolutely Afghanis. I must have observed a thousand Afghanis during my tour in that God-forgotten place. The men I saw here seemed to be doing a pre-operational reconnaissance."

"Pre-operational? You think they're going to conduct some operational thing here in the zoo? Why?"

"I suppose they're some kind of animal terrorist outfit...but it doesn't really fit. Guess maybe they're tied up with some radical animal Taliban. Well, that's above my pay grade, Detective."

He had an uneasy feeling about this. In his gut, he believed her.

"Could you postpone that night's ceremony until..."

She was shaking her head the moment he started talking. "No way. Officials from China are flying in to be here on that date. There's been massive publicity and the TV networks have reserved time for us and..."

"Okay, okay, I believe you, Rachael."

Hudson looked closely at the young woman. She was attractive, with luminous, dark brown eyes and she was quite feminine. But he saw a vein of iron, a determination that she must have developed in the army. Could she be trusted to...

"Well?"

"Well, what?"

"Well, what have you decided? Christ, you're hardly subtle. When you get your eyes full, open your mouth."

Hudson exhaled. "That's not why I was staring at you. Because you're attractive. I was wondering..."

"You were wondering if you can trust the information I've given you. And if you should tell me something about why you're so bloody hot and giggly about a giant panda debut, and at, of all places, a zoo."

Hudson swallowed back his anger at being patronized and mocked by this girl. He smiled.

"Guilty as charged, Rachael."

They sat on a bench and Hudson gave her a filtered version of reasons why the zoo might be a target. She listened quietly, nodded a couple of times when he asked her to look out for specific things. She had no questions.

Hudson was relieved when he walked out of the zoo, certain that Rachael would be a valuable asset.

If Hudson could have seen Rachael an hour later, when she took her break and met a young man in a refreshment area, the man's dark hair, eyes, features, his mannerisms, and overheard her telling him what she did—and not in English—it would have left him far from relieved.

"Qazi was right," Fahim mumbled under his breath. He sat at a table on the outdoor patio at the Pit Fire Pizza located at 2nd Street and Main Street. He had his note pad and camera in hand.

Every undercover officer walked outside from the new police headquarters building, across the street right in front of him, towards the parking garage. Several minutes later, they all drove right by him, sometimes stopping at the light just yards away from his. Fahim took notes and photos of every undercover car and officer he could, including car descriptions and license plates. He figured he could do this for a week straight before he had almost every Los Angeles Police Department undercover officer and vehicle identified.

Fahim caught something out of the corner of his eye and quickly looked up. His heart skipped a beat and his adrenaline surged. It was Captain Wade, the infidel whore who commanded the Anti-Terrorism Division. He quickly looked down and his breathing became short and choppy. She was walking into Pit Fire Pizza for lunch with some other officers.

"Did she recognize me?" he said outloud to himself. Panic set in and he decided he had to get out of there quickly. Working undercover was still new to the young and inexperienced student who was bound to make at least some mistakes. Fahim walked quickly away without paying his bill.

Yasmine stood in the women's room, mouth slightly open, and listened, with disbelief, to what this Muslim woman was telling her. Every minute or so, Yasmine glanced over her shoulder, in fear that Mahmood might rush through the door.

The woman was a nurse at the same hospital where Yasmine had her sonogram. Apparently, she had been told by another nurse of Yasmine's situation.

"Yasmine, you know you are a dead woman when your husband is presented with a baby girl. You can leave him now, right now, and be protected and sue him for half of his estate and…"

"No. You don't know my husband or the power and influence he wields with everyone, the police, the courts…"

"Not here, Yasmine. Not in Los Angeles. In his own community, yes, and with weak infidels. But we have our own influence and you just witnessed your husband back down from mine."

The door suddenly opened. Yasmine stumbled back and tripped. She was trying to stop the fall with her hands on the tile wall. She gasped, "No, revered husband, mercy," before realizing that it was another woman.

Ryan and Rodriguiz were surprised by Frank, the Getty Museum official that met them by the door. He had a brush cut and was big as an offensive tackle. He had the voice to match.

"Welcome to the Getty. You said on the phone that this was just a routine visit to check our security situation. Also, you want a rundown of our security arrangements."

"Yes, we'd appreciate that," Ryan said.

The official obliged and the policemen soon realized that, because so much priceless art was involved, the museum's security arrangements were impressive, down to the fact that they used more than one security company and alarm system, "in the highly unlikely instance that one firm might employ someone dishonest," said Frank.

"Now, your annual big dance is coming up, isn't it? Any special arrangements for that?"

"Well, of course, though most of the museum will be locked up and secured, as usual. We will have extra security staff, including two off-duty police officers."

"And the only way in and out of the museum is the gate where we entered?"

"That's right," said Frank.

"We'd like a list of all your security people, including the policemen, for the night of the party. Actually, of everyone who'll be here that night."

"Including guests? Well, gentlemen, that decision is over my head and I'll have to talk to someone about it. That list is usually kept private."

"Here's my card," Ryan said and added as casual as possible. "Has your staff noticed any unusual looking visitors lately? Someone taking unusual pictures or maybe, drawing diagrams or something?"

"Unusual looking visitors? Detective, this is Los Angeles," laughed Frank. "We get the best dressed, most elegant visitors and those who are practically in rags. Many people take pictures and it's not unusual to see people sketching. Could you be more specific?"

Gonzalez shook his head. He too, tried to sound casual. "No, no, these are just routine questions."

"Then I'll talk to my superiors about the list you asked for. We'll be in touch within a day or two."

Jennifer Wade joined the squad's meeting late but she made no apologies.

JC brought her up to date on the squad's activities, concluding with the detectives' visit to the museum.

"They're always security conscious," Gonzalez said. "And they'll have extra guards, including a couple of off duty cops, the night of the gala."

"And we'll keep checking back with them," Ryan added. "We're waiting for a list of their employees and the guest list."

"Sounds good," Jennifer said. "What were the results at the Villa?"

She looked at a circle of blank faces. Finally, Riley said, "What Villa?"

"The museum Villa," Jennifer said. "Out on Pacific Palisades. Also a kind of educational place. They're trying to attract young people. They're having some kind of affair that same Saturday night."

More blank looks. Heads shaking.

"We'll check it out, Captain," JC said,

Fahim followed Jennifer Wade to her isolated home out in the suburbs.

He closed his car door silently and moved without sound, just like they had practiced during stealth movement training on the grounds of the Islamic Center. He saw no other car, no sign that anyone else lived there. And no sign of a dog.

Lights went on. It was a one story house. All the better. No alarm system, as far as he could tell.

Fahim cursed as Jennifer pulled the curtains closed in a back bedroom. He knew she was taking off her clothes. That's all right. There'd be other nights.

As he drove away, he began to think about what it would be like if they could use the female captain to gain access to a police station. He wanted to make an unforgettable statement. To occupy a police station, kill all the cops and destroy it, would be a further blow to American confidence and sense of security, along with the destruction of the other targets.

Yasmine stood spellbound as she listened to the second young woman in the rest room. Her name was A'amira. She had been married to a man who sounded much like Mahmood and she had simply run away over a year ago, with the help of the organization of Afghani women to which A'amira now belonged.

Though she was digesting everything A'amira said, Yasmine was also remembering her life before marriage, in a family that was devoutly Muslim, but completely opposed the Taliban. Yasmine was a good Muslim girl but had certain freedoms that she took for granted. Her father never once hit or kicked her.

Yasmine realized that she and A'amira were now alone. She glanced anxiously at the door, then her stomach tensed at the gentle kicking from inside of her.

She knew that she could wait no longer. Regardless of how these ladies coerced her, she had to make the most important decision of her life and make that decision fast.

Mahmood was leaning over and talking to the fellow businessman at the table when the man's wretched wife returned, alone.

"Where's my wife?"

"Still a little sick. She'll be back shortly."

The woman stared Mahmood down and it was all he could do to refrain from hitting her. He sat on the edge of his chair. Tense. Coiled.

Without a word, he shoved back his chair and jumped up. The chair crashed to the floor. People gasped. One woman screamed.

Mahmood hurried to the back of the restaurant and he was shoving open the door to the women's room.

Empty. So was the men's room. Mahmood dug nails into flesh as he stood in a quiet fit of indecision.

He ran past the rest rooms, into the dark kitchen. He cursed in two languages and finally his frantic fingers found a light switch.

Empty. He bellowed Yasmine's name. When he got this little bitch home, he would…

He saw a door and ran to it, pushed open the bar and found himself outside in the dark. Rain soaked him in seconds. He called his wife, each shout followed by profanity. Mahmood shoved at the outside bar. The door didn't budge. He pounded and kicked the door and shouted. The only sound was the rain.

He trotted around to the front of the restaurant. The front door was locked. No response to his pounding and kicking and shouts.

The door had thick glass paneling at the top. Mahmood picked up half a brick and slammed it against a pane of glass. Nothing. Again. Nothing.

"Sir, what are you doing?"

Mahmood whirled around. He faced two policemen.

"My wife's in there."

"Looks deserted to me."

"Sir, put down the brick."

"She's in there."

"Have you called her cell phone?"

"She's my wife. She doesn't have a Goddamn cell phone."

"Put the brick down. I'm not telling you again."

Mahmood stood there holding up the brick in the rain, staring at these cops. Mere policemen. Confronting him. He longed, just for a few moments, to be in Afghanistan, where the police knew how to treat people who mattered.

A policeman took a step forward. Mahmood hurled the brick….

Fatima and her husband were entertaining Omar at dinner again. This was a common way to spend an evening by now and they were all comfortable with each other.

By the time Omar revealed that he was actually an undercover policemen, they were hardly surprised. Actually, they were more comfortable than anything else. They felt they were really a part of this new country.

Fatima was grateful to have a new friend, an official friend, who listened to the story of her ordeal so sympathetically. One who offered to help her get the revenge and retribution she craved. Now, she could speak openly of Hurrah's murder. She did not discuss the rape. She did not need to. Omar already assumed the atrocities that happened.

Omar had encouraged Fatima's husband to attend radical Islamic meetings and to get to know some of the more militant leaders. Soon, Fatima and her husband were working as Confidential Informants (CI) for the Chicago Police Department, code named Romeo and Juliet. They were being fast-tracked as CI's, which can lead to trouble, but Omar felt that the terrorist threat warranted such action.

Dawud Ali Nazari was getting settled into his new assignment at the JTTF. To ease what he perceived as anti-Muslim bias amongst his co-workers and to better gain their trust and acceptance, Dawud used his initials to give himself the American nickname of "DAN." He had touched base with Detective Hudson, who briefed the new Special Agent assigned to the case. Hudson drove Dan around the various locations, explaining the case and parts of the city as they went. Afterwards, Hudson took Dan to a little Italian Deli and sandwich shop in Canoga Park for lunch. The Italian deli was known for some of the best and freshest Italian meats and sandwiches around. The little handmade cannoli provided an extra bonus for desert on the way out. Steve ordered his favorite hot Italian sausage with green peppers and melted cheese. The seasoned detective's observation skills were high and it did not go unnoticed that the new Muslim agent ordered only a vegetarian sandwich with cheese, lettuce, tomato, onion, mustard, mayo, and Italian dressing. Nothing that would have had any contact with any form of meat. They got there right before the lunch crowd and were able to get a small table out front.

Hudson discussed the case and the findings of their "trash runs." Also called, "trash covers," these were investigative techniques where the police collect a suspect's garbage. As long as garbage was on private property, it couldn't be searched. Once off private property, as commonly placed on the street the night before scheduled pick up service, anyone could pick through it. This technique, while not glamorous, could yield valuable pieces of information such as notes, phone records, credit card statements, medical conditions, as well as establish habits which over time could provide valuable leads, evidence, and intelligence. Hudson and his team were giving anything placed outside the Islamic Center special attention.

The conversation turned to personal likes and activities and Dan told Hudson how his family owned a hookah smoke lounge in Long Beach and how he spent his weekends and off time helping run the family business. He also spoke of his brother, who was a SWAT team member for an agency back east and Dan bragged of his prowess as a mixed martial artist. Hudson's bullshit detector was registering pretty high and it was clear the young agent was trying to impress the veteran detective. But it wasn't just the bravado and tough talk that made the hair stand up on the back of the detective's neck. There was something more in the stories that Dan told to the detective that just didn't ring true. Something else the veteran detective just couldn't put his finger on….

Tony was explaining to Qazi why it had been so difficult to locate Mahmood.

"Mahmood was…in jail? How can this be possible?"

"It's this wretched country, revered Imam. The police even roughed him up, I'm told."

"I know influential people. Someone will pay. But why did our brother take his wife to that dinner?"

Tony was telling Qazi about the business necessity when the Imam interrupted him. "Our brother, Mahmood, has made the mistake of letting his business become more important than his primary mission on this earth."

"Yes, holy Imam. He should be here shortly."

Mahmood's anger almost caused a wreck more than once on the way to the Islamic Center. He cursed every living creature he saw and a few he remembered from the past.

Once more, Mahmood' unpardonable ordeal played itself out in his mind: He was merely throwing down the brick but, in his fury, it almost hit a policeman in the leg. Suddenly, he was attacked with batons, handcuffed, pushed into a car, and shortly thereafter, thrown into a cell. Him! Mahmood Erdogan.

And, then, to be confronted by Detective Hudson, who he knew had been trying to find him. Fortunately, his lawyer spewed some legal mumbo jumbo and Hudson backed off. Mahmood was told not to leave the city.

The two detectives slouched down in the car and sipped at tepid coffee. They watched, with a bored, detached professionalism developed over years of such surveillance work. Their experience allowed them to simultaneously relax while they noted everything they saw.

Mostly, they saw an angry, impatient Mahmood walking in and out of his mansion, ordering people around, talking on his cell phone. He seemed a man in the process of taking some action, but they had no idea what.

It had taken hours for his damned lawyer to get him out. Hours lost that he could have been trying to find his bitch whore of a wife. He would have killed her where he found her, but she was still carrying his child, a son.

But he couldn't find her and as his rage sobered, his thoughts moved to his crucial part in the upcoming holocaust. He had gone home to change into fresh clothes when that bastard Tony found him, that convert whose mother was an infidel.

He almost hit a woman with a baby carriage and his thoughts were silenced. Two minutes later, he squealed into the driveway of the Islamic Center.

This time, Jennifer Wade showed up on time for the meeting of JC's squad. Hudson started the meeting and he did most of the talking.

Everyone had agreed that the overwhelming chatter from various sources meant that something was about to happen. The problem was that nothing was confirmed and there were a variety of targets.

"Chatter only," Hudson emphasized. They decided to focus on what they knew. Hudson employed a simple but effective technique to organize an investigation. Lay everything out in three columns: (1) What you know. These are the facts that you can admit into evidence and are generally undisputed. (2) What you don't know. These are the questions that need to be answered and will steer an investigation. (3) What you think. This is based on your expertise and provides useful analysis into an event, situation, or investigation. These categories typically involve each person's expertise as to gang activity, narcotics behaviors, and other insight into an investigation. Two probable weekend threat assessments had emerged: The museum gala and the debut of the zoo's panda with the Chinese delegation.

"Christ," Jennifer said. "In a city such as Los Angeles...ball games, movie premiers, there could be scores of places."

"Yeah, I suspect that's what the bastards are counting on," JC said.

"There's also, well, we can't count out red herrings," Hudson commented. The bottom line was that they didn't have any actionable intelligence. At this point, all they knew was rumors and innuendos. They needed to vet out the information to verify and confirm it. They decided to employ more aggressive investigative tactics.

"Do we have any indication that the Islamists are working with any of the domestic animal rights groups?"

"We haven't seen anything to indicate this," JC answered.

"Anything from the Bureau?" Jennifer asked.

"Nothing," responded JC.

"What else is new," the Captain stated in frustration, not asking a question.

"Steve, I think we need to expand surveillance coverage and deploy the specialized electronic surveillance team at this point," JC stated. "Are they available or are they on another assignment?"

"They will be available. I'll get them on this right away. Call them in or change days off if we have to. This is what they signed up for. I won't hear any bitching or moaning. JC, if you get any grief from their team leaders, you let me know."

"Yes maam," JC replied smartly.

"Steve, who do you want followed and where do you want to place cameras and tracking devices? We will need a list so we can move on this. Time is of the essence. Overtime is approved. I have a sick feeling we are behind the eight ball on this one."

No one said anything but they all agreed.

"I want this kept close at hand," the Captain stated. "Keep this in house until we have something actionable. We don't need any distractions."

In the relatively short time since the small family operation moved their cake making business from home to a small store, the little Cuban Bakery & Cafe had become a well-known and well-respected place that drew all kinds of people to the much larger facility they now occupied in Glendale. The bakery and café was so successful, they expanded to the neighboring cities of Burbank and Downey. The family's success since their arrival from Cuba with nothing more than the clothes on their back was a story that illustrated how immigrants in America could succeed.

On any given day, the place would be jammed with office workers, students, city workers, movie stars, actor wanna-be's, government employees, policemen, firemen, and the list went on and on, all of them enjoying many of the popular favorites such as the meat pies, guava and cheese pastries, or the traditional Cuban sandwich.

Steve ordered his favorite Cuban sandwich, the Medianoche Preparada. It was a regular Cuban sandwich on a sweet roll and lined with a ham croquettes. Steve found a table against the back wall and sat down with the other detectives in his squad, Ryan Riley and Pedro Gonzalez. Steve's case was spinning up quicker and quicker and he would need all the help he could find. They listened intently as they bit into the fresh homemade plantain chips that were served with every sandwich. Riley and Gonzalez were more than willing to assist Steve in any way they could and he brought them up to speed, explaining the case. They were given the green light on all available resources available to the specialty detective division including GPS tracking devices, pole cameras, and surveillance teams. All of them would reach out to their sources for any reporting or word from the various Muslim communities, Islamic centers, mosques, shops, halal markets, and restaurants.

"They are full of sin and degradation," the Imam continued as he ranted of Western decadence which was consuming the infidels.

Qazi was speaking with a fervor about some of the massage parlors which had seemingly popped up overnight in the San Fernando Valley. Everyone knew they were only fronts for organized prostitution rackets and Qazi was using the opportunity to warn his students and show how the time for the rebirth of Islamic rule had arrived.

Fahim's thoughts wandered to his lust for the infidel whore. He dreamed of raping her repeatedly before slitting her throat. He had taken to driving by her home several times a week, looking for an opportunity, combining his fantasy for sex and violence into one bloody incident. Perhaps he would drive by tonight after the preacher's lesson. However, he was tired after a long day at the hospital. Tonight, he would settle for washing his face with cold water.

"Hudson," Steve answered his cell phone. It was the leader of one of the surveillance teams. The team had decided to put a physical surveillance on the Islamic Center to identify additional players and learn more about the activities occurring there.

"Ok Detective, we followed a promising target to the Playboy Mansion. He's been in there for a couple hours and we have all the exits covered. We couldn't make entry for obvious reasons. It is pretty well protected and surrounded by high walls, trees, and bushes. We're almost off duty and going end of watch unless you want us to stay on this on an overtime basis."

"No, I have a feeling we're going to need you guys a lot. Why don't you and your team go home and get some rest while you can. I'll follow up there in the morning and see what I can find out."

"Ok thanks. We will email you our surveillance logs in the next couple of hours."

"Good job. Thanks for your efforts."

Hudson thought, as much as that Imam hated Western decadence and constantly railed about it in the mosque, the Playboy mansion could be ground zero for his minions.

At the Mansion the following morning, Hudson talked to a lady in a severe black business suit who, could have at one time had been a former Bunny. Her name was Maria. It turned out that she had, indeed, been a Bunny, while getting a business degree from nearby UCLA.

Hudson said that his visit was simply a routine check and in the course of the subsequent conversation, he learned that a large party was on tap for Saturday night and that it was to be a particularly lavish occasion, with fireworks.

Hudson had trouble showing no emotion when Maria said. "It'll be an Arabian Nights theme."

The mansion had some 29 rooms and 22,000 square feet and the grounds were five acres, with another mansion across the street for Bunnies. Security at this place would be a nightmare. The head of security was not available and Steve didn't want to give Maria any cause for alarm. He casually downplayed a request for the security head's name and contact information. Steve was relieved when Maria mentioned that the security head was an ex-cop from New York.

Maria gave Hudson a tour: Wine cellar, zoo, aviary, pet cemetery, tennis courts and, in a separate house on the property, a game room that included far more than one room and a movie theater.

They passed a barbecue area, the famed grotto, sauna, wishing well and, finally, a patio and swimming pool with bikini-clad Bunnies lounging around.

Hudson saw two Muslim men and asked Maria about them.

"Oh, that guy standing around with the clippers is…don't even remember his name. He's a gardener. And a creep, always peeping at the girls around the pool."

"Is he a threat to them?"

"Hardly. If the girls said 'Boo' to him, he'd run away. Oh, I remember now, his name is Farooq."

"And the other one?"

"That's Abu. He's security. Nice guy but kind of serious. Formal, you know."

"The company that sent him…was it Muslim?"

"No. Guy that owns it is Italian. I know because his cousin's been out here a couple of times. Don't know the owner's name but the cousin is named Tony…something. Can't quite remember…oh yeah, Tony Marino."

"Saturday night of the big party, what about security arrangements?"

"Well, a bigger security staff. Abu will take care of that. Guys from his firm have always been reliable. But nothing really special. Do you have any idea how many occasions like Saturday night have been held here over the years, the decades?"

Hudson allowed her to believe that he was certain it was an impressive number. He didn't want to discuss security further with her yet. Maria tried to get Hudson to have a drink at the pool side bar but he said he'd have to take a rain check.

"Don't be a stranger." she called as he walked out.

Hudson drove through adjacent UCLA and the well manicured mansions of the Holmby Hills Area and tried to collect his thoughts. That Italian name, Tony Marino, was vaguely familiar, though he couldn't, for the life of him, remember why.

Trying to relax and get his mind off work for a bit, Hudson paid attention to the homes he was passing. What would it be like to live out in this area? To have some regular, well-paying job? To teach at UCLA. To have the leisure to sit around the Playboy pool with the Bunnies. Or stroll hand in hand to the grotto with Maria and spend a leisurely, exciting time alone there with...

He couldn't maintain the fantasy, as his restless mind resumed its digging for the name Tony Marino. As Steve drove into the Sepulveda Pass, he couldn't help but notice how dry the brush was in the steep hills.

Tony, as always, felt renewed when he left the Imam's presence. He walked with a new purpose now, his stride brisk and confident. When he passed a place such as a massage parlor, behind a smeared plate glass facade, or some second-rate pole dancing club or a sleazy theater showing porn movies, he felt unclean and wanted to rush home and take a long, hot shower.

He longed for the day when he could start dressing in the garb of a true believer but when he brought it up with Qazi, he had said that, for the present, he was more useful wearing the Western clothes he had always worn, that they should take advantage of his look.

"By your devotion to me and by your actions in our upcoming endeavor will you cleanse your body and your soul," the Imam had told him. They planned to destroy the Playboy Mansion, an iconic American location that represented the worst of the infidels. They would kill as many sinners as possible.

He had then revealed to Tony for the first time some specific operational information: Destruction of the Playboy Mansion while hoards of infidels wallowed in sin there.

As Hudson drove, his mind kept almost grasping, then losing, the name "Tony Marino." Hudson was certain he'd heard the name before, more than once, in the context of an investigation.

He was turning a corner when he had a "Eureka!" moment. Tony Marino. Of course.

Hudson had been seconded to another unit to provide manpower and assistance for another investigation. For a couple of days , it had seemed that there might be a citywide motorcycle gang rumble, complicated by the gangs' ties to major vice—porno, drugs, pole dancing places.

Nothing had actually happened but in the course of Hudson's participation, the name Tony Marino had come up more than once. The man was involved in porno films, pole-dancing places, motorcycle gangs and—though never proved—quite probably narcotics.

Hudson returned to the office and checked out the latest on Tony Marino. Interesting. Marino seemed to have gone straight… relatively speaking.

He had acquired a gun permit while still partner in a second-rate pole dancing club and then gone to work for his cousin, who owned a security firm, which seemed legitimate. No trouble with the law.

With a relative such as Tony Marino on the payroll, that was likely to change, Hudson told himself.

Ah, yes. Surveillance units had seen Marino visit the Islamic center on numerous occasions. Now, that could hardly be a coincidence.

But, why? Why would this Catholic man be tied up with the Imam? And what could the radical Muslims want from Marino?

Hudson needed more about Marino.

Jennifer called JC and Hudson into her office to, in her words, "Decide if this information holds water."

To Jennifer it seemed important. To JC and Hudson it did not. There could be hundreds of those sleazy massage places, some muscle and three or four girls. Terrorists wouldn't waste time on such penny-ante shit.

"Yeah, Jennifer," Hudson said. "And those Muslim radicals would have to damn well know that the massage parlors were connected to various organized crime groups. Even the most radical terrorist wouldn't draw their wrath knowingly." It was bad business. Detectives at this level were aware how the various underground criminal networks coordinated with each other.

"Where'd you get this information?" JC asked. "Is the source… is it a proven asset?"

"I don't know. I guess it's just a hunch at this point but I want it checked out. I don't want to leave any stone unturned. Remember what happened on 9/11, we can't afford to be wrong."

Despite how he was treated at the Playboy mansion, Farooq's mood was greatly improved as he went through the motions of clipping shrubbery. Last night, he had finally been able to get the tickets to the regular Saturday night fights—but a very special Saturday night of MMA, when part of a big-budget Hollywood movie would be filmed in the arena.

The director was known for his insistence on absolute reality and he had decided that there was no way that this arena, with its crowds and boxers, could be replicated in a studio. The film's two stars would both be there.

Farooq was so enthralled about his upcoming Saturday night that he paid no attention to what he was doing and clipped the hedge far too low. He swore aloud and stood ready to hurl the clippers as far as possible when a soft, firm voice so startled him that he almost stabbed himself.

"Farooq, what have you done now?" Maria was saying. "Where

did you learn to trim shuddery? The Marx Brothers School of Gardening?"

"Don't you dare talk to me in such a way...you, only a woman who..."

He bit off the sentence. The whore wasn't alone. A man stood behind her, a man that Farooq, who had had unfortunate experiences with the law in more than one country, knew immediately was a policeman.

Farooq looked past Maria and into a face that revealed nothing. The man flashed a badge and said that he was a detective and that he wanted to talk to Farooq.

With something resembling a chill, Farooq realized that Abu stood deeper in the garden, staring at him.

Fahim moved through the dark with stealthy, self-satisfied confidence. The thrill of the hunt was surging into a kind of heat.

It had been so easy to follow the bitch home to this isolated beach cottage. He had given her enough time to fall asleep. The lights had been off for almost an hour.

Fahim crept around the house. No alarm system. No burglar bars. Quite an expensive address for a woman with a limited income. Perhaps there was more to the bitch than he realized.

Well, soon, he would learn everything about her. Soon, she would be groveling to tell him anything he wanted to know about her life or about her confidential police work. Qazi had been teaching them basic interrogation techniques and he was eager to put his training to practical use.

Residential houses, even those of law enforcement, weren't designed for security and were relatively easy to break into. Fahim slipped silently into the house. Paused. Listened to the quiet darkness. He activated all of his senses.

Fahim nodded and let out his breath. No hint of danger. Even better, there were no signs of any dogs. Good, he was afraid of dogs.

He moved down a central hallway. Slowly, peering around the edge of a door…he saw her.

Jennifer Wade lay half naked on the bed. She wore only a shirt and it was twisted up above her waist. In the dim ambient light, Fahim couldn't see much detail but his imagination filled in the blanks.

Jennifer twisted in her sleep and exposed the area between her thighs—as though displaying it for his pleasure. He tried not to linger on what he saw. She was in fine shape, body toned, slightly muscled.

And she would supply her own handcuffs…

Tony strolled around the old neighborhood while he waited for Abu, who had called to tell him that he would be late due to typical L.A. traffic and a massive traffic accident.

Tony felt truly blessed as he passed the spot where his old pole dancing place had been located. It now housed a cheap Chinese restaurant that looked to frequented by the same Hispanic clientele who had paid to watch the girls pole dance.

"*Alhamdulillah*," he said aloud. Allah be praised.

The blessed Imam had saved his life and, thanks also to Abu, his shepherd to the promised land, and to the paradise that, he was confident, awaited him.

As he walked hurriedly along the street, he saw Abu climbing from his car. He was wearing his security company uniform.

"So, Glendale was a nightmare, Abu?"

"Yes, brother, one more place that should shame the infidels."

"It should be wiped from the face of the earth."

"*Inshalla*, brother." In Allah's time.

The door to the old arena wasn't locked. They walked past the empty ticket booths and down a long, dim hall. The place reeked of age and smoke and sweat and something else disgusting, but Tony was thankful not to know what.

An old rent-a-cop came hobbling toward them in a faded and frayed blue uniform. A name tag said that his name was "Marv."

"Place is closed, guys. Nobody allowed."

"Hey, we're in the same game, pal. Work for a security company." As Tony spoke, he dug a twenty dollar bill from his pocket. "Andrew says, 'Hello,' Marv, take good care of my pals here.'"

"What, oh, I, uh, thanks."

"Marv, we'd just like to take a quick look around."

"We're part of the movie crew that will be here Saturday night for the filming."

"Sure, guys, anything you want. I was just going to take my break."

"That's fine, Marv, enjoy your break."

Marv shuffled off and Tony and Abu walked briskly into the arena, dim-lit and deserted. They discovered a couple of fire exits but they were locked and looked as though they hadn't been opened in years.

"So, the crowd can only get out that one way — the way we came in."

"Yes, this will be…what do you Americans say? A piece of cake."

A phone suddenly rang and so startled Fahim that he gasped aloud. Jennifer didn't move for a minute, but then bolted up in the bed, sheets sliding from thighs and rendering her naked from the waist down.

Fahim stepped back as she fumbled for the phone. Her conversation was muffled by her half-asleep voice but he picked up enough to understand that something serious had happened and that a police car was on the way to pick her up.

Taking a risk, he peered around the door again and watched Jennifer, naked now, walk unsteadily into what he assumed was the bathroom, which was confirmed a moment later by the sound of running water.

He cursed. Anything he could do to her now would have to be done so quickly that it would lose all purpose—and all pleasure.

Fahim eased himself out the back door.

Qazi knew that America had fought a great Civil War but he had never heard of either Robert E. Lee or the Battle of Gettysburg. It was a history lesson he would have been well served to know.

General Pickett, who was to lead the doomed charge up Cemetery Ridge and told Lee: "General, no 12,000 men ever assembled in the history of battle could take that hill." Lee ignored him, believing his soldiers, his beloved troops, could take any position and win any battle.

The restaurant had closed an hour earlier but Qazi and the members of his Council remained in a back room. The meal had been served and now the Council would hold an informal meeting to discuss developing issues. The Imam, like Lee, stubbornly indicated that his handpicked and indoctrinated followers could not be daunted, no matter how large their mission.

"But, Imam..." The Imam held up his hand to cut off Ziya Gokalp's protests. The accountant was a faithful follower and devout Muslim but, like all accountants, was too cautious and lacked faith in the young zealots the Imam had indoctrinated and already sent to Pakistan for additional training. The accountant was concerned that Qazi was expanding his new stateside recruits too rapidly, without proper screening, and sending them overseas for the next phases of training too quickly.

Normally, no one directly contradicted Qazi in a council meeting. To do so was to contradict Allah's direct servant, the 12th

Imam. He had allowed the other council members an exceptional privilege today by letting them express their true feelings. But he had heard quite enough dissent for one day.

"I agree with you, revered Imam," Mahmood said. "Since you have personally chosen and instructed these young soldiers, they will be able to do anything, perform any tasks assigned to them."

Mahmood knew he sounded sycophantic but after the debacle following his wife's disappearance, he was desperate to retain the Imam's favor. Each servile comment stoked resentment in Mahmood's gut.

Habia Khan seemed uncertain, so he had little to say. Hussayn Helmandi backed the Imam, but with little fervor.

It wouldn't have mattered. The Imam knew what he wanted to happen and so, Inshallah, it would happen.

Qazi was going to Chicago as he had planned.

Jennifer had the oddest feeling as she strapped on her weapon and headed out for the waiting police car. Gonzalez was coming to pick her up. JC and Steve were interviewing a woman who had come in with information on Mahmood. The woman was scared to death and would be in need of police protection and from the information she was providing, she would deserve it. Jennifer would need the influence of her rank to ensure that the detectives received the resources they needed.

Fatima and Khaleed—or, Romeo and Juliet, as they had been code named had integrated themselves into a radical mosque in Chicago. Because they were devout, practicing Muslims born overseas, they were quickly accepted and entrusted into the inner radical circles.

When the mosque Imam approached Khaleed and asked for a

special favor, Romeo gladly complied with the request. Khaleed was to use his taxi cab to pick up a special guest who would be arriving from the West Coast. Khaleed understood this arriving preacher to be of renowned importance, and who regularly spoke in front of millions at the annual Muslim pilgrimage known as the Hajj. He was arriving to help with local fundraising and internal politics of the mosque. Rumors that the mosque had been infiltrated by American law enforcement and intelligence services had increased. The result had been the cause of discontent and the challenging of the leadership of the Chicago facility. Khaleed, or Romeo, would gladly help out in any way he could.

"Hey JC," Steve answered.

"Steve, can you call this guy from Chicago PD? It looks like they have some information or questions about Qazi. I'm not sure what it's about but they called here earlier looking for some information."

"No problem, boss. I'll get right on it."

After Dawud had met with the Los Angeles detective, he decided he would look in to the activities of the Woodland Hills Islamic Center on his own and head to the Friday Jumma services. He had donned his traditional Islamic garb which included a brown flowing robe-like covering and a black vest. The Friday, mid-day, Jumma service was the big Muslim weekly sermon much like a Sunday mass for American Christians. However, the Jumma service only lasted about 20 minutes.

"Better to not tell my supervisors about this," Dawud said to himself out loud as he got dressed.

Dawud arrived early and sat in the front row. In fundamental traditional mosques, the front row was reserved for special guests and people of importance. By sitting in the front unannounced and uninvited, he was sure to draw attention to himself which was what he had planned. He would need to get Qazi's attention. An imam of Qazi's stature and reputation would not intermingle freely with other worshipers and would hold himself out of reach. Dawud would need to streamline the procedure to be recognized by the Imam quickly.

It worked. Immediately, he drew harsh stares from Qazi's students who were accustomed to sitting in the front. When Qazi also looked at Dawud, the agent met the Imam's eyes and held them. Qazi inquisitively looked upon him and made a note to meet this newcomer immediately after prayers.

A.J. made no attempt to hide his status as an FBI Special Agent, a practicing Muslim, a fan of Qazi, and a potential friend of the Imam.

Qazi would have liked to spend more time with his new guest, but he had a plane to catch.

News of Qazi's arrival to the Windy City had prompted a call to LAPD for some information on the guest of some importance. Steve managed to fly out ahead of Qazi to meet and strategize with Chicago PD.

"This is what we know..." Steve continued on with his investigative briefing with the Chicago police. He detailed Qazi's ties to the Taliban, information from Vick's son, and now what they had learned from Mahmood's wife, Yasmine. So far, there wasn't any confirmed information to merit discussion on already high profile targets such as the Getty Museum, the Playboy Mansion, or the LA Zoo. Steve let out an uncontrollable yawn. Everyone in the room knew the detective had flown the red-eye from Los Angeles to Chicago after getting off the phone with the Chicago policeman. After being picked up from O'Hare Airport by a Chicago police escort, he was briefing Omar and the other Chicago police detectives working counter terrorism. Steve learned that Qazi's flight would be arriving later that evening. Omar filled Steve in on their informants Romeo and Juliet and explained that hidden video cameras and microphones had been installed in Romeo's taxi cab.

"Well, you guys in Chicago PD really are Number Two but don't tell NYPD that because I already told them that they were Number Two," Steve and all the detectives laughed at the friendly jousting and bantering between some of the country's biggest policing agencies. A joking and friendly atmosphere was at the surface of what everyone sensed to be an underlying sense of urgency and seriousness.

Farooq didn't even notice the misting rain as he walked aimlessly around the grounds of the Playboy Mansion. His face still stung where Abu had slapped him and demanded to know what he told the policeman. He hadn't told the bastard policeman anything that he didn't already know. But Abu would never believe that. Neither would that fucking Imam and the other sanctimonious assholes at the Islamic Center.

The rain fell harder but Farooq remained oblivious. He had done nothing wrong, had done everything he had been told. They were still dissatisfied with him, though, and Abu had made that abundantly clear.

I'm...what do the infidel Americans say? Dead meat, he thought. He had known they were squeezing him out of operations here at the mansion. Now, he feared they planned to kill him. Abu had all but warned him.

It was only when he stepped into the bar and out of the rain that he realized he was wet. He cursed. In his quivering mind, it was as though the heavens were pissing on him. Allah had abandoned him. That was unfair, too.

He ordered whiskey neat, with a beer back, changed it to a double. He sank into a seat at a table in dim light, fingers drumming on the table.

The juke box was playing an upbeat song as he sat in his booth alone. Well, what was he supposed to do with his time off? His so-called brothers at the Islamic Center had hardly welcomed him with open arms.

After a second round in his isolated, dim corner. Farooq found himself checking his pockets for coins with which to make a phone call, before promising himself that, no matter how bitterly he had been wronged, he would never betray his brothers.

Finally, Khaleed was invited to pick-up the Imam, whose holiness and radicalism were well known in Chicago's radical Muslim circles. He hoped by volunteering to pick Qazi up from the airport, that Khaleed would remain his personal tour guide and escort for the weekend, while Qazi was to be in town.

Qazi was immediately impressed with Khaleed, who had grown up on the streets of Karachi. Khaleed had a physical and mental toughness to him which Qazi immediately sensed. Qazi could use the native Pakistani's life experience and maturity, to his advantage, including as a mentor to some of his younger students. Khaleed spent the weekend entertaining Qazi at various sites, restaurants and, of course, the local mosque. Qazi made such comments as, "We can take down the Sears Tower and John Hancock Building just as we did the Twin Towers," as they drove down Lake Shore Drive. Khaleed had become a master at hiding his true feelings and when Qazi invited him to his compound in Los Angeles, Khaleed had responded with humility and gratitude. He appeared incredibly honored to be in the presence of the man who was able to communicate with the Prophet and Allah himself.

By the end of the weekend, Qazi was recruiting Khaleed to

move to Los Angeles to join his group of elite students. Qazi explained that his training would include a higher understanding of the true word of Allah and would also include preliminary paramilitary training, including formal hand-to-hand combat, firearms, and basic infantry squad movements which they regularly practiced through paintball training. Graduation from his program would be a pre-requisite to being sent overseas for additional training at one of the many training camps in Pakistan's Northwest Frontier Provence.

All of these conversations were overheard and captured on tape by the detectives from Chicago and Los Angeles police departments.

Steve's "To Do List" was growing and all in different directions, as he checked the voicemail and email messages which had accumulated during his trip to Chicago. Rachel from the zoo had called and requested to see him. He also wanted to plan a trash run at the Woodland Hills Islamic Center for the next day. He would need to brief his squad members, JC, as well as a write up summary for the Commanding Officer. He didn't have a choice but to keep the Bureau up to speed and include them in the recent advancements of the case. He would set something up with A.J. for later in the week. Maybe the zoo would have something further on any threat assessments for the upcoming Chinese delegation.

Hudson parked at the zoo. As he walked from the parking lot, he picked up the animal smell that always permeated this whole area. He found it discomforting and wondered how the zoo employees coped with it.

He found Rachael supervising work over the seating for panda domain, when the panda arrived from China.

She looked up. "Detective." She looked back down and ignored him. This didn't win her any points. Obviously, she didn't care.

"All right, now, detective. It's been a madhouse around here. Seems the panda might arrive a little earlier than we had thought."

"You seem like a lady who'll make sure everything's kosher when the panda gets here."

"Panda. China. Kosher. Afghanis. Pakistanis. A whole United Nations here at our little zoo. Now, what can I do for you?"

"You're the one who called...Rachael."

"So, I did. One of your Muslims showed up here again. Scary looking guy. No pictures or drawings. This guy seems more like, you know, a leader or something."

"Scary looking, how?"

"Big, burly guy. Dark features. Face made it look like he was suffering from terminal constipation. Wasn't shy or wary like the others, either. Came right up and asked me questions."

"What kind of questions?"

"Curiously—for him—about kids, would they be safe in a big crowd...you know, safe from all the people? Would there be plenty of guards? Like that."

"Yeah, good. Thanks for your vigilance, Rachael. It's quite helpful. Now, I have to... Before, didn't you tell me you were originally from Long Island?"

She waited a couple of beats before answering. "Yeah. Why?"

"My sister lives on Long Island. In, well, I can't quite remember but, well, that's beside the point. I mean, have you been to Pasadena's Old Town since you came out here?"

"No, I've heard about it but haven't found the time, I guess. Why?"

Now he hesitated...took the plunge. "I'd like to get back there, haven't been there in a while and I was wondering if, you know..."

"Christ. Detective...Steve Hudson, just go on and ask me for the date."

"Yes, would you have dinner in Old Town with me? Say, Thursday night?"

"Sure, why not? About seven? Here."

"Uh, yeah, sure. But I can pick you up at your home."

"No, too far away. I only get off at six and I'll have to change and all. Or, if you really want, I could just wear this uniform."

"Surprise me! See you, Thursday, Rachael!" He turned and started walking away.

"Okay, Detective," she said winking.

He was too distracted to notice the dark-featured man waiting for Rachael on a nearby bench.

Steve left the zoo and drove out to the Valley. He sipped a cup of coffee as he walked around the Balboa Lake trying to put his thoughts together. Steve always felt drawn to this area. During WW II, this part of the San Fernando Valley from the Sepulveda Basin to Balboa was used as a staging area for American G.I.'s. There was still a heavy military presence to it and one could recognize the old military style barracks nestled in and around the Van Nuys airport and Balboa Park area. He finished his coffee and decided he needed something to eat. Without a craving for anything in particular, he went through the Inn-N-Out drive thru ordering a famous Double-Double Cheeseburger combo. Steve drove northbound down Woodley Avenue across from the Van Nuys Fly Away. Abutting the south side of LAFD Fire Station No. 90, was a tiny alley like roadway.

Steve pulled down this tiny unmarked street and followed it to the end where it dead ended at the eastern fence border of the Van Nuys Airport. Unknown to most people, there was a small park and viewing area of the airport runway complete with a sound system broadcasting all of the Air Control Towers transmissions. Steve sat at one of the picnic tables and downed his "gut grenade" fast food meal. He was watching the small planes land and take off when an old Huey helicopter took off from one of the hangers behind him. A flood of old Army memories and counter terrorism training raced through his mind.

Everyone liked to focus on the radical Islamists' ability to detonate a nuke on U.S. soil. The reality was that it was an unlikely scenario. Of course, anything in the kill zone would be destroyed. Radioactive fallout would impact the rest of the country for any affected areas for forty-eight hours afterwards. The jet stream would carry the fallout in an easterly direction. Any nuclear attack on the East Coast would carry the fallout into the Atlantic Ocean. For maximum effect, a nuke would have to be detonated somewhere on the West Coast. However, if a dirty bomb or nuke detonated a couple of miles off of the Southern California coast it would create a radioactive tsunami that would flood the coast from San Diego to Santa Barbara and wipe out the entire Los Angeles region. Of course, there were a small amount of extremists always vying for this option but none the less it remained a difficult task.

The more likely scenarios would be soft targets. Western cultures put their values on their children. You hit the enemy where it hurts the most. Target their kids. The Israelis learned this first hand on May 15, 1974, when Islamic terrorists killed 26 including 21 children in what was to be known as the Ma'alot Massacre. Vowing not to let this happen again, the Israelis started providing armed security to protect their most young and vulnerable. This was something his fellow Americans refused to acknowledge, despite more recent similar incidents. Steve believed that the best predictor of future events was to look at past incidents. After the Soviet's withdrew from Afghanistan, the extremists didn't stop fighting. They were able to regroup and take the fight to the Russian homeland. In September of 2004, Islamic militants took over 1100 people hostage, including over 770 children at a Russian school. The result was the death of 334 hostages, including 186 children.

"That's it!" Steve exclaimed to himself. "The Chinese delegation at the zoo was never the target at all. The real target is the families with their children who will go to see the heavily advertised rare panda exhibit."

With the combination of food and caffeine, and the excitement of his date with Rachel, Steve found a renewed energy and excitedly drove back downtown to his office.

He found Gonzales and Ryan already off duty or known as, "End of Watch" and having a beer at the Justice Cafe. The Justice Café, or "Justice" as it was referred to was an upbeat and urban modern pub that catered to guests of the Double Tree Hilton, Little Tokyo, and City workers, including any number of cops who worked inside police headquarters. Many of which went to Justice for happy hour specials or going away parties. It was a comfortable, relaxed, and always fun.

"I should've known I'd find the two of you here," Steve called out.

"Just finishing another hard day's work," replied Ryan.

"Your day may have been hard but I doubt 'work' had any part of it," laughed Hudson as he pulled up a seat and helped himself to the end of the nacho boat, now soggy and cold, but still good. No one can sit at a table with nachos on it and not succumb to a nibbling binge that coated the fingers with grease that was never easy to wash off.

Steve filled in the two detectives in on what he was thinking. Both Ryan and Gonzalez were impressed with how Steve was progressing with the case. They also noticed exhaustion in their partner and volunteered to take care of the 3 a.m. trash run at the Islamic Center so Steve could get some rest. Steve nodded his appreciation and told them he would meet them later the next morning and then he gladly headed home for some much needed sleep.

Tony and Abu had followed Farooq to the bar where the mixed martial arts movie had been filmed. How stupid for this son of an infidel whore to not only be seen but then filmed drinking and acting like a foolish child cheering and shouting for this staged corrupt MMA event.

"This fool's usefulness is reaching its end," Abu told Tony. "We will have to consider our options to rid of Farooq soon."

"God Damn, you stink!" exclaimed Ryan. "Did you not think to bring a change of clothes?"

Ryan and Gonzalez returned to the office after their trash run and had to clear some space to spread out their finds. Trash runs are part of the arsenal of sensitive undercover investigations. They entail collecting a suspects trash after it is put out for regular trash collection. People don't typically think of what they are throwing away and the information recovered by law enforcement can be quite valuable despite the potential of unpleasant finds. The room was in need of a good cleaning. Old cups still holding coffee, remnants of fast food breakfasts, lunches, and dinners, a motley of papers covered almost every chair, desk, and tabletop and oftentimes extended onto the floor.

Because the squad's work was so secret and because sensitive papers were sometimes left out, the cleaning staff had been barred from coming into the room. The room's detectives were particularly good at what they did as well as any number of other things, but keeping a room clean wasn't in their job description.

Captain Wade was the exception. Her office was always

immaculate. It wasn't because she wasn't there more or less than the others but because she was simply more fastidious than the others. The fact that she was a woman, being largely in a men's fraternity also had something to do with it and was all the explanation needed.

As Ryan and Gonzalez shifted through the papers, they realized that they didn't recover any "golden bricks" as they say from their trash run. Things were never that easy. They did find some papers with the names, Nassim al Waqqas and Yunus Banah. The names didn't ring a bell with Hudson but he decided to conduct a full work up on the names to see what came up. He decided he would give the names to FBI Special Agent Dawud, aka Dan for two reasons. One, to see if anything came up and two, to gauge the level of cooperation and assistance they could expect to receive from the federal agent.

Dawud didn't want to be bothered by the detective's request for a meeting to discuss this case but he needed more information from him. He was disgusted that the police were investigating Qazi. Qazi was a hero who was being persecuted by those who were waging a continued crusade against the religion of Islam. One day they would all pay for their misgivings and Dawud would help to see that day. The Bureau relied heavily on access to classified information and in this case, there wasn't much to go on. The local detectives had been digging up information not captured within the national databases. He didn't have a choice. He had to meet with the locals. However, he did have a choice on how much of his actions he would reveal.

JTTF Supervisory F.B.I. Special Agent Tom Floyd and Dan listened intently as Steve and JC briefed them on the developments of the Qazi case, including the informants, Chicago trip, and early morning trash runs. Dan sat quietly and took notes under the supervision of SSA Floyd. At the conclusion of the meeting, SSA Floyd offered the full cooperation and resources available to the

Bureau to support this case. Everyone agreed to meet on a weekly basis.

This was the proudest moment of Tony Marino's life—except that he was no longer Tony Marino. The blessed Imam had honored him by bestowing a Muslim name on him. As Tony entered the grounds of the Islamic Center and headed for the Mosque, he tried out the new name aloud: Rasheed Shari.

He touched his new beard. Coming along nicely. He would grow a long, full beard but with no mustache, in the Salafi tradition. He remembered, back when he was a child, he had an older cousin who grew a beard, a long, scraggly thing, and everyone derided him and called him a hippie. This beard was different. This beard marked him as a most devout Muslim.

The Imam emerged from the mosque, followed closely by Fahim. Tony was struck by the reverence, the adulation that flowed, almost incorporeal fashion from the people on the grounds, toward their beloved Imam. When Qazi looked directly at Tony…Rasheed Shari…the one whose mother was an infidel and glowed with satisfaction.

Qazi's gaze lingered on Tony for only a moment, then the Imam turned to watch a woman in full *jibaab*—a large cloth that covered her outer garments and *khimaar* or head scarf, walk hand in hand with his young son. They came from the small school on the Islamic Center's grounds.

Perhaps one day, Qazi would help arrange for Tony…Rasheed Shari to take a Muslim wife….

After the meeting with the locals, Dawud found himself in an especially foul mood. He hadn't expected the effectiveness of the detectives in the LAPD. All of his training told him that the local police were nothing more than knuckle dragging hired guns who were incapable of handling complex investigations. Dawud quickly found this not to be the case and he began to realize that he under estimated the LAPD. Unknowingly, he was experiencing some of the reasons the LAPD was so well respected around the world. The briefing by the detectives' developments in the Qazi investigation proved so much. Dawud also received news from South Carolina. His brother was facing a seven-year sentence on a plea bargain deal offered by the prosecution. It was enough to cloud the new agent's better judgment.

Dawud sped through the city streets towards the Woodland Hills Islamic Center in his government issued car with tinted windows. He was hell bent on warning Qazi and to urge more caution. Qazi knew better, but by leaving names in the trash was a sign that the Imam was getting complacent and sloppy with operational security.

Qazi was meeting with Mahmood in his office on the grounds of the Woodland Hills Islamic Center. It was turning out to be a day of meetings for the Imam.

"His name is Khaleed and he is a good candidate to join our group," Qazi was telling Mahmood. "I foresee him traveling back to Pakistan with the speed and blessings of the Prophet. Here is his contact information. Invite him and his wife to visit us in Los Angeles. Tell him of the benefits of living here such as the Muslim community and the weather. Invite him to stay with you and your family. By the way, has your wife returned home to you yet?" Qazi asked.

The conversation was interrupted by the arrival of the FBI Special Agent who urgently insisted on speaking privately with the Imam.

Qazi looked on Dawud with a new level of admiration.

Dawud didn't have enough information to reveal with any certainty the complete identities of any of the Confidential Informants. The agent was entering into a dangerous game of playing both sides of the fence. Double crossing was common place and he also had to take caution to protect himself. Dawud provided Qazi only with enough non-specific information to warn the preacher.

"Things are getting dangerous," Dawud advised. "I will not be coming onto the grounds of the Islamic Center again. I will communicate to you through other means until it is otherwise safe to do so."

"In Shallah. It is the will of Allah that you were sent here to look out for us," Qazi replied.

"Go with God, my revered Imam."

JC and Steve didn't provide every detail about the case at their briefing. They conveniently left out that LAPD had an active surveillance team monitoring the Woodland Hills Islamic Center and that the surveillance team was assisted with a hidden camera which had been installed on a telephone pole outside the mosque. The camera was capturing all vehicle traffic coming and going from the Islamic Center and was pre-positioned to capture vehicle license plates.

..... The officer at the wheel could tell Jennifer little about what had happened, only that Vick's son had been struck by a hit-and-run driver and was now undergoing surgery. The detectives were feeling guilty. They were overdue with a meeting with their original informant.

At the hospital, Jennifer found JC and Steve Hudson. Sitting over to the side and clearly avoiding the police, was the boy's father.

"He's out of surgery," JC said. "Broken hip. Sprained wrist. Some bad cuts and bruises. He'll be all right but it'll take him a while to recover."

JC walked over to Vick. The father looked up and stared at Hudson defiantly.

"I blame you for this. He could have been killed. I should never have allowed him to return to the mosque. Well, we're finished helping the police."

"Vick, I'm so sorry. And we don't even know who the driver was. Perhaps it was just a drunk..."

"You know damned well who's responsible for this and you won't, or can't, take any action against the Imam. Will you?"

Hudson started to launch into another attempt at apology but returned to the detectives instead.

"Still no word on the driver?"

"Nothing," JC said. "This has gotten far more serious faster than we anticipated."

"Make sure the boy and his father are guarded around the clock," Jennifer said. "I want to run down all possibilities on this. Enough said."

"Time for a meeting," she said.

"Yeah. Tomorrow morning. Eight. My office." Jennifer was clearly disturbed, as she walked away. How was this boy found out?

Fahim was finishing up his shift at the hospital. As he walked from the hospital room into the hall, he heard Jennifer's familiar voice. He stepped into a janitor's closet just as she and some man— it had to be another policeman—came around a corner.

Why was Jennifer here? Qazi's suspicions were correct. The police presence verified it. The boy was a traitor, an apostate, a stool pigeon for the police. He had embraced the religion and now renounced and vilified it. How much did the swine know?

Forsaking caution, Fahim stepped from the closet to get another look. This time, the Police Captain saw him. But more than that, he knew immediately that the veteran officer recognized him.

The hair on the back of her neck stood up. Jennifer said something into the room but caught Fahim duck down the hallway. She quietly and quickly followed Fahim out of the hospital.

At first, Jennifer thought that Fahim was just driving around randomly. It had been some time since she followed someone and she was a little rusty, a little unsure of herself. But it all came back after the first few miles.

Eventually, Fahim made his way right to the Islamic Center. Jennifer's faith in his innocence was hanging by a thread. Jennifer knew about the increased surveillance at the Islamic Center and stayed far enough away but close enough to see when Fahim left.

Something else struck Jennifer: Was it the Muslim terrorists who had run the boy down? If not, what would they think now that they had seen the detectives visiting him in the hospital? She was glad she had ordered police protection for the boy and his family. A flood of possibilities entered her thoughts when she saw Fahim's car leave the Islamic Center.

Panic began to set in on Jennifer. Her heart rate sky rocketed and she felt her vision narrow as everything seemed to close in on her. Jennifer did not know how Fahim knew where she lived as she followed Fahim into her neighborhood. She watched as Fahim parked a block away and exited his car wearing dark clothing and heading towards her house on foot.

Jennifer felt exhausted and beaten as she drove away from her neighborhood. She was not sure what to do or where to go. She did not want to go straight to her team. She did not want to show weakness. She hadn't felt this alone since her mother suddenly died while she was away for her freshman year in college. Divorced, she lived alone, and she never really confided in anyone. She had thought briefly about calling Jimmy Butler, her ex, for help. He had also been promoted up to the rank of captain and was the commanding officer of one the Valley patrol divisions. Although the marriage had been done for some time, the final straw was an affair he had with one of the young female sergeants under his command. They had moved in together after the separation.

She abruptly decided against calling for help. She had stopped only to pick up a bottle of gin and tonic to calm her nerves and she soon afterwards found herself sitting behind her desk with a stiff drink.

Qazi sat alone, sipping tea and enjoying this rare solitude. Things were progressing as planned. He had a steady flow of students with a wide variety of expertise and access to critical infrastructure including law enforcement, local security, hospitals, business, education, religion, construction...you name it. It was sheer genius on his part to insist that the selected students have a variety of backgrounds. There were plenty of covers and access to information. Several of his students had moved on. He was able to send them overseas for additional training and the routes of travel and cover stories had held up without drawing the attention of any law enforcement or intelligence agencies. They had done well at the training camps in Pakistan, and this reflected favorable upon him. Now they had returned home ready and waiting for any sign or order for a direct-action mission. Both they believed were imminent.

Finances were never an issue for the Islamic Center. Helmandi remained a financer of operations as a way to launder his illegitimate ventures. Qazi had also secured a steady flow of money from Saudi Arabia. All he had to do was periodically show how he was spreading the Salafi or Wahhabi Islamic traditions. It was easy enough to record any number of the sermons he regularly gave, preaching hatred of Western decadence and the coming of a new Age of Islam. There were also others overseas who paid handsomely for photos, maps, and information on any number of high and low profile infrastructure and tourist locations in and around major American cities. Qazi and his family lived quite comfortably on the Islamic Center grounds.

By Qazi's wishes, Mahmood had arranged for the purchase of airline tickets for Khaleed and his wife. They would visit their hosts in Los Angeles and Qazi would ensure through Fahim and Mahmood that they were well taken care of. Khaleed would be an asset for Qazi and serve as a good role model for his younger students. It was essential that Khaleed fill one of his open spots as soon as possible. The other students were watching and waiting the arrival of the next chosen one. Qazi had trained them to believe they were in fact, chosen. Some of his critics might call his tactics brainwashing or cultlike. He believed it to be the will of Allah.

His thoughts flowed fluidly from one to the next as he enjoyed a rare Valley morning breeze. He reveled in the arrival of the new FBI Special Agent. He had done some homework on the newcomer and learned that his family owned a hookah smoke lounge with a cousin of Ziya Gokalp. It truly was a small world, after all. Ziya had vouched for Dawud's family as devout and dedicated Muslims. The new agent could be trusted and that was what mattered. The information provided would be useful.

He was informed that Fahim had arrived. It was important that he have a long talk with his favorite and most promising pupil. He needed to ease his mind and counsel him again on not letting his hatred get the better of his judgment. Fahim was quick tempered and eager for action. He would have to work on teaching Fahim patience and clear thinking. While anger was easy to manipulate it could also be the cause of costly mistakes, if not managed properly. The challenge would be in getting Fahim to learn this.

"Tell me, my young friend, what did you learn last night after leaving the Mosque?"

At 8 o'clock, JC, Steve, Ryan, and Gonzalez arrived with fresh coffee for their meeting. Jennifer was not there and she had not contacted anyone.. JC looked at his watch annoyed.

Sensing JC's growing impatience with their Captain, Steve offered to go check her office.

Steve found Jennifer at her desk. She had a fresh pot of coffee going and was already busy working.

"Let the guys know I'll be right there, if you would. I'm just finishing this up." Having used her authority as the Captain, Jennifer had already called in the heads of her surveillance teams in for a 7 o'clock meeting. She wanted 24/7 surveillance coverage on Fahim. She insisted on being updated directly from the teams on any change, at any time, in his movements or locations. The officers and detectives on this detail were sworn to secrecy, and given her status as the commander of the anti-terrorism unit, they obeyed without protest.

"No worries, everyone is just walking in now," Steve replied. The half empty bottle of gin on the back shelf did not go unnoticed. No reason to make any mention of the bottle. She was entitled to a drink just like everyone else.

The meeting kicked off at 8:15 a.m.

"Let me hear your thoughts," Jennifer said, opening the meeting. In most police circles, information went one way, down. There wasn't a lot of room for two-way exchange of information. However, at ATD, the value and expertise of everyone in the room was too high. It was the reason there was such a rigorous screening and background to even make it into this elite LAPD Division. Information and ideas went lateral. Nothing was left unturned and everyone contributed. There was too much at stake and Jennifer made it a point to let it be known that egos and rank were to be left at the door during these meetings. Although the responsibility and final decision was always hers, she made her best management decisions by listening to everyone and based on having all the information, good or bad.

"Well, we have no proof that last night's accident was anything more than just an accident," JC started.

"But something just doesn't seem right," Ryan finished for him.

"And we have to account for everything," JC added.

"AND we owe it to Vick and his son. We can't abandon them," Steve continued remembering the Ranger Creed in which Rangers vow never to leave a fallen comrade behind.

"On another note," Steve continued, "I took a call from Chicago PD this morning. Apparently, Qazi is pretty insistent that the Chicago PD CI's, Romeo and Juliet, come to Los Angeles for a visit and to view their operation. Qazi is recruiting Romeo to be one of his students and how he can sell his cab and move to Los Angeles. Qazi already paid for plane tickets for both of them. The Chicago detectives are on board and willing to come out with the CI's, if we can accommodate them."

"I like it," JC replied. "This case is moving forward quickly. We need to stay on top of things or we may miss something. Steve, let me know if you need more manpower on this. We need to follow the players on this and not be distracted by any red herrings. I think we should bring in the Joint Regional Intelligence Center (JRIC) to help with threat assessments."

The JRIC was the regional fusion center which bore the responsibility for producing and distributing regional threat assessments and informational bulletins.

"I'll place a call to see what they have on the Getty Center, the Playboy Mansion, the LA Zoo, as well as anything new on any of the same traditional high profile targets.

"We will need to brief the F.B.I. on this operation and invite them to play," Jennifer added, "BUT I want this to be an LAPD operation. There's too much at stake on this and we can't afford to have the Bureau screw up this up."

"Chicago will let us know the details when they get more information," Steve continued. "It's not confirmed but it looks like they'll be staying with Mahmood and arriving early next week."

"We still have Mahmood's wife, right?" Jennifer asked.

"Yes. She is still in a safe house. We are working with some of the abused women shelters and other Non-Government Organizations (NGO's) to help her out. She is giving us good but limited information. She just doesn't have a lot of detail. Her husband couldn't hide everything, but he did keep her in the dark on a lot of things."

"We should get a layout of the house from her," said Ryan. Ryan was a former SWAT cop and always tactically oriented. His SWAT training, like Hudson's military training was not to be discounted, nor was the mental mindset this training and background fostered.

"OK, Ryan and Gonzalez, Steve's got his hands full. Can you guys free up your schedule?" JC asked. "We will need a whole operations plan while we have the CI's embedded with the bad guys. Let's get a pole camera up on Mahmood's house and additional GPS tracking devices on Mahmood's vehicles. Let the surveillance teams know to plan for some long days ahead. We will need those CI's in pocket 23 of the 24 hours a day."

"Since this investigation primarily revolves around the Valley, we should set up a Command Post (CP) nearby," said Gonzalez, who had remained quiet was on a roll. Everyone knew Gonzalez to be an analytical and thorough thinker, so they let him talk without interruptions. "We should use that new CP vehicle so we can access all computer and video systems. How about setting up at the new Davis Training Academy? They have a big parking lot, any resources we may need…bathrooms, locker rooms, power, fuel… it is out of sight, won't draw unwanted attention, freeway friendly, has armed security, and is right up the street from the new Mission Division Patrol Station, in case we need additional man power or resources. There is also a helipad in case Air Support Division needs to land a helicopter."

"I like it," JC said. "I was Academy classmates with one of the Captains over there. He's an old friend. He'll give us whatever support we need."

"OK, Steve, keep me posted on updates as they come in from Chicago. It looks like you guys have this handled. Let me know if you need anything from me." Jennifer started to excuse herself. "Oh, most importantly, I need to get my city car in to the motor pool for service. They want it today, of all days. Ryan, if you wouldn't mind driving me home today after work? Steve, can you pick me up in the morning?"

"Sure boss. It won't be a problem," both Steve and Ryan agreed.

It was a productive meeting. A plan was coming together.

No one in the room was aware how crucial their planning would become.

Rachael looked up in annoyance as the small, private plane dropped toward the zoo. It frightened and unsettled the animals. Second time that bastard had flown so low. Rachael filed the plane's numbers in her mind but knew she'd never follow up and report the pilot to… She didn't have any idea where or who to report him to.

There must be hundreds, probably thousands, of private pilots with their own planes in the Los Angeles area. And, the police had their hands full.

She returned to her work supervising the men from the tent company. They were measuring the area so they could bring the right sized tents for the arrival of the Chinese delegation. Actually, supervising was the wrong way to describe what she was doing. Mostly, she worked to stay out of the way.

At times such as this, Rachael thought again that she might well have made the wrong decision when she came to work for the zoo. She loved animals, had a degree in animal behavior from UCLA and was halfheartedly working on a master's degree. But these sets of events took her away from the animals as she became more and more a coordinator. She'd have to give this serious re-consideration.

Her gaze wandered to the empty panda quarters. She felt intense pity towards the panda being shipped from overseas. Pandas didn't adjust well to change.

Rachael had strongly suggested that the panda's debut be put off until the bear could adjust to its new surroundings and its new handlers. Not a chance, she was told.

Some 99% of a panda's diet was bamboo and the zoo seemed to

have plenty of bamboo but hadn't yet secured the food items that were special treats in captivity: Honey, yam, fish, eggs, oranges, shrub leaves and bananas.

Rachael wondered how long the panda would live in captivity. There were only some thirty-five pandas in zoos outside China, some 240 in China. No one knew exactly how many pandas still lived in the wild. Estimates ranged from two to three thousand. In any case, the giant panda was on the endangered list.

"Hey, sweetie, could you go get us some coffee?" one of the tent men called.

"I could—but I'm not going to."

The word he muttered in reply was muffled but Rachael was certain it started with a "C."

Jesus, it was hot today. Hot and dry. She'd lived in Seattle before coming down here. Seattle. Cool, mild, damp. Here, it could get up to a hundred and ten degrees plus in the summer. Constant danger of fire in the surrounding forests. Before she arrived, a raging fire had almost reached the zoo, just yards from where she was now standing.

Rachael shook her head. She sighed wearily and trudged toward a bench where a dark-featured man sat. She was reminded of Steve Hudson and her upcoming date.

Hudson was frustrated. No one could find Mahmood anywhere. Surveillance was trying to pin him down so they could plant the GPS tracker under Mahmood's car. With a tracking device, they would be able to pick up his car anytime and anyplace.

"Can't find the bastard anywhere," he stated out loud to whoever would listen. "He's gone to ground or he's dead." Steve knew Mahmood had an unpredictable schedule and that it wouldn't be long before he showed up at either the mosque or his house. He would just have to give it time. The install team would just have to be on a stand by status and ready to roll out at a moment's notice.

Steve was right. Mahmood hadn't travelled far. He was stuck on the 405 Freeway, in typical Los Angeles traffic. Mahmood had gone to the Getty Center in a futile attempt to regain his lost catering contract with Gerard Chaudry. He couldn't even get in the door and all of his phone messages had been ignored. Mahmood was seething. Every day brought the man more frustration and anger. As he sat motionless on the freeway, he watched the high Santa Ana winds whip across the dry brush of the Sepulveda Pass.

The Santa Ana winds are strong, dry winds that impact Southern California. These winds can exceed 40 m.p.h. with hurricane force gusts. They have been sometimes called the "Devil Winds" and are infamous for fanning regional wildfires.

He thought of how this would be a really bad place and time to be stuck in a brush fire. A fire through this dry, steep, overgrown terrain could easily become a disaster. Or, could it become a.....

"This is Kevin," Supervisory Special Agent Floyd made the introductions at the JTTF.

It was clear, everyone at LAPD liked Floyd. He came from a police background. His dad was a SWAT Commander and he had started with a local agency in the Midwest before joining the Bureau. Floyd knew how cops thought and he also knew how to talk to them. The best feds were always the ones with prior police experience. Everyone knows there is a big difference between police and federal agents and most think that it is because the feds are better educated. However, the real reason is actually the 4th Amendment. The 4th Amendment requires a warrant before any search or seizure which includes arrests.

However, the judiciary determined a long time ago that in the interest of public safety, they would make exceptions to the warrant requirement for the police to do their job effectively. It was determined that the police have three contacts with the general public: consensual encounter, detentions based on reasonable suspicion, and arrests based on probable cause. The police can arrest someone without a warrant if probable cause exists. Probable cause is generally defined as a set of facts or circumstances that would lead a reasonable person with similar training and experience to believe that a crime was about to occur, was occurring, or had just occurred. The layman's standard for probable cause is "more likely than not." If you can answer that "more likely than not," a certain offense occurred, you have probable cause. The mathematical equivalent to probable cause is 51%. If a cop can articulate 51% from all of the surrounding facts and circumstances, he can make a lawful arrest without a warrant. The result is that street police officers become pretty good at looking at the totality of circumstances in order to justify lawful arrests. They do it every night.

Probable cause to a federal agent is a chapter in a textbook. They learn it in the academy, or in school, but rarely will they ever make a probable cause warrantless arrest. When the feds get a case, they take it to an Assistant U.S. Attorney who directs the case through the investigation all the way through to prosecution. The U.S. Attorney's Office will then seek a grand jury indictment, and thus securing federal charges prior to making any arrests. Federal agents regularly fail to see how each of the individual circumstances combined together paint a full picture of what is really happening. A grand jury indictment is also a timely procedure. It is why local law enforcement can move at such a faster pace than their federal counterparts.

JC had called SSA Floyd and requested that they meet sooner than they had previously planned. Things were heating up. It was better to meet in person as it was considered poor operational security to speak openly on unsecured telephone lines. JC had worked with Kevin before on another previous case and Steve had seen him at a couple of meetings and classified briefings. There was an immediate mutual recognition by the way each carried himself. As each carried an aura common with that of special operations training background.

Dan was the only new face. Kevin went only by his first name. Everyone else always gave their title and agency at formal introductions. However, the CIA was prevented by law from conducting Agency sponsored investigations on U.S. soil. When the Agency was involved, they had to be careful not to cross any legal boundaries. They were part of the JTTF. for assistance and intelligence capabilities. Any actions or active investigations had to be coordinated with their designated federal law enforcement agency, the FBI. Neither side was happy about this policy and neither side came even close to trusting the other. It was a rocky relationship, at the very least.

JC started, "This is LAPD Investigation nicknamed *Operation Q-Tip...*"

Everyone, except Dan, chuckled. Both JC and Steve noticed and made note of how tense Dan was throughout JC's case briefing.

If Qazi was sending people to terrorist training camps overseas, the CIA needed to be involved. The Agency had established good overseas operational capacity. The fact that the LAPD and Chicago PD detectives had infiltrated this silent cell, using good old fashioned police work, with the potential of identifying Taliban and likely Al Qaeda connected camps in Pakistan was not only of interest to the experienced but mysterious case agent but it also openly impressed him. Of course, the Agency would need to verify everything and start its own overseas investigation. Kevin was well versed at hiding any emotion, or giving away body signals but he openly showed an admiration for the LAPD, while casting a scowling eye at his federal counter parts for their regular practice of incompetence.

"I'm not saying but I'm just saying, this is the kind of thing that gets predator drones and cruise missiles launched into sovereign countries. Keep us posted…and by the way, good job, *Detectives*," said Kevin.

The JTTF is a classified facility. As such, national security rules and procedures prohibit bringing in any cell phones, personal lap tops, thumb drives, or any other recording or digital electronic recording or storage devices. The idea is to prevent the intentional or unintentional removal of classified information from the facility. Before entering the secured area of the building, everyone places a post it note on their phones and leaves them in a drawer. Cell phones are prohibited inside. While JC and Steve sat inside the meeting with SSA Floyd, Kevin, and Dan, they missed the several urgent phone calls from one of the surveillance detectives assigned to the investigation. Surveillance teams had identified Special Agent Dawud Ali Nazari as having at least one time having entered the Woodland Hills Islamic Center.

Both detectives sat stunned and speechless for several minutes after retrieving their messages. There were too many unanswered questions. What exactly happened and what exactly did this mean? Whatever it was, they both knew something wasn't right.

Jennifer felt better about staying home now that Fahim would remain under 24 hour surveillance. She was a trained and decorated police veteran. She felt confident she could handle Fahim. He was still, after all, just a boy. Plus, it was re-assuring that a team of specialized detectives would be within a moment's notice of Fahim had he tried anything foolish. None the less, she asked Ryan to make a quick stop before dropping her off at home. She was getting used to at least one, and usually more, stiff gin and tonics to take the edge off every night.

Fahim took an early break and headed for Karim's room. A policeman stood at the door. This stopped Fahim up short, his mind whirling. Jennifer had said the boy's father was a friend of people in high places. Fahim asked himself if he could believe this.

The father was a caterer and much respected. His business might well have gained him powerful friends.

Still, Fahim needed more proof of his innocence...

"Hey, Buddy. Yeah, you there. What you doing here?"

Fahim had forgotten the policeman. He contained his anger at being challenged. "I work here at the hospital. See, I'm in my scrubs."

"Yeah, I'm not blind. Why you loitering around this room?"

"I didn't realize that I was loitering, officer. I'll leave immediately." Fahim did, but with the slowest passable steps.

Silence in the car as Hudson and Rachael drove to Pasadena. Hudson realized that he hadn't had an actual, old-fashioned date in an eternity. Not that he hadn't been with women, but... He snapped off the thought.

"So, Rachael, things at the zoo about ready for your panda?" He knew how lame that sounded before he had finished speaking the words.

She shrugged. "I suppose so, though much of it has to be taken care of Saturday afternoon. How's your work going?"

"The usual routine, well, all right, we're working full tilt... about Saturday night, you know, at the zoo."

"You don't know anything more than you did? How about all those suspicious Afghani men?"

Now, he shrugged. "We're working on that. And I want to thank you again for your help there. But there are so many Muslims in the Los Angeles and no more than a few of them are militant."

"May I make a suggestion for the evening? Let's not talk shop."

"Works for me, Rachael." He hoped he had added a tone of levity as he added: "What else do we have to talk about?"

"There's always truth and beauty, detective."

"'Detective is talking shop. Call me Steve."

"All right, now, back to truth and beauty."

"Sure, though lately I've been seeing little truth and even less beauty." He glanced around at Rachael and their eyes met and he felt like biting his tongue.

"Don't even try to wiggle out of that one, Steve." The good-natured, teasing smile that crinkled around her lips made him smile, also.

Perhaps this date would turn out to be all right, after all.

As Hudson was looking for a place to park in Pasadena's Colorado Old Town Colorado Street, JC and Gonzalez were sipping Dewar's at Justice Cafe.

"I love this place," Ryan said as he joined them after driving their Captain home. "Reminds me of the old Irish bars in New York." Ryan was a fourth generation police officer. A bad divorce and a dislike of winter had brought him out to Los Angeles.

"We're not sure what any of this means. We met with the Bureau earlier. They didn't' say anything or give any other indication that Qazi was working for them as a CI or giving them any information at all. The Agency has nothing, either. I think they are out of the loop completely."

"Could be that the Bureau has a mole. A dirty agent." It was half-question and half-statement.

"We have no proof of that. We have to be careful about any accusations, especially without any solid evidence."

"Either way, we have to confirm those reports. I want to see those videos and surveillance logs for myself," JC responded. "I'm starving. I need to eat, and then I'm heading back to the office. Anyone care for some overtime hours tonight? I could use some company, and the help..."

"Can I get you another round?" the pretty young waitress interrupted.

"Better make it three large coffees," Ryan answered.

Jennifer dragged herself through the front door and mixed a tall, lethal gin and tonic. In the living room during the last light of dusk, she stepped out of her shoes, stripped off her holster and sank into an easy chair. She took sharp little sips and savored each rush of gin.

She closed her eyes in the fading light and ignored the faint sounds in her house...

Hudson and Rachael were sipping margaritas at an outside table just off Colorado. Hudson rarely drank such mixed drinks but he was actually enjoying the spicy margarita, ordered at Rachael's suggestion.

"I really like this area, Old Town. I'm so glad we came."

"So am I, Rachael." He'd found that he and Rachael had a good deal in common, including overseas military service.

The waitress had just served their first course when Steve couldn't believe what he was seeing. He rubbed his eyes thinking that this case was really starting to get to him but there was no mistaking that face. "Oh shit! Do you see that tall, scary, Afghani man over there? He's talking to that other equally as ugly ...."

Rachel waited a couple of beats, then looked around casually, as though looking for their waitress. Her look back at Steve showed her surprise.

"I've been looking for him all week. That's Mahmood Erdogan, aka, 'Mike the Terrorist.' I can't be sure but I think he's with someone else my team has been looking for named Yunus Banah. Whatever it is Rachel, these are bad guys and are involved in some heavy stuff. We have a lot of things spinning up over these two. I've got surveillance teams actively hunting them. I'm going to have to make some phone calls."

"Why do you think he's here, this particular restaurant?"

Hudson shook his head. "I don't know. Could be anything…"

"Perhaps he's on recon," she quickly added.

"Rachael, why do you say that?"

"Force of habit? Some old gut feeling? Maybe he simply always looks like he's up to no good. Well, Big City Detective, the way I see it is to do the math. Your surveillance team is probably off duty and scattered all over the County. By the time they get here, across town, and likely against late rush hour Los Angeles traffic, you are looking at AT LEAST an hour turnaround time. It doesn't look like you have that much time. You can let him go or we can follow him and call it in to the cavalry."

Just then Mahmood shoved back his chair, as though about to get up. Hudson saw that the bill for that table had already been paid.

A potted palm shielded Hudson and Rachael as Mahmood emerged from the exit with Yunus Banah. Hudson thought Mahmood was making a phone call, then realized he was taking pictures with the phone's camera. Mahmood took out a pad, jotted down some notes, pivoted and walked away.

Hudson knew he had to follow Mahmood but what was he to do with Rachael? Suddenly, she was on her feet.

"Come on. You'll lose him."

Hudson stood up, threw some bills on the table and caught up with Rachael.

"I'll have to put you in a taxi or…"

"Don't worry about me, Steve."

"But I can't jeopardize your…"

"You think I can't take care of myself?"

Hudson saw that Mahmood was already driving away. He and Rachael followed. If anything did happen to Rachael…

"This is one bad son of a bitch, I take it."

Hudson nodded. "Oh, yeah. Bad."

"And there's a lot more going on here than something happening at the panda debut."

"There's always a lot going on in police work, Rachael."

"Okay, don't tell me. Let me guess."

"This is no fucking game, Rachael. And pardon my French."

"Oh, I can speak that kind of French, Steve. How about *merde*?"

"*Merde*?"

"French for shit. Which is what I'm being fed here."

Hudson didn't reply. He concentrated on Mahmood who, for some odd reason, was now driving along the forest that bordered the highway near the zoo.

Why was the bastard taking this route? What was he going to do with Rachael if something went down? What if he had missed out on something the squad was involved in this evening? He knew he should have stayed at work but JC insisted he go out for some down time. JC needed a clear head and Steve needed a mental break. Some break.

"We're not that far from the zoo."

"What? Oh, yeah, you're right."

Silence in the car. Mahmood turned off the highway and seemed to be heading home. But he didn't go there. He drove into an even shabbier part of town, finally into a warren of what Hudson assumed to be derelict warehouses.

Mahmood's car eased to a stop, just in front of a pickup truck. Hudson also stopped, behind the cover of a loading dock.

A man climbed out of the truck's cab and into Mahmood's car. Steve couldn't be sure in the faded light but if he had to bet, he would put his money that this was Nassim al Waqqas. What was going on now? Uniformed Patrol was such an easier assignment...

Rachael moved closer to Hudson and in a soft whisper, "It's like we're in a bad gangster movie."

Hudson nodded. Closer now, he inhaled her lilac scent and became aware of Rachael, the girl, which added to his uneasiness about having her along.

"You got a backup weapon, Steve?"

"What? No way, Rachael."

"Sweetie, I'm qualified in a range of weapons. I can probably out-shoot you."

"Well, you're not getting the chance tonight. Christ, I must have been out of..."

The front doors to Mahmood's car opened. Both men got out. The trunk opened. The man from the pickup loaded two large boxes into Mahmood's trunk. Mahmood then returned to his car and he drove away, leaving Nassim al Waqqas and Yunus Banah standing outside of the pickup truck smoking cigarettes.

Hudson waited a full five minutes, then backed away.

Mostly inane talk on the way to Rachael's house. Hudson walked her to the door. They stood there. Lilac perfume. Her breathing. Rachael, the girl. All girl.

"Steve, you sure know how to show a girl a good time."

"I enjoyed tonight, Rachael."

"Oh, I enjoyed it, too. Well, don't be a stranger. If you need me, just follow the panda."

Her lingering kiss on his lips surprised him. She pulled away, stepped inside, and closed the door without looking back. Date over.

Hudson stood staring at the door for an extra moment, inhaling lilac, exhilarated in a lazy way…that slid into a more alert tension. He sensed something in the shrubbery. He stood stark still.

Nothing. No movement. No sound. He exhaled.

Hudson headed to his car and drove away.

Dawud had to do something but he needed to be cautious. On hindsight, driving directly onto the grounds of the Islamic Center was foolish. He was trained and aware of the effectiveness of the FBI forensics team and crime lab. They were capable of linking typed letters to specific printers and computers. Dawud went out of his way to an old Salvation Army store where he found and purchased an old typewriter. His plan was to use the typewriter one time and get rid of it. He would dispose of it where it would have no chance of being found for years to come. He took great care in the handling of paper and used latex gloves. He would be sure not to leave any trace evidence or DNA on this letter. However, he made two careless and costly mistakes. He failed to take the same caution in the handling of the letter's envelope and didn't think to use a wet sponge to seal the envelope before mailing it from a post office processing center on his way to his family's hookah lounge.

Hudson's tail lights disappeared and a figure slipped out from bushes at the corner of the house. The figure also exhaled. Slowly it moved to the window. Rachael could be seen kicking off her shoes, and calmly stripping down to her bra and panties.

She walked into the kitchen and took a bottle of white wine from the refrigerator, poured a glass and moved into the bedroom.

The figure was now watching from outside the bedroom window, watching, indecisive, fondling a short metal object.

Mahmood logged into the shared free yahoo account which had been created and checked the "Save Draft" section. Sent emails could be easily, and oftentimes were, intercepted by American law enforcement and intelligence agencies. One way to avert this was to not electronically send any messages. Instead, you could communicate covertly by composing a message and then simply save it as a draft. Everyone would have access to the account, which could be logged into with a common user name and password, enabling everyone with access to log in from any coffee house internet connection. Log in, check the saved drafts, receive the message, and either log out for others to read the message or delete the draft. The accounts were easy enough to create using fictitious names and locations.

Mahmood created a draft message confirming and providing details from what the three had discussed. Qazi was confident that he and Fahim were competent enough to handle the task, but Nassim al Waqqas and Yunus Banah had received a higher level of training. Plus, Mahmood suspected that Qazi wanted to keep him and Fahim, the newest assassins close at hand. He didn't want to chance them going rogue or freelancing on their own. It was risky.

The new special agent would have benefited by having knowledge of this method of covert communication.

Steve parked in front of Jennifer's house, while wondering if she'd been hitting the bottle at home again. Rumors of her recent increased drinking were starting to unfold.

He shook his head. It wasn't like Jennifer to let a few drinks and complicated case ruin her reputation and her chance for promotion, if not jeopardize her whole career.

Hudson's hand was moving to ring the bell but, instead, it moved to unholster his gun.

The front door was cracked open.

He shoved the door open and stepped inside, holding the pistol with both hands, pointing up. To his left, the living room looked like a portrait of decadence; an empty gin bottle beside a broken glass on the hardwood floor. Amid dried blood stains, a trail of scattered clothes down the hall, ending with bra and panties, at the bedroom door.

No sounds came from the bedroom...

Hudson waited another tick, checked his gun grip, and then stepped into the bedroom, steeling himself for what he might find.

He found a sheet-covered mass that resembled a body and there was blood on the sheet. After making certain that no one else was in the room, Hudson approached the bed.

He found himself taking small steps and was breathing with shallow breath, as though he might, at any instant, reach a point near the bed where his olfactory sense would detect a decaying corpse.

Steve Hudson had seen more than his share of corpses, of mutilated bodies, in his army and police careers. But, he wasn't sure he could do this.

He hesitated, then with his left hand, he reached for the sheet. The wail that escaped from under the sheet made him shiver with a kind of fear he'd never encountered, the kind of fear and sound he'd take to the grave.

He had recovered enough to reach for the sheet again...

It moved and what emerged was a living form, or something once human: blonde hair damp with blood stuck to a bloated face. Her blue eyes were blood shot and drool was oozing from her bloody lips.

The eyes narrowed. Lips quivered.

"Steve?" A gutteral whisper, barely audible.

"Jennifer...are you...what happened?"

Already, Hudson's mind was forming an image of the young Muslim punk that he would go out to find and destroy...

"Who did this to you?"

"Did? Nobody did. I did. Oh, shit, I'm sick. Don't stand too close. About to throw up."

He stepped back. She pulled off the bloody sheet and he saw that her foot had been cut. He snatched up the cell phone on her bedside table. Battery dead.

The whole thing became disgustingly clear: Jennifer had come home alone, drank herself into a stupor with gin and cut herself on the broken glass.

He stepped back as she lurched toward the bathroom.

Hudson tried to be patient as he waited for Jennifer in the emergency room while her foot was being stitched, just as he had been patient while she got cleaned up and tried to make herself look reasonably put together.

Jennifer had done a fine job with that, although there was still a puffiness to her face and her blue eyes were still bloodshot. She could walk relatively normally.

Unfortunately for her, Jennifer drank gin, not vodka. And she still reeked of gin, as though sweating gin. There was no mistaking that smell.

He glanced at his watch. They were cutting it close and Hudson had let her know that he wouldn't be late because of her. However, he wouldn't contradict her story but neither would he tell any lies for her.

She hobbled out a minute later, forcing a smile that was almost pitiful. He helped her to the car. When he drove off, she still hadn't said anything.

Finally she broke the silence, "Thanks for all your help. And concern." It was a soft little voice, void of all feeling.

He shook his head. "Forget it."

They remained silent all the way back to the police station.

JC, Ryan and Gonzalez glanced up as Hudson walked into the room.

"Where's Jennifer?" JC asked. "Is our illustrious captain going to be late yet one more time?"

"Give her a break," Hudson said. "I saw her just a minute ago. She's right behind me."

There was no comment. Jennifer hobbled into the squad room a minute later. The harsh ambient light did her no favors and the dilapidated state of her face was obvious.

"Jesus, what happened?" Gonzalez asked.

Jennifer eased down into her chair. "Stupid accident. Dropped a glass, it broke, I cut my foot."

Again, no comment. JC sat closest to the desk and Hudson winced as he watched JC's realization of the gin smell seeping from her body.

It took her a full minute to speak. "All right, guys. Let's discuss what's happening and where we stand now."

JC stood abruptly and stepped away from the desk, as though revolted by the way Jennifer smelled. "Where do we stand... Captain? Oh, just a routine week. While you were out partying, we've been here all night. We managed to infiltrate a silent terror cell, identify additional members of the cell, and uncover a potential mole within the FBI."

Hudson was startled by the venom in JC's tone. Jennifer responded as though she had been slapped. A nasty confrontation seemed inevitable. Jennifer decided to let it go for now. She didn't have the energy. She would deal with JC in private.

"Tell me more."

Steve jumped in to cool things off. He explained what he had seen last night. He left out Rachel's involvement. "Work ups on Nassim al Waqqas and Yunus Banah revealed they both had numerous parking tickets outside of the Islamic Center but they were dated and over 18 months old. Nothing recent. They both shared the same address which was a one bedroom apartment in the heart of Canoga Park. A search of DMV records revealed twenty different people were currently using the same address. The building was owned by Husayn Helmandi. Looks like a safe house. Immigration & Customs Enforcement (ICE) have confirmed their overseas travel to Pakistan for several months. Timeline is right after the last ticket received at the mosque. They haven't been seen at the Islamic Center since. They emerged last night with Mahmood."

"It's looking like we just identified a couple of the Imam's students who were sent overseas."

"What's that about a mole?"

"Special Agent Dawud Ali Nazari. He goes by the nick name Dan. A new Muslim agent. We have him travelling to the Woodland Hills Islamic Center and meeting with Qazi right after one of our meetings at the JTTF. Of course, we don't know what was said, but Mahmood left right after Dan arrived and Fahim arrived shortly thereafter. It doesn't look good. We made some calls back East where he said he was from. Looks like he has a brother who was in law enforcement."

"*Was?*" Jennifer asked.

"Correct. Was. He is currently in custody awaiting sentencing. The official charges include a forced arranged marriage with a fourteen year-old girl. The local sheriff is looking into unofficial charges that he was training known radical and extremist Islamics in advanced firearms and SWAT tactics. The group is affiliated with Jamaat al Fuqra."

"JAF...that's the Pakistani group which was tied to the

beheading of that journalist Daniel Pearl a few years back," Jennifer said remembering.

"Ya, that's them," JC contributed. "They've been in the news also for a training camp they are running in upstate New York. They call it Islamberg. It is a real mess over there."

"It's also turning out to be a scandal for the sheriff, who is facing a tough re-election campaign in South Carolina," Steve continued. "That's not all. We started looking into Dan's family. Looks like his family owns a hookah parlor near Long Beach."

"O.K....," Jennifer said, following along.

"Well, one of the business partners is Ziya Golkap. He's been identified as a close associate of Qazi's. He is a member of Qazi's top Council."

"So," Jennifer summarized. "Let me see if I have all of this right:

The FBI Agent, Dawud or Dan, is consulting with terrorism suspects, his family is in business with the same, and his brother is under suspicion of aiding and abetting and providing support for terrorism.

We believe we have identified a silent terror cell which is sending and has, we believe, sent at least two people overseas to terror training camps, and we have infiltrated this cell with informants from Chicago and are cooperating fully with Chicago PD.

Does the FBI know any of this yet?"

"They know everything except that they have a mole in their ranks," JC answered.

"JC, what do you have planned for today?"

"Well, we've been here all night. I was going to go home and get some sleep. Chicago PD will be arriving in a couple of days and we are all going to need some rest."

"Grab some coffee. We are going to have to brief this up the chain of command. This has the potential of embarrassing the Bureau and is about to get real political real quick. It's time to advise the chief of Police. I am going to need you there. Also, we are going to have to let the Bureau know about this. We need Dan off this case immediately. Plus it will give me a chance to sing all of your praises. This is one of the best cases ATD has ever seen."

"No rest for the wicked," JC responded and headed off to the locker room for a shower, a fresh shave, and change of clothes.

One of Qazi's young minions had brought him the daily mail. As he shifted through all of it for anything interesting, his eyes fell on an envelope written in a child's writing. It was postmarked from Long Beach, California. "Long Beach?" Qazi said to himself as he opened it …

Dear Qazi,

I cannot reveal myself to you. I am a friend. You know who I am.

DO NOT trust your visitors from Chicago. They are spies for the F.B.I. They report on your activities.

Tell brothers Mahmood and Fahim to look into their rear view mirrors. They are being followed.

Tell them to look under their vehicles. Their every movement is being tracked electronically.

Look up from the Mosque. There is a camera watching you.

As Salamu Alaykum

Qazi's blood began to boil, his face flushed in anger, and he saw everything in a haze of bright red.

That night, Abu and Tony had made sure they were the on-duty security detail at the Playboy Mansion, as planned. Farooq was also in the security office, although they kept him at arm's distance, when one of the motion detector alarms went off near one of the high walls on the street side of the Mansion.

The Mansion was a regular target of the nearby UCLA fraternity houses, who found it common sport to breach the grounds of the Mansion. Half the time, they were drunk. The high stone walls that separated the grounds from Charring Cross Road led any would be intruders directly into a steep uphill incline, which was covered with heavy foliage rendering the grounds pitch black. Any would-be trespassers would find themselves immediately disoriented and thrashing around the underbrush. Activated motion alarms would alert security officers and the noise never made it hard for them to locate the intruders quickly. Security threatens to arrest all trespassers but the local frat boys were often times detained at the security office and released after being identified.

"Farooq," Abu commanded. "Go chase those boys off the grounds. Take this flashlight with you."

"But…"

"Go. Do what you are told instead of arguing like an insolent little woman." Farooq, mumbling under his breath and looking down at his feet, did as he was told. He approached the area he was directed to and half-heartedly shined his light into the darkness.

Yunnus Banah and Nassim al Waqqas, wearing all dark clothing, had scaled the wall right at the spot they had been directed to and travelled up the hill to an opening in the brush. They waited motionless in the shadows. Everything was as detailed in the message.

As the individual with the light clumsily approached their position, Yunnus threw a handful of stones in the other direction.

Surprised, Farooq jerked his light and turned his attention towards the sudden sound. He didn't see the red dot which had been sighted on his upper back. Suddenly, two darts penetrated his skin instantly sending 50,000 volts of electricity through his body. Farooq shook violently where he stood for five seconds, from the M-26C Taser attack before falling to the ground. When he hit the ground, the impact dislodged one of the taser darts. As the two assassins approached they initiated another five second dose of electricity. However, they did not realize one dart had been dislodged. For a taser to be successful, both darts have to penetrate the skin to establish a complete electric circuit.

Nassim approached the disabled gardener first to silence him for good. Although he had no formal training, Farooq's reaction surprised even himself. His love for mixed martial arts grappling had pre-programed a response. From the ground, the gardener explosively delivered an instep kick to Nassim's knee, causing the first assassin to bellow out in pain as he fell forward. The gardener instinctively wrapped his legs around his attacker and pulled him into his guard. Twisting to his right, Farooq reversed his position and took a mounted position over the assassin, better enabling a ground and pound counter attack.

The gardener was unaware that there were two attackers. While grappling remains an effective martial art, it has severe limitations against numerous attackers.

Yunus grabbed Farooq's hair from the scalp and yanked his head backwards violently. He then slid the edge of his steel blade across the gardener's throat. The gardener immediately fell to the ground as the second shadowy figure tended to his fallen partner. Adrenaline pumped through Farooq's body but he refused to give up. He got to his feet and escaped into the darkness holding the open wound which was pumping blood and making a pulsating sucking sound.

"Why are you punishing me so, Allah? I know I drank the prohibited alcohol, like an infidel but…" The Imam and all of them had dismissed him as one to trust at this mansion, had humiliated him and tossed him aside, even for the one whose mother was an infidel.

The gardener ran to a hidden side delivery gate near the zoo and escaped onto the street. He could hear Tony and Abu yelling and cursing him from the darkness behind him. The untrained laborer tapped into a survival instinct that he knew nothing about other than the will to live. He ran and ran until he found himself on Sunset Boulevard. Barely seeing him, a passing car squealed to a screeching stop and then ran to the dying man's aid.

Officers and detectives from the West Los Angeles Patrol Division responded to the Ronald Reagan UCLA Medical Center Emergency Room for a male with a slit throat. The emergency room doctors said that the victim sustained a knife wound to the neck area and had lost a good amount of blood. However, the wound was superficial and he was expected to survive. He was being sent to the operating room. Farooq was unable to talk but wrote the name "Detective Hudson" on a piece of paper before losing consciousness.

Steve left early to account for traffic delays on the 405 Freeway. The 405 was known for its stop and go traffic almost 24 hours a day. He wanted to stop at the Ronald Reagan UCLA Memorial

Hospital to see what the cause of his 2 a.m. phone call was. He gave himself plenty of time before picking up Omar and his partner from Los Angeles International Airport (LAX).

He met with the officers standing guard. Farooq had made it through surgery and doctors said he was able to talk, only in short spirts. The problem was that Farooq would not talk to anybody except for the detective he had requested. West LA Division was able to track down Steve's phone number through RACR Division which also served as a 24 hour departmental command post and information center.

"Jesus! What happened to you?" Steve asked. "I gotta tell you, you were the last person I expected to get a call from at two a.m." Farooq blinked his eyes open.

Criminals cooperate with law enforcement and give up information typically for only a few reasons: money, to eliminate criminal competition, to work off a criminal charge, and for revenge. Farooq had been betrayed and set up and Steve knew it. "I told you, Brother Abu, that one more time and I would end you," the gardener thought to himself out loud. Their failure to kill him would be their undoing. Farooq talked, and talked, and talked. Even when the doctor came in and told him to stop, he refused. He was on a mission fueled with anger and determination for revenge. He stopped only when Steve cut him short.

Steve hated to leave Farooq but he needed to get to LAX. He had an operation to run. He needed to pick up the Chicago detectives and get them situated. Romeo and Juliet were arriving later that afternoon and would be picked up from LAX by Mahmood and Fahim. Gonzalez and Ryan had done a great job on the Operations Plan and had every angle covered. They had arranged, with airport police, for the surveillance team to gain access behind the secure TSA lines in order to have "eyes on" Romeo and Juliet from the moment they stepped off the plane.

181

Farooq lay in the hospital bed as IV tubes pumped fluids into his arm. He was drowsy from the pain medicine but he could feel an emptiness in his stomach. A taste worse than bile crept up from his stomach. He turned his head to find something to vomit in but only dry-heaved. What had he done? Had he actually talked to the police and ratted out his Muslim brothers?

He glanced up and then quickly down. His chin sank into his chest, ashamed that Allah might look into his face.

Farooq's embarrassment slowly turned to fear when he realized how vulnerable he was in the hospital and in his helpless condition. Would they try to find him and kill him again? Did they know where he was? He had to get out of here but where would he go? He couldn't go back to the Mansion. What would he do? How could they do this to him? How could Allah let this happen to him? He drank the prohibited alcohol but didn't deserve this. He had been betrayed.

His fear gradually turned to anger. His so-called brothers at the Mosque had hardly welcomed him with open arms. No, he had done the right thing, he convinced himself. He vowed to make them pay for turning on him. They would regret not having succeeded in killing him.

Qazi summoned Fahim and Mahmood into his office after morning prayers. Abu and Tony were already there waiting.

"Tell me again, what exactly happened," Qazi demanded. It was not a question. Abu did the talking and explained the failed attempt to eliminate the ousted former student, Farooq, by Nassim and Yunnus, two of Qazi's formerly prized students.

"Did I not provide them with the best guerilla training available? How could they be so incompetent that they could not take care of a simple gardener?" Qazi asked in disgust. The other students were envious and awaited their turn to be chosen to attend this schooling in the crafts of the trade....explosives, automatic weapons, surveillance, target elimination, and on and on. Qazi was still fuming at the events of the recent days and he unwillingly let his emotion and frustration show, something he rarely allowed himself to do. Part of the imam's image was to be viewed as having super human abilities.

Qazi produced the letter which he had received in the mail. He watched each student's face as each read the script. The preacher thought he knew the author but he wanted to be sure as he studied the emotions of those in his office.

Fahim always craved for action, and Mahmood never missed an opportunity to inflict pain. Driven by an inner cruelness, they called for the heads of any blasphemous traitor. They needed to send a message to anyone who would work against them and turn on the true meaning of Islam. The Quran and Hadiths, the written collections of the revered Prophet Muhammad, were clear on what was to become of infidels and non-believers.

Fahim and Mahmood would still pick up their out of town guests as planned but their activities would change.

After their discussions, Qazi gave the letter to Tony. "Rasheed, do you think you can get rid of this for me?" Qazi asked, more of a sarcastic direction than a question. Tony accepted the letter and envelope, crumpled them up, and stuffed them in his pocket. Qazi wanted the letter and envelope disposed of off the grounds of the Islamic Center.

Qazi's intent was lost upon Tony, who placed the crumpled papers in a covered trash can in the parking lot outside of the mosque.

Steve picked up Omar and his partner, Chicago PD Detective Jeff O'Mally, from LAX. O'Mally was a seasoned veteran who had spent the majority of his career working narcotics. He was serious and had a good nature to him which he carried on a muscular frame forged from years of weight lifting. After 9/11, he had been recruited into Chicago PD's counter terrorism efforts. O'Mally was a cop's cop and the Los Angeles detective immediately took a liking to him. The three stopped for a beachside lunch on the famous Venice Beach boardwalk and then headed back downtown for introductions and to discuss some complications which had arisen.

As they pulled in, Steve saw FBI SSA Floyd pulling out of the underground parking structure. He was talking on his cell phone and didn't look happy.

It didn't turn out to be a light-hearted meeting. They all knew they had to let Chicago PD know that there was a potential breach in the case by a possible rogue agent. They didn't have any direct evidence but they all agreed it wasn't good. The FBI was pissed but they didn't say if they were pissed that one of their own was being accused, if one of their own was dirty, or if someone other than the Bureau had discovered a bad agent in their ranks. The Bureau was big on ego, image, and perception. They didn't like being shown up by anyone. Jennifer was smart to make sure the chief of police had been advised in advance.

The next issue was what to do. Romeo and Juliet were already on a plane and as such, the investigation was already in an operational stage. If there was a breach and the informants landed and turned back around, it would be seen as a confirmation that they were working with law enforcement. The FBI wanted to call the operation off but the final decision would be Chicago PD's. It was their informants and a half a dozen Chicago cases were already spinning off of the work of Romeo and Juliet. Chicago PD asked how LAPD had set up the operation. After a briefing by Ryan and Gonzalez, an impressed O'Mally gave the green light. O'Mally had a ton of experience working with informants and felt comfortable working through the operational issues.

"Keep the operation going. We all sign up for a certain degree of risk," he said to the group.

After evening prayer services, police surveillance observed that a large number of cars remained in the Islamic Center parking lot.

Inside the mosque, Qazi preached to his students who were all in attendance for their special guests who had arrived. Fatima, "Juliet," immediately fell into her expected role and remained with the other women cooking and cleaning. She was made to feel welcome. However, Khaleed, "Romeo," while greeted cordially and friendly by the other students, had expected a warmer feeling. He sensed something wasn't right.

All of the students listened intently when Qazi spoke. Qazi chose all of his words carefully as he vividly told of a dream he had not long ago in which a devout Catholic woman came to him. She was lost as she wandered through the religion she was born into and could find help in her new religion. Qazi demonstrated masterful oratory skills and his students took in every word. The next day, the woman visited him at the mosque and they engaged in a long conversation. Immediately afterwards, the woman converted. Today, the woman remains a devout Muslim who has found true meaning through Islam, the one true belief system.

After the sermon, the men all gathered in the back parking lot and got into their cars. Fahim and Mahmood directed Khaleed to the Italian convert's car. They had been warned. They had parked their cars towards the front of the Islamic Center to be easily seen from the street. Decoys to throw off any monitoring police.

After leaving the Command Post, Jennifer had gone home to get some rest. She was exhausted. She was glad she reconsidered her decision for a security detail. Her surveillance team had been reassigned because they were needed for the Romeo and Juliet operation. Instead, Jennifer had some of the elite tactical officers from Metropolitan Division provide her security around her house. Metropolitan officers were regularly assigned to provide VIP protection details and security to credible threats against officers. Jennifer could sleep well with them outside her house.

"Point on. The gathering inside appears to be breaking up. There are a lot of cars all leaving the grounds. No movement on target Vehicle 1 or 2. All units stand by for further instructions."

Neither Mahmood, Fahim, or Qazi actually saw any surveillance vehicles outside the Islamic Center as they left the grounds various vehicles owned by other students but they fully believed there were eyes out there watching them. They all sped away in a single file line from Woodland Hills Islamic Center and headed straight for the 101 Freeway northbound. They exited at Malibu Canyon Road and took the windy and dangerous two lane mountain pass highway to the ocean. The Imam and his cadre of young students had been here before so this was no surprise. They drove fast enough to be classified as extremely reckless both to scare Khaleed as well as to ensure they weren't being followed.

Khaleed was relieved when they arrived and parked on a small dark deserted road. The sign said they were entering Zuma Beach. They were alone under the midnight moon and they sat in a circle in the soft sand around Qazi, who was meditating. They were all there, Mahmood, Fahim, Abu, the Italian Convert, and several others. How did the Imam get there so quickly? They sat silent taking in the salty sea air and the sound of the waves gently rolling onto shore, unitl Qazi ended his meditation.

Khaleed had received good training from Omar and others

within the Chicago Police Department, including mind control techniques common in cults, street and prison gangs, organized crime. They also studied how pimps and traffickers control girls and force them into prostitution. The leader seeks to control an individual's behavior, intellect, thoughts, and emotions. Mind control seeks to create an obedient servant whose goal it is to please the controller or leader.

Khaleed quickly noticed how Qazi had created a cult-like atmosphere with his followers. There were many rules the imam had put in place, such as limiting those the students could associate with outside of the mosque, diets, controlling and enforcing strict grooming regulations which were consistent with fundamental Islamic traditions. One being each member to don a long beard with a shaved upper lip area. Dress code included white traditional Pakastani and Afghani outerwear and turbans. The turbans were black and one of the younger students had earlier bragged to Khaleed how the style of turban was the same worn by the Taliban. Qazi's students wore them proudly to pay homage to the Taliban soldiers overseas and to be recognized by others in the mosque as one of Qazi's specially chosen students.

Qazi disseminated a good level of propaganda and discouraged any competing viewpoints or other sources of information. Names were changed, and an "us versus them" mentality was apparent in this group. Khaleed immediately recognized this group as being manipulated and controlled by Qazi. He was clearly charismatic and they were all completely brainwashed by his sermons. This group was becoming quite dangerous and the detectives would need as much detail as possible about each of the individuals present tonight.

Qazi began speaking and told of how important it was to remain in good physical condition. Gracefully, Qazi stood, his white robes flowing in the ocean breeze and glittering in the moonlight.

Suddenly, the Imam pulled up his robes and started running

through the soft sand, running faster and faster. His students were panting as they followed him.

The Imam continued his sprint, never slowing or taking a break. When he finally stopped far down the beach, he stood there with a benevolent smile, neither sweating nor gasping for breath, although his students were. The winded students collapsed at Qazi's feet. They could only stare at the Imam in amazement. They believed the preacher who claimed to speak to others in his dreams, he who communicated directly with the prophet, he who had supernatural powers. They believed in the mystique and greatness of the man, or was he more than just a man?

"No change on point." The surveillance detail was so focused on Fahim's and Mahmood's cars that they did not notice as the entire group quickly left in different vehicles and caravanned away from the Islamic Center. Unknowingly to the surveillance detectives, the targets has slipped the surveillance and the police had no idea where their informant was.

The information SSA Floyd received from LAPD turned a counter terrorism investigation into a counter terrorism, espionage, and treason investigation, with one of his own agents as the prime suspect. Floyd knew that as Dan's supervisor, this could kill his career and reputation. Floyd wasn't too concerned about climbing up the FBI bureaucracy but he was a good agent and expected a respectable career path and the admiration of his peers. He could not overlook the threat to public safety being caused by *his* rogue agent. It would have been better if the Bureau had discovered the compromised agent rather than another agency, and a local one at that. He would have to answer for a good portion of this mess but he would have to deal with that at a later time.

Right now he had to do the right thing and the right thing at this point was to bring in the FBI's Counter Intelligence (CI) Section. It was late by the time the meeting finished and exhaustion was setting in. Floyd had an emptiness inside. He took Dan's betrayal very personally. He hadn't eaten all day, nor was he hungry. He felt like he was punched in the gut ...*hard!* CI would start immediately. National Security Letters and all the powers granted by the Patriot Act would be put into motion. The agents of counter intelligence would start tracking all of Dan's phones, financial transactions, personal and work emails, and run internal checks of every keyboard stroke Dan made on any Bureau computers. They wouldn't leave any stone unturned.

The Bureau didn't look favorably on corrupt G-Men. In fact, their reputation was that no FBI man could be corrupted. Some agents actually believed this despite the infamous scandals involving disgraced dirty agents such as Robert Hanson, the agent who had leaked secrets to the Soviet Union, and John Connolly, the compromised agent who for years protected Boston's Irish mob leader Whitey Bulger.

The word "dislike" has many cousins, all of them far more rabid than the first. There's hate, which means to feel intense, passionate dislike for someone. Despise is perhaps a second cousin, to feel contempt or a deep repugnance for. Detest is right there in the family and it suggests looking down with great contempt and regarding the person as mean, petty, weak or worthless. Loathe is a cousin and means to feel utter disgust toward someone.

As he stood in his usual pose of benign, Allah-sanctioned serenity, Qazi was about to run the gamut of dislike's cousins as he addressed his students.

"To be disloyal to Islam is among the worst crime and deserving of the most severe, cruel, and hateful of punishments."

Khaleed's heart skipped several beats. His face went pale. He started breathing heavy and shallow breaths, and he felt a bead of sweat forming on his brow. He felt like his chest was about to collapse. "Get a hold of yourself," he told himself. He started taking forced deep long controlled breaths to regain his composure. No one noticed, except for Fahim and Mahmood who had been watching his every move.

It was getting late and after cleaning and then waiting around gossiping, the ladies at the Woodland Hills Islamic Center needed to get home. They felt it bad hospitality to leave their guest alone, even at her hotel room, so Fatima was invited to go and stay with one of the other women for the night. They promised that they would all go to the market in the morning and then drive her over to her husband at the hotel. The ladies chattered and gossiped about Mahmood and why the man's wife had disappeared. That information was not supposed to have been known but the women watched, listened, and gossiped, and like women everywhere, they often knew plenty about the happenings of their men. Besides, Mahmood was a cruel, mean, and ugly man. Fatima was warned to stay clear from him.

The team of detectives were gathered at the Command Post. Jennifer Wade had stopped by earlier to check in but then left the operation to the detectives. They knew what they were doing.

It was quiet. The tension inside was building in leaps and bounds. There was still no word from the surveillance team or from Khaleed.

"He should have called by now," Hudson said to no one in particular.

"I told him to call and check in every two hours…no more than every three hours," O'Mally replied. Everyone already knew this.

Omar wasn't saying anything. He was visibly nervous and alternated between sitting tapping his feet and pacing back and forth in the command post.

"We have to stay calm," JC responded. JC was starting to get worried but he couldn't let people panic and make rash and bad decisions. JC nervously thought to himself, "What if the Bureau was right? Did they have additional information they weren't telling us? No. SSA Floyd was shocked at the findings. He didn't think Floyd knew much of anything. On the other hand, Floyd didn't call with any updates on his end. What if Dan knew more than they did? Could Romeo and Juliet be endangered?" They had run through this earlier but decided that it was a small chance. They took a calculated risk. Was it the right one?

Khaleed was relieved to be leaving the beach. He had an uneasy feeling as he entered the front seat of the Italian convert's car. Mahmood and Fahim sat in the back and the Italian drove off like a bat out of hell through the windy mountain pass back to the San Fernando Valley. The Italian turned off the headlights as he took a sharp turn way too fast for Khaleed's liking. After coming out of the turn, the Italian suddenly slammed on his brakes causing the car to skid and slide to a stop. Khaleed was holding the door with clenched fists and his face had turned white. The smell of burning rubber engulfed the car. Mahmood, Fahim, and the Italian burst into laughter as if they were seventeen years old, immature, teenage boys joyriding in one of their father's sports car. Khaleed let out a long breath, relieved to be alive.

"I have to take a leak," the Italian stated crudely as he exited the car.

"Allah may have saved you by converting you to the true way, but you remain as crude as a barnyard goat," Fahim lashed out.

Khaleed was just starting to relax from the car ride when he suddenly felt Mahmood's breath on the back of his neck. Before he could react, Khaleed, who had survived the mean streets of Karachi, felt a thin wire with knots in it wrap tightly around his neck. Pain stabbed at every part of Khaleed's body.

"Fuck you and die you apostate traitor," Mahmood whispered into his ear with a wicked smile. He was enjoying every moment of this. "You should have kept your mouth shut. This is what happens to those who betray Islam." Mahmood continued to twist the wire until is was buried deep into Khaleed's neck.

Khaleed wiggled and squealed as he groveled for every diminishing breath. In the four minutes it took him to die, Khaleed heard what the three men had planned for his wife. He died scared for her life.

"Get him out of here," as Mahmood directed Fahim and Tony to remove the spy's body from the front seat. They dragged him out as a small but steady stream of blood started draining from the traitor's neck and onto his own clothing.

"Don't leave any evidence in my car," Tony pleaded. He was thankful the blood seemed contained, as to not link his car to a murder. They dragged Khaleed's lifeless body to the side of the road and pushed him over the cliff. It was at least a one hundred and fifty foot drop of treacherous terrain. The mountain lions, coyotes, or other wild creatures would surely find him and feast on his body. It was unlikely he would be found anytime soon by anyone else.

The radio crackled.

"Ok, we have movement. Looks like our caravan is returning." The surveillance detectives watched as the cars sped back into the parking lot. They couldn't make out individuals but they could see people shuffling about in the back parking lot, before slowly returning to the other cars and leaving on their own. Everyone on this detail knew they had been burned. No matter how good you were, undercover operations were always dicey and there was always a chance of getting burned or losing a surveillance target. They all knew they should have split the team in two, and that their mistake may be very costly.

Could have, should have, would have.

Fahim and Mahmood went into the Islamic Center to find Fatima only to find that the lights were all off and the place deserted. Mahmood started to seeth. He raced back out to Tony's car, Fahim following closely behind.

"We have to find that worthless bitch!"

"Calm down," Fahim said. "We know where she went." Since, Mahmood's wife hadn't returned, Qazi did not want their guests to stay with Mahmood. Finances were never an issue for the Islamic Center so Qazi had insisted on renting them a hotel room nearby. Qazi had paid for everything beforehand and had sent Fahim to register ahead of time. More importantly, Fahim was to obtain extra electronic keys, one of which Fahim was to keep for himself.

"To the hotel room?" Tony asked, already knowing the answer.

"Yes," Mahmood stated calming down.

Fahim was smarter than Mahmood. Mahmood's anger and temper had regularly gotten the better of him causing ill-fated actions. Fahim wondered why Qazi kept him so close to him and internally questioned the imam's wisdom on this choice. While Fahim pushed for action from the group, he didn't encourage blind action. He wanted an organized plan.

Five minutes later, they arrived at the hotel. Fahim had Tony pass the hotel and make a quick right turn. Concerned about the possibility of a police surveillance they couldn't see but were afraid could be nearby, Fahim directed Tony into and around a closed McDonalds. The parking lot was dark.

"Make sure you aren't being followed. Wait for our call." While Tony Marino, aka Rasheed Shari, the Italian convert, had gained their trust, he still hadn't gained their respect. Only time and actions would cure that.

Fahim and Mahmood jumped out of the car and slipped into the darkness towards the back of the hotel. Fahim's heart was racing. He had never killed anyone before and in one night he would be responsible for two murders. He felt like he was in a dream as he moved towards the room he had rented earlier. Everything was in slow motion and hazy. He bit onto his lip to make sure this was all real. He watched Mahmood, who was emotionless and acted without any regard for human life.

It was as Qazi had said, "...infidels are less than cows. They should be sent to the slaughter." Mahmood embodied this emotion. Maybe this was why Qazi kept Mahmood as a member of his inner circle and trusted confidant.

Now, Fahim wanted to prove himself. He wanted to be the one to dispatch this wretched whore to an eternity in hell. However, he was still apprehensive. It was one thing to take part in a killing but another all together to do the killing with his own hands. It required a new mental state and Fahim had doubts whether he could actually carry it out. Another reason to carry this murder out now was because it was a woman. An easier target. Less likely to fight. Easier to control. Plus, Mahmood would be his back up. If he failed, Mahmood would have no problem taking care of his shortcomings.

Fahim slid the electronic card into the hotel door. The light turned green with the quiet clicking sound of the releasing lock. He carefully and slowly creaked the door open. The room was dark.

"Better if the whore was asleep," he thought as he entered into the room with Mahmood almost on top of him. They crept into the room. Stillness. The room was empty. She wasn't there.

Mahmood's instant tempter took over, again. "Where the fuck is she?" he cursed. "Where could she have possibly gone?"

"She went with one of the other women," Fahim responded. "It is the only place she could have gone." Fahim was relieved but disappointed at the same time. He had wanted to test himself just like he wanted to test his abilities against Jennifer. Now, once again, his test would have to wait.

"Which one of those bitches took her?"

"I don't know. But let's get out of here before we're seen."

The detective in the Command Post knew something was wrong. They had lost contact with Romeo and Juliet and had no idea what was happening. Neither of them had called. It was time to start making contingency plans. "OK, we need to acknowledge that the surveillance team has been burned," Omar finally stated. "We need to find them and take them out of pocket." Being "in pocket" was a police term used when an undercover or informant was in with the bad guys. Omar was afraid for his CI's safety. He was responsible for them and wanted them out at all costs.

"I agree," said O'Mally. "Something is not right. We need to plan our next move." Everyone in the room nodded in agreement. "What are our options?"

The laws varied from state to state on what actions law enforcement could take and what the required procedures were that they needed to follow. California varied from Illinois law and procedure.

"Romeo and Juliet both have cell phones, right?" JC asked.

Omar nodded.

"Give me the numbers," Steve stated. He was already on it.

He knew what JC was thinking. As Omar read off the numbers, Steve ran them through the web site Fone Finder. The prefix would tell him who the phone provider was. Some phone companies were friendlier than others when dealing with law enforcement. Some would require a court order while others wouldn't. A law enforcement emergency was not necessarily a phone company emergency. Especially since the phone companies' law enforcement contact dealt with police across the country and manned their support desk, with minimal staffing during off hours.

"It will take a couple of hours at least," JC explained to the Chicago detectives. "We'll need to write it up and email it to the District Attorney Command Post. After the on-call District Attorney reviews the court order, he will wake up the on-call judge. The warrant will be faxed to the judge who will read the warrant. After he reads it, he will call the DA back. From a three way call, Steve will swear in and the warrant will be signed and sent back. Once we get the signed warrant, we send it to the phone company. Once they get the warrant, they will start "pinging" the numbers. Depending on the company, pinging in the San Fernando Valley has a margin of error ranging from two feet to two square miles."

Pinging a phone is a law enforcement technique to find the location of a cell phone. It relies on the signals a cell phone sends to the cell phone transmission towers. As the signal bounces off the towers, it can be triangulated to locate the area where a phone is. Depending on the company, sometimes the phone location can be pinpointed exactly. It requires that the phone be powered on to receive a signal. From past experience, results of this technique in the San Fernando Valley varied. It was their best option at this point.

"Hopefully, they'll come back on our radar before-hand, but we need to start this process now."

"God damn it," O'Mally stated, exhausted and frustrated. The two detectives had been up for over twenty four hours and it was looking like they wouldn't be getting any sleep anytime soon.

"Why don't you guys try to get some shut eye," JC said, recognizing their exhaustion. "This is all procedural right now and there is nothing you can do. I'll let you know when something develops."

JC was doing his best to remain optimistic but everyone had an empty feeling in his or her guts. They all wanted to know what went wrong with the surveillance team but knew that there were more important issues at hand. There would be plenty of time later to critique what went wrong.

After leaving the Islamic Center, Fahim didn't want to go home. He was hungry for a kill and blinded by his burning desire to continue the hunt. He needed a target of substance. "Aaahh… that whore Captain, Jennifer Wade!" he exclaimed out loud to himself. He would try her again. First, he would extract as much information from the blonde-haired infidel whore. The taser in his pocket would assure him of this. When he was done with her, he would be sure to take with him any of her equipment from which he could benefit. He made a mental list: her police radio, uniforms, badges, handcuffs, cell phone, and of course….her gun.

"We have one birdy away from the nest," the surveillance detective broadcast into the radio. The team knew they couldn't afford to make any more mistakes.

The Team Leader spoke, "Listen up. We're splitting up. First half on the mover, second half stand by for the remaining birdy. I want intel on both targets. Don't screw this up."

They were on the move. The detectives had good information

on both Fahim and Mahmood. It was late and they expected Fahim to go home.

"I don't know where he's going but we are entering the 405 southbound transition. I got him. Ok, target is away southbound and transitioning to the number one lane," said Team One.

"We are with you. You have plenty of help behind you," responded the number two surveillance car, letting the lead know he could leave point whenever he was ready.

"Hello," the still half asleep voice answered.

"Sorry to bother you, Captain, but we are on Fahim. He is moving and we just got off the 405 freeway and are heading to your neck of the woods. Wanted to give you a heads up," the voice reported.

Jennifer sprang up out of her bed reaching over her gun, which was loaded and on her nightstand, by her cell phone.

"Better let Metro know we are going to have some company," she said out loud. The sound of her voice gave her confidence in her otherwise quiet and lonely house. She was thankful she hadn't had anything to drink before going to bed, as she quickly got dressed. She double checked all the doors and windows in the house, turned out the lights, and then sat down in her living room and waited. Jennifer never felt so lonely.

The next call from the surveillance team on Fahim was to the Command Post where JC and Steve were finishing up with the court order process.

"Ok, we have both Fahim and Mahmood away from the Islamic Center. They left alone. We never saw Romeo or Juliet leave the location. Not to say they haven't left in another car."

"Thanks. Do you guys have anything else?"

"Ya, Fahim is on the move but he's not going home. Looks like he's going to Captain Wade's…"

"What!" JC demanded.

"Ya. Metro is pulling security there. They have been advised. Your second guy, Mahmood, is on the go. It appears, he is not going home either. Team Two is following him. He's been to a bunch of houses and apartments we've never seen before. He approaches and within five minutes he leaves."

"Are you guys keeping logs with addresses, including apartment numbers?"

"Ya, we are recording everything for you guys."

The kind lady who had opened up her apartment to Fatima had gone to the back bedroom. She had made a bed for Fatima on the sofa. However, Fatima was worried sick about Khaleed. He was far overdue in contacting her. She had no way of contacting Omar either. For security reasons, they had decided between themselves that only Khaleed would carry Omar's phone number. They knew Omar would be upset, but they decided the decision was theirs because they were the ones taking all the risks.

Fatima couldn't sleep and she sat on the edge of a straight back chair. Her fears seemed to grow in her anxious mind. When she heard a car screeching into the parking lot, flashes came of her days back in Afghanistan. Her mind gave way to the first time she saw the list of new prohibitions imposed by the newly-powerful Taliban. She had a flashback of the poor girl whose finger was cut off for painting her nails, not to mention her own trauma.

A pounding on the door drew Fatima's body up tight. She felt she dared not breathe.

Again, another pounding. Suppressed memories and fears burned through her mind of that dreadful night long ago when the Taliban broke into her home, raping her and killing her brother.

Her host came running in. She was careful not to make any noise. "Sshh. Don't make a sound."

"Fatima! Open this door. I know you are in there. I want to take you to your husband."

Her host knew it was Mahmood. He had no business coming here unannounced. It was bad manners. Furthermore, Mahmood knew her husband was away this week. Nothing good could come from his unannounced visit. She would not open the door.

At that instant, Fatima had no doubt that Khaleed was dead. She was alone and in peril for her life. She was so terrified, she could not think clearly. She knew she had to get away.

Suddenly, the pounding stopped. After hearing Mahmood climb into his car and drive away, Fatima sobbed uncontrollably into the darkness.

Fahim was heated with rising excitement as he made his way around to the front of the house. Delights for what he would do to the infidel whore. He stopped to savor every picture in his mind. He was moving toward the front door when a set of headlights startled him. He propelled himself back into the cover of shrubbery. Silent curses filled his mind. A uniformed officer was standing outside of a dark blue Ford Crown Victoria with tinted windows. It was clearly an unmarked police car complete with side alley lights. Due to the dark windows, Fahim couldn't tell if there was another officer inside the car. If there was, he was probably sleeping he thought to himself. Police officers were fat, undisciplined, and lazy. His dislike for police clearly leading his thoughts.

"Why would there be a uniformed officer? Surely, Jennifer didn't know that he posed a threat to her. It must be something else, but what?"

More curses. He had to get his hands on the whore and soon. Fahim melted into the shadows and watched silently. The cop seemed in good shape, wiry, muscular. He looked like he could handle himself in a fight, for certain. And, he was armed. Other cops might be right behind him. But he, Fahim, had the advantage of surprise. Surely, he could strike from the back and overwhelm the infidel bastard. Except...

"AAAHHH..." the officer screamed out as the electric current hit jolted through his body. He spammed backward only seeing a dark figure in the shadows holding a taser.

Jennifer was going for her weapon when the figure stumbled back and started running. Jennifer looked down at the officer who motioned for her to pursue the attacker.

Fahim ran to the shadows. He was fast. So was Jennifer. His legs were longer, his lungs obviously younger.

Jennifer called one time for him to halt and, when he didn't, she fired. He disappeared and she didn't know if she hit him. But she found no blood. She bent down, caught her breath, then jogged back to the detective. She had no doubt about who the attacker had been.

"I knew it!" Mahmood exclaimed to himself. He had returned to the woman's apartment and waited for what was left of the night at the far end of the parking lot. Now the woman and Fatima were leaving, driving away somewhere. "You won't get away from me this time..."

As he followed them out of the parking lot, he was still unaware that he wasn't the only one following someone this morning.

Fatima was terrified and exhausted. She had cried all night, knowing in her gut that she would never see her husband again. Since that night in Kabul when the Taliban burst into her house, her relationship with Allah and his prophet had been tenuous. But she had still considered herself a devout person, even if making unforgiveable mistakes in his eyes. She had longed for that softer, more loving Allah she remembered from childhood.

Now it was done. What would she do with what was left of, she knew, the short time she had left to live?

The woman who had been so kind knew that she was upset but had no way of knowing the extent of what was happening.

"Please go with me to the farmer's market?" she asked Fatima. "I need some fresh foods. Afterwards, I'll drive you back to your hotel and to your husband. If the men were out late, it may be best to let him sleep in, anyways. You both must be tired from the long trip."

She went on describing how the Warner Center Park in the middle of Woodland Hills was now hosting a weekly open air farmer's market. Many merchants from the Indian sub-continent who had been quietly moving into the San Fernando Valley sold their goods from many of the booths there. She could get fresh fruits and vegetables and spices such as cardamom, saffron, and turmeric.

Fatima nodded in agreement, knowing that it was too dangerous to return to the hotel, but not knowing where she would go from there. She was too tired to even form words. She was safe for the moment but she would not be able to stay with this kind woman much longer. She was exhausted and devastated but desperately needed to think clearly. Fatima knew nothing of the Afghani and Pakistani communities in Los Angeles.

The ladies arrived at the market before the busy morning rush. Fatima was cowering under the full veil that covered her and was supposed to give her anonymity. She didn't feel anonymous and felt that everyone was glancing at her.

Each breath brought the smells of Kabul's markets, smells that brought nostalgia and a vivid reminder of the dinner she was cooking that night when the Taliban had knocked down the front door. The Taliban had killed her entire family in Afghanistan, had killed her soul, and now, she was certain, the Taliban had killed her husband. Her fear of falling into the hands of the Taliban was more than she could handle. She knew if they found her, she would die soon after, but maybe it was time.

Fatima glanced around the market when she also realized that a man was staring at her. His face seemed a mask, hiding—not very effectively—a hard heart and black soul. A chill tormented her.

She hadn't survived this long without developing sharp street smarts and every instinct she possessed shouted at her to flee the market.

Moving faster than she ever had, Fatima made her way through the people crowding stands and stalls. She knew, without glancing back, that she was being followed.

Fatima had already started to develop the heavy feeling that her life was over, that she was a fleeing corpse. After her family's murder, her rape, her husband's murder, what did life hold for her?

She only hoped that she could get away. She didn't know where to go. She was lost, afraid, and alone.

Once outside the market, she dared a glance over her shoulder. "Allah, save me." She saw the heavy set man with the dark soul face who was pursuing her.

And he was gaining on her with each step…

When her pursuer was only a few steps behind, Fatima turned into a large store and found the sign for women's rest room. The man could almost reach out and touch her as she pushed open the door.

Such a man might follow her, even into such a place. But he didn't follow. This was a momentary relief. There was no other exit. How long could she stay in this place?

Fatima locked herself into a stall and dove face first into the toilet bowl, throwing up. She needed to gain a hold of herself and think quickly if she wanted to get out of this alive.

Mahmood glanced at his watch again. What was the whore up to? Streams of infidel women had come and gone from the toilet but no woman in Muslim attire.

One slowly materialized…but she was short and fat.

Mahmood stopped her and obviously frightened her. He thrust a twenty dollar bill into her hand as he instructed her what to do, implying that she was in no way to be hurt or humiliated—unless she failed to do what he demanded.

The woman demurred at first, glanced around fitfully. She gripped the bill tightly and walked into the toilet. She returned to Mahmood a couple of minutes later and handed him Fatima's *jibaab*.

The woman hurried off as a bitterly angry Mahmood slammed the garment to the floor. The whore had come out of the toilet in infidel dress. She had outwitted him. Him, Mahmood.

"Hey, you can't throw that thing on the floor. You have to pick it up."

Mahmood whirled on the slack-jawed, balding store security guard in his shiny blue uniform. It took the last ounce of his self-control to stop himself from planting his fist in the man's face.

He pivoted and walked away. The store cop said nothing, just picked up the garment and threw it into a garbage can.

"There she is. We got her northbound Topanga Canyon on

foot from the Macy's heading towards Erwin Street, east side of the street."

"Is she alone?" the male voice asked.

"Yes, it appears that way."

"OK. I want her taken out NOW!"

"Get her before she gets to the Citi Bank. We don't need any armed bank security guards playing hero."

Fatima nervously walked across the street. She felt like she was in a haze. It was like she was in a dream, a bad dream. She had no idea where she was or where she was going. Then she realized it was the first time in her life she wore Western clothes out in public. She felt naked and exposed, an abomination in the eyes of Allah. She was an emotional and physical wreck.

As she crossed the street, a dark colored minivan with tinted windows suddenly came to a screeching and skidding stop. Her heart almost stopped. She was paralyzed in fear when the side door violently slid open.

"FATIMA!" Omar called out reaching to her from inside of the van.

From behind the van, two scruffy men jumped out of a dark Ford Expedition, also with tinted windows. To the sudden surprise of other motorists stopped at the intersection, one with a drawn handgun and the other armed with a short barreled tactical shotgun.

Despite the early Saturday morning rising temperatures, they were wearing blue jeans and blue nylon jackets stenciled in large white print were the words POLICE. The men all had overgrown beards or mustaches and long hair. The body armor they wore underneath their raid jackets gave the already muscular and serious looking men an even more imposing presence. They looked like they meant business as they scanned and covered the immediate area from behind dark sunglasses while Fatima was whisked into the van.

It was like clockwork. The whole procedure, in an out, took less than forty seconds. The extraction of Juliet was complete. The ping on Fatima's cell phone coupled with surveillance on Mahmood had paid off. Now they needed to find Romeo.

The two business partners were sharing some tea in the hookah lounge, which they owned.

"How are your other business ventures?" the younger man asked. Dawud knew that his business partner had his hand in a number of enterprises. He was also a major shareholder in some related incorporations which were permitted to run several adult gentlemen's clubs in Orange County. How better to demoralize their enemies than to do so in their own backyard and through the abuse of their children, especially their daughters. It was a tactic as old as war itself. The man enjoyed the cruelty of providing the stage for the daughters of the infidels to parade their sinful and unrepentant morals. These women represented the decaying societal values of the West, and would bring Allah's wrath and the return of the Age of Islam to the world. It was orchestrated by these businessmen and others around the country just like them. Even better if the whores became addicted to the drugs which were brought in and distributed through these clubs. To these men, it was justified in the name of their religion.

Down to business. "Thank you for those names," the FBI agent said politely.

"Were you able to find anything?" Ziya asked.

"I looked into it but didn't' find much. Travel records from Immigration and Customs show only the two going to Pakistan."

"But they were questioned by customs," protested the more cautious elder.

"The only thing in the system reveals a secondary screening from customs agents. Nothing was uncovered which would have triggered any additional investigation. They have nothing to worry about."

"Maybe not from their travels but they have plenty to worry about now."

"What do you mean?" Dawud asked.

Ziya Golkap explained the failed murder attempt of Farooq to the special agent. He was hoping the federal law enforcement officer would be able to learn if Farooq had talked to the police. If so, perhaps there was a way to somehow interfere with the investigation. They had spent a lot of money and resources on these two muslims. Plus, they had a lot of information and Ziya, always the worrier, did not want to run the risk of exposing either of them to intensive police interrogations.

"I'll look into it and see what I can find out," Dawud concluded.

"One more thing," Ziya, the accountant, continued. "What do you know about any drug investigations?"

"The Drug Enforcement Agency, DEA, handles most major narcotics investigations. Why?"

"Can you run this address through your systems to see if there are any current investigations?"

"Yes, but why?" Dawud questioned.

"It's better that you don't know all the details just yet."

"I'll see what I can do," he agreed. A variety of businesses, strip clubs, attempted murders, and now narcotics, Dawud thought to himself. Maybe the accountant wasn't as cautious as he had originally thought. And, maybe he wasn't as smart as everyone had given him credit for.

They parted ways knowing that it was safer for them to meet at the hookah lounge they shared rather than with Qazi or even on the grounds of the Islamic Center.

The aroma of hash browns coupled with an array of breakfast sandwiches filled the room. Three large McDonald's bags sat in the middle of the conference room table. A large box contained fresh coffee and handfuls of creamers, sugar and sweetener packets, napkins, and plastic stir sticks were piled loosely onto the table. The detectives needed food and coffee. They had been up all night and weren't going home anytime soon.

Fatima had been successfully extracted from the operation.

"This is still a rescue operation," JC said out loud.

Nods around the room. It needed to be said but everyone knew that it would end up being a recovery mission. Rescue implied that Romeo was still alive. Recovery was for dead bodies. Recovery meant forensics and prosecution for a murder charge. Recovery was dealing with a family's grief for their lost one. "Rescue" gave hope and encouraged a positive sense of urgency. JC was right to state it this way. JC was as tired and worried as everyone else. Still, he managed to set the tone for staying inspired and focused. Even the Chicago detectives picked up on it…. true leadership.

They needed to know exactly what Fatima knew so they could try to find Khaleed.

"All the men left late in the evening." They had concluded correctly, surveillance had been slipped. Fatima gave as much detail as she could but she had learned little. Fatima described Mahmood and included the gossip from the women. She recalled the previous night's events and how Mahmood had chased her from the Farmer's

Market. How she had hid in the bathroom and escaped before they had found her.

"I want to get her out of town," Omar stated. "She is still in danger as long as she stays in Los Angeles. Plus, we need to front load our Chicago investigations and do damage control. People are going to start talking."

O'Mally nodded in agreement. "I'll stay here until we get Romeo."

There were no objections form LAPD. FBI didn't have a seat at the table.

"We don't know the extent of this network," JC added. "They slipped our surveillance easily enough and now we have a missing CI. Unfortunately, they are more sophisticated than we originally thought."

"Do you think they have people at LAX?" Omar asked.

"I don't think so but we can't be sure. I just don't know and it is possible," JC responded. "It's better to be safe than sorry. I think we need to get both of you out from either Long Beach airport or Burbank airport."

"I'm pulling flights up now from both airports," Steve replied as he manipulated his laptop.

"...Morning," Jennifer said as she entered the room. There was nothing "good" about what was happening. Her unit was on the defensive and police preferred to be on the offensive, causing reactions not the other way around.

The captain was briefed on the action plans. She had no objections.

"Got one," Steve said. "Flies out of Burbank in three hours. Better to get them out ASAP before Qazi or Mahmood realize we have her back."

"I have a contact at Airport Police," Ryan who had been sitting quietly, stated. "I'll give him a call and get VIP boarding. I'll have him get a passenger list also with some runs on the names."

"Might be nice to see if there are any Air Marshalls on board also," added Gonzalez. "Extra security would be comforting. I'll make a couple of calls."

Steve's phone silently vibrated. It was Rachel, again. She had called a few days ago and he didn't have the chance to get back to her. He was going to have some explaining to do. Rachel wouldn't put up with any bullshit from anyone and he really did want to see her again. He sent her a quick text message.

Hi! Still at work...in a mtg....u free for breakfast in the morning....

Her response was almost immediate,

First, I'm not free. Second, what makes you think I'm spending the night with you to even eat breakfast?

Steve smiled at her play on words. She was a spitfire and he loved it.

I'll pick you up at 9am....

Don't be late, was the response. For the first time in two days, Steve smiled as he re-entered the discussions...

JC was talking, "This is what we know... the last ping was off Malibu Canyon." A lost cell ping could mean a number of things: dead battery, disabled phone, or the phone simply powered down.

"Phone reception is at best, weak and sporadic, through any of the mountain passes," Ryan said.

"That is the Sheriff's Lost Hills Station area," Gonzalez added.

"I'll give them a call," said Jennifer. "Maybe we can get some air support fly overs and observations. I think we need a patrol unit out to the location of the last ping. Also, find out if they had any unusual calls in the area last night. It's not much but at least it is a starting point. Plus, they have some really good search and rescue teams who know those mountains and canyons better than anyone."

Ryan added, "Let's see if we can get some plain clothes officers from the Valley to set up on Romeo and Juliet's hotel room just in case Romeo returns or someone pays a visit."

"Great idea, Ryan," JC added. "OK, let's break, make it happen. We'll meet back here in an hour."

Heavy traffic is routine in Los Angeles. Congestion on the 101 Freeway South towards Los Angeles was snarled bumper to bumper.

Mahmood crawled along slowly, heading towards the Sepulveda Pass. The quickly rising Valley summer temperatures did not help his foul mood. He burned up inside and out. How could the bitch get away from him, "Mike the Terrorist?" What kind of man allows two different women to escape from him? He knew he failed Allah. He wanted to start over.

The nearby hills south of Ventura Boulevard were dried up and brown. A summer heat wave was coming and would consume the Valley areas with well over triple digit numbers for the next week. Mahmood fled he was being equally consumed by guilt.

Suddenly, Mahmood started to smile. It was a twisting and churning smile which turned into wicked laughter the sight of which would have been a fright to behold.

It only took a couple of hours before they received the first call at the Command Post. Omar and Juliet were already on their way to the Burbank Airport for their flight back to Chicago.

"Detective Carter, this is Sergeant Hicks over at the Los Angeles

County Sheriff's Department, Lost Hills Station. I'm the Watch Sergeant today."

"Thanks for getting back to us so quickly. Do you have any news?"

"Actually, ya. One of our LASD Air Units observed a body in a ravine about 150 feet down from Malibu Canyon Road. It is too soon to make any positive identity but I was asked to contact you."

"Ok, thanks for the call. Do you have your homicide people rolling out yet?"

"We have our Search and Rescue Team on their way. It's too soon to tell if there is any foul play. It's probably a hiker who fell for all we know."

"No. This is going to be a homicide. You should probably make the notification so they don't lose any daylight. Let Search and Rescue know they will be entering a crime scene. Any video or photos they can take in the ravine will be helpful."

"Will you guys be heading out there?"

"Yes, we will have a team on the way from the Valley."

"Ok, but this is an LASD murder case."

"Of course. This will be your murder investigation. We are not trying to interfere but the victim is going to be an LAPD and Chicago PD Confidential Informant. He went missing late last night, after getting by one of our surveillance teams. Let your detectives know we will talk to them out at the scene. Thanks for the call," JC didn't wait for a response. He felt he didn't need to add, he died after the surveillance team lost him.

JC turned to everyone at the Command Post. Their eyes were already locked on him. They had heard him take the phone call.

"Bad news guys..."

Jennifer reached home and sat in her car a minute, trying to clear her head of the clutter and clatter of this work-day Saturday. It had been a long sleepless night and day.

LASD Homicide was already at the scene and the body was quickly positively identified by Detective O'Mally as Romeo's late in the day.

The scene was horrific. After making her way through the tangle of deputies, detectives, and crime scene technicians, she saw the body. She had to immediately look away to keep herself from vomiting.

Romeo lie there face up, wire twisted and embedded deep in the neck, which had been nearly snapped off. The face was a rictus of suffering, tongue hanging out. A strong, nauseating stench almost turned Jennifer away again as she remembered the conversation with the deputy...

"What in Christ happened here?"

"Been garroted, Captain. Never seen anything like it. Who kills by garroting? That just doesn't happen around here."

She wondered what kind of world it would be if the Islamists had their way.

"Hey Captain, are you OK in there?" the Metro Officer asked. After last night, the Metro security detail would be increased. Although it was unlikely that Fahim would return again, she welcomed the extra protection.

Jennifer planned on a good night's sleep with the help of a few strong drinks. She had insisted on everyone taking Sunday off. She told everyone to press their "reset" buttons and get some rest. They would need to be clear thinking come Monday morning. Plus, she had started to feel alienated from her unit. She needed to figure out how to fix that. If the head of the Anti-Terrorism Division was being talked about by her own people, it certainly wouldn't add to the unit's credibility or her career.

Tony strolled around the grounds of the Playboy Mansion, his leisurely, slouching walk a stark contrast with his writhing insides. It was an uneventful Saturday night at the Mansion. He walked the path from Hugh's game room and movie theater, passed the zoo and around the yard towards the pool and famous grotto. There were a few barely dressed, young women lounging around. Tony enjoyed the quietness of the grounds. It was a stark contrast to the party which was planned for the next weekend. He stopped at the security guard house at the top of the driveway where Abu was speaking to some uniformed officers from West LA Division.

"Hello Officers," Tony, aka Rasheed, greeted.

"Hey, what's up?" one of them asked. "Big party next weekend," he continued. No doubt looking forward to the few hundred dollars in extra income he would earn from the event. The officers worked off duty security during some of the big planned events and parties.

LAPD officers were required to obtain a work permit for all off-duty work. Working at the Playboy Mansion was prohibited because it was considered a conflict of interest due to the questionable sexual conduct and rumors of rampant drug use associated with the location. The policy violation could very well cost them their jobs but they didn't seem to care much about what they considered petty Department rules and regulations. They seemed to like the mystique of working at the Mansion. Of course, it made them susceptible to corruption and manipulation.

"Hey, I have a question for you," Rasheed asked.

"Go ahead, shoot." Rasheed noted the play on words.

"What is that big number "8" on the back of your black and white?" Tony asked.

"That is the number of our Division. West LA was the eighth police division created so the number designation is '8.' It also preempts our radio call sign. For example, our unit number and call sign is 8A53."

"So what is the 'A'?" Rasheed interrupted.

"Well like I was saying…"

What an arrogant and cocky son of a bitch, Rasheed thought to himself. He noticed Abu's slight smile. They were both thinking the same thing. Maybe one day they would see if he just was as good as he thought himself to be.

"The 8 means West Los Angeles Division." The cop was talking slowly and deliberately in an attempt to patronized Rasheed.

He only made himself look more and more foolish to both Rasheed and Abu but he was giving them information into police operations they did not otherwise have. Being talked to in this manner was a small price to pay for the insight they were receiving.

"The 'A' means a two-man patrol response car. In LAPD, we roll with two officers to every radio call. Sometimes, if there is an odd man, we will run a one-man car but they are in a support role and are not assigned to emergency response radio calls. You with me?"

The more of an audience he had the more it fed his ego. They both nodded so he would continue.

"The '53' is our beat. The division is broken into various patrol beats and given a numeric designation. Different units use different letters. Like gangs uses a 'G' so their call sign would be 8G21 or something."

"And Detectives use a 'W'," his partner chimed in.

"Got it," replied Rasheed. "I always wondered."

Abu continued to make small talk with the officers, fishing for any information that the officers had about the failed attempted murder of Farooq, any news of a murder victim off of Malibu Canyon, a missing Muslim woman, or any other information which would link them to any of their recent events. Unbeknownst to the officers, they could also be used as character witnesses in their defense if they were ever charged in a crime. It wasn't the first time that Rasheed noticed how Abu really was much smarter and more cunning than his simple-minded nature revealed him to be. Rasheed kept quiet until the officers left.

"Do you think the police know anything yet?" Tony asked.

"I don't think so. At least those two fools don't know anything."

They agreed, this probably meant that no one had talked to the police and implicated them.

"Where are you taking me?" Rachel asked.

"Have you ever had Cuban food?"

"Where?"

"There is a little Cuban place over on Brand Street in Glendale. It's the best bakery in Los Angeles. For breakfast, they have something called a Machaca Wrap. It has eggs, roasted pork, roasted potatoes, cheese, tomatoes, bell peppers, and onions all wrapped up in a flour tortilla. They are the best!"

"Sounds yummy!"

"It is one of my favorite little spots. Afterwards, I figured we could go for a little hike. Have you heard of Hermit Falls?" He would wait to see how the day went before inviting her over for a swim later in the afternoon when the heat wave would be in full force. It was never a bad thing to get a good – looking girl into his condo with little to no clothes on. The day definitely was starting out to be a good one.

"No, where is that?"

"It's a trail off of the 210 Freeway near Arcadia in the Angeles National Forest. Roundtrip is only about two and a half miles. It leads to a little waterfall and swimming hole. That is, *if* you are up for the challenge? We should go before it gets too hot," Steve lightly mocked her. There was a nice pool in his condo complex in nearby Pasadena.

"Watch it, Army boy. I can hang with the best of them."

"I'm counting on it," he said smiling.

"You are clearly delusional, Detective. I thought you had to pass a psych exam before joining the police department?"

"Good enough for government work!"

"Aren't you just full of energy this morning. I thought you were supposed to be soooo tired from your long week at work..." she laughed.

They parked and as they approached the entrance of the bakery, Steve reached out in front of her to open the door.

"A real-life gentleman," Rachel exclaimed. "Do you do this all the time?"

"Nope, that gentleman thing is just a common myth," he replied. "We only open the door for you girls so that we can catch a look at your ass without you catching us. And yes, I do it all the time!"

"I got your number now. Don't get any ideas," she warned.

"I already have them," he chuckled back. The light teasing and laughing went on throughout breakfast. "So, I have to tell you..." Rachel stated after a pause in the conversation.

"Uh oh, here it comes..." Steve replied.

"I went back to the warehouse the other day and..."

"You did WHAT?" Steve interrupted. "Rachel, are you out of yo...."

"You heard me," she cut him off. "I went back to the warehouse." She didn't like having to answer to others nor did she like being interrupted. "Call it curiosity."

"Rachel. You are going to get hurt. Not to mention compromise my case."

"I don't know anything about your case and I'm not that stupid

217

as to get myself hurt. Now, do you want to know what I saw or not?"

There was going to be no arguing with this one, he thought to himself. "Go on," he sighed.

She smiled at his submission. Both were stubborn and neither liked to give in. She also liked keeping score.

"I drove by and saw two young Mexican kids out there. They had shaved heads, white baggy t-shirt, and some tattoos."

"Gang members. Did you see the tattoos?"

"No. I didn't get that close. One of them had a gun under his shirt."

"Did you see the gun?"

"Well, kind of…"

"What do you mean 'kind of'?"

"Well, I definitely saw a bulge and then a partial dark shape…. No, it was a gun. Everything about it screamed GUN! Look, just because I'm not a big city police detective…"

"No, trust your gut feeling." Steve said, wanting her to continue. He had been around long enough to know that when the hair stood up on the back of your neck, it was your sixth sense. Your sixth sense was all your other senses screaming to you that you were missing something. Stop, re-evaluate, and take a second look. "Go with your instinct. What were they doing?" His tone had changed. He was very direct, focused, and methodical in his questioning without being overbearing. It was the sign of a seasoned detective.

"I saw them because they were standing at the loading dock of the warehouse. There were others behind them, further inside. They weren't white-white but like dark-white with Middle Eastern features or brown like Mexican or Hispanic. I couldn't be sure but the ones inside had beards. It looked like they were loading boxes or crates or something. The two Mexicans … do you really think they were street gang members?"

"Well, I won't know for sure but yeah, based on your description. Sounds like they were posted up as lookouts."

"Yeah, that's it exactly. What do you think it means?"

"Drugs."

"Impressive. Maybe you are smarter than you look," she said grinning. She was impressed. "Let's go there now."

"NO WAY! I have to do some research on who owns that facility first. They are going to be suspicious and on the lookout for strange cars coming by. We have to be careful."

"Well if you thought you were going to get me to go skinny dipping at some waterfall…" She hit him playfully on the arm.

A red flag warning had been issued. Searing triple digit summer temperatures were rising quickly and humidity was expected to drop below fifteen percent. Wind gusts over twenty-five miles per hour from the Santa Ana winds were supposed to continue through the week.

The heat wave continued through the day and the night. The early morning hours didn't offer any relief to the two detectives who, acting on a gut feeling, decided to conduct another trash run on the Islamic Center. Maybe they would find something that would connect the Mosque to the murder investigation.

They arrived in the area, turned off the radio, opened the windows, and drove slowly through the neighborhood as they looked for any signs of activity in the sleeping neighborhood. Sweat began to form on Ryan's forehead as a single bead rolled down his nose. He let the drop drip off his nose. He had already donned a heavy-duty pair of latex gloves and the gloves had a powder coating he preferred not to get on his face.

They stopped their undercover Ford Ranger pickup truck half a block away and turned off the ignition as they watched the stillness from the shadows. After about five minutes, without saying a word,

Gonzalez started the truck and with the lights off coasted to the trash cans which were left out on the curb. He pulled the truck bed right next to the cans as Ryan got out. Ryan quietly lifted and placed several of the bags in the truck bed as Gonzalez covered him. They quietly got back in the truck cab and without slamming the doors, coasted away as quietly as they came in.

"There's a shopping plaza with a Rite Aid drug store and a Ralph's over on the northeast corner of Topanga Canyon and Ventura Boulevard. Let's go to the back and go through this garbage."

"Good call, partner. There should be some good light and we can just throw everything in one of the dumpsters when we're done."

"Bzzzz. Bzzzz. Bzzzz." The cell phone was vibrating on the stand next to the clock which read 3:30 am in bright red LED lights. Steve tried to get his bearings.

"What now?" Steve asked himself as he rolled out of bed to grab the phone. "Hudson," he answered, half asleep, already knowing it was Ryan on the other end.

"Sorry to wake you buddy."

"No problem," he replied. He knew Ryan would not call him at this time unless it was something big. "What's up?"

"Holy Shit!" Steve belted out. Ryan was reading the contents of the crumpled-up letter they had recovered from the trash can. His body was instantly wide awake. Steve reached for his pants, which had been hurriedly strewn on the floor. Again, "Holy Shit!" His breathing was rapid and shallow like he had just received an electrical shock to his entire system. "Who else knows?" He was trying to think clearly and quickly.

"No one, yet," Ryan responded.

"OK, let's keep it that way. Call JC but no one else right now. We have to be sure about this. Suggestions?" Steve asked.

"This is too sensitive. We can't process this through the system through normal procedures. It needs to be hand carried and in *our* direct chain of custody throughout the process. We're on our way to SID right now."

Scientific Investigation Division, SID, is the LAPD crime lab. Unlike, television, SID employees are civilian criminalists. They are not police officers, they do not carry guns, they do not make arrests, they do not interrogate suspects, and they certainly do not take point on SWAT team entries. They ARE highly educated scientists with advanced degrees in biology, chemistry, physics, and the other physical sciences. The training they receive in their respective fields of expertise is equally extensive. They are some of the most dedicated, highly trained, and quiet professionals operating behind the scenes and receiving little, if any, of the credit, glory, or accolades. Their job is to analyze evidence objectively. Most times, they do not even know what their stuff is related to.

"Ok, I'll meet you there. I'm rolling now." Steve hung up the phone and started looking for the rest of his clothes.

"Does this happen all of the time?" Rachel asked, covered only in the sheets she was wrapped in. The question stopped him in his tracks as he admired her long brown hair outlining her features in the ambient light.

He glanced over at the clock, as if looking for permission, before dropping his pants back on the floor, and he crawled back underneath the sheets.

Steve turned onto the entrance driveway leading to the campus of the California State University, Los Angeles (CSU-LA), and made a right turn into the first parking lot which housed the Hertzberg-Davis Forensics Science Laboratory. The new regional criminalistics lab was a joint venture between the LAPD, the Los

Angeles County Sheriff's Department, and CSU-LA which ran state of the art criminal justice and forensic science academic programs at the facility.

JC was already there and they were all waiting out front when Steve arrived. The civilian personnel hadn't arrived to work yet. The lab was typically backlogged but ATD would need an emergency priority rush on this request. JC was there to facilitate the request and Captain Wade would also be calling the Commanding Officer of SID any time now to ensure they didn't encounter any obstacles.

Only Ryan handled the letter and every time he handled it, he put on a new pair of latex gloves from the same box. There was no way he was going to cause any contamination on this piece of evidence. He laid it out on the hood of the truck. Everyone read it and stood in disbelief.

"This stays under wraps. No one says a word outside of this circle and the Commanding Officer. That's a direct order." The fact that JC never gave direct orders in this manner made the command that much more serious.

"We got you, Dan, you traitor son-of-a-bitch!" Hudson said excitedly.

"We can't jump the gun on this. We need conclusive evidence," JC reminded everyone.

But everyone already knew they had him. It was bitter sweet and everyone smiled. Everyone was thinking the same thing, "He is a traitor. Fuck this guy!"

"No one knows what happened," JC began. "It's an LASD open homicide case. Chicago PD is pretty pissed."

"Here you go," Steve said as he passed out four Grande sized Starbucks coffees. "It's been a long few days. We figured we would share the wealth. Plus, we know you Bureau guys get lost every time you leave your office," Steve said jokingly.

JC and Steve had arranged a last minute meeting at the JTTF between SSA Floyd and Dan. They wanted Dan acting natural and didn't want to tip their hand. They didn't want Dan spooked at all. The meeting was as much to fish for information as well as to keep the two agencies talking to each other. It was a low key meeting.

But, JC and Steve had another intended purpose.

They made small talk and no real information was shared. They made a couple of investigative requests with no real substance after the meeting and followed Dan back to his cubicle. Dan finished his cup of coffee and threw it in the trash can under his desk. When Dan stepped away to use the bathroom, JC took out the cup and placed it into a brown paper bag which was folded up in his pocket. JC replaced Dan's cup from the trash with his own identical coffee cup and walked away.

Noticing the quizzical look on the supervisory agent's face, JC stopped in to SSA Floyd's office.

"Listen, Floyd," JC began.

"JC, the two of us go way back…"

"I know. We go way back and I want to keep you in the loop as much as possible. I can't go into it right now. We have a lead we are trying to substantiate. I'll call you later today, probably after hours when I have more information. I promise, you will be the first to know. Do me a favor, keep your agent close by and act normal."

"JC, I'm trusting you on this one. I'm going to have some

answering to do so don't fuck me over. This shit comes down on me."

"Floyd, this is a good case and it will make both our agencies shine. I've been doing this a long time now and I couldn't ask for a better team of detectives on this one."

"Call me. I don't care what time it is."

JC nodded.

"Is this your target sample?" the SID DNA criminalist asked.

"Yes, sir," JC responded, showing the civilian as much respect and appreciation for this priority request as possible.

The letter and envelope had first been photographed. Then they were both processed for trace evidence and DNA samples before being sent to latent prints for additional. Each phase of every process was ordered videotaped for good measure on the order of the Commanding Officer of Scientific Investigation Division.

SID had recovered a DNA sample from saliva used to seal the envelope and entered into CODIS, the computerized data system for DNA matches. Matches on CODIS must be confirmed with a live sample from your target.

JC and Hudson arranged for the meeting at the JTTF specifically to obtain a confirmed target sample from Dan. By taking his coffee cup to the lab, they would compare DNA recovered from the cup with that of the saliva sample from the envelope.

It would be a few more hours and Ryan and Gonzalez were already exhausted. They had watched any and every move anyone at SID made with that letter. Up to this point, they weren't letting it out of their sight. No way.

JC and Steve relieved them so they could go home. Their job had been done and now they were just awaiting the confirmation that would confirm Dan as the writer of the letter. FBI Special Agent Dawud Ali Nazari, aka DAN, had compromised their case and cost Romeo his life at the hands of Qazi.

While they waited, Steve and JC discussed the possible outcomes and various sources of action. Steve also caught JC up to speed on what he uncovered at the warehouse and the possible nexus to gangs and narcotics smuggling.

"Great. This is what we have been fearing. A nexus between street gangs, prison gangs, and terrorists. Common denominator is money. The profits from the drug trade. This will give our Middle Eastern friends direct connectivity to the criminal underground and access to stash houses, weapons, stolen cars. The list goes on and on. Our job just got a little bit more complicated."

"Yeah but it will also give us a criminal nexus to exploit," Steve continued. "Dopers talk. Gang members talk. Plus we have probations and parole search authorities. There may be some angles we can work."

"I like how you think Steve. Like a real street cop."

"Detectives," the chief analyst announced entering the break room they had been waiting in.

"Yes…"

"We have your results. The saliva sample from the envelope is a match to the saliva sample from the coffee cup. Match is positive to approximately a ninety eight point seven certainty. It's about as good as it gets."

PART III: TWO FOOTED

As promised, JC's first call was to Supervisory Special Agent Floyd.

"Hey, it's JC. You have any plans tonight?"

"Would it change the outcome of the call if I said yes?"

"Probably not. We need to meet...tonight. Can't talk on the phone but notify your Counter Intel people. We need them there."

"Can it wait until the morning?"

"Not unless you want to read about an LAPD warrant and arrest of one of yours. If you want a say in how this goes down, we are going to need you there."

"Shit. Dan?" Floyd asked.

"Unfortunately, yes." No one wanted to find out that one of their own was a dirty cop. LAPD had its share over the years. JC knew how Floyd felt.

"Can we do this in Westwood?" Floyd requested.

"No problem," said JC.

The Federal Building in Westwood housed all the main offices for the FBI Los Angeles Field Office. Floyd would have to go all the way up the chain on this, as would he. But that would be Captain Wade's job.

Time to give her a call.

"I think that went pretty well. How about you?" Steve asked.

"I think it went about as good as we could've hoped for," JC replied.

"They stacked the house full of their brass. I didn't expect the LA Director to be there."

After a quick introduction between the LAPD detectives and FBI Directors and a summary of the case, the working agents had taken control of the meeting.

"It's a good thing Captain Wade was there. She did a good job of representing our command staff. And, I like the plan."

"Me too. I think it will work. Good to know the Bureau's Counter Intelligence people took our information serious. They have been busy."

"Yeah, but how did they hire this guy in the first place? I can't believe the FBI background didn't catch any of this. I mean, I can understand the brother getting through a small local agency, but I expected more from the Bureau."

"As with most things, perception is nine-tenths the battle."

"Yeah…but really? An arranged marriage with a fourteen-year old girl? What the fuck is that about? And then the training of militants…"

"At least the state police back east were on top of it." Steve always respected how JC always managed to find something good to say. "You can always count on the 'Staties', they have a lot of juice back east."

"Yea, they do. They are typically an impressive bunch."

"But I tell you, Steve, this is your case and that is clear. You are impressing a lot of people here. None of this would have been uncovered without you. Even this strategy to disseminate disinformation is based on your information. No one had any idea Qazi was in Morgantown, Virginia. There was even a big case, the Virginia Jihad, that came out of there and Qazi never got linked into that. You have to ask yourself, 'why not?' Qazi being linked to the Imam at that mosque is sure to trigger a response."

The strategy was dissemination of disinformation. Create a trackable false story and catch everyone up in acting on it. It was an old wiretap trick called "tickling the wire." They needed to initiate reactions on the bad guys. They wanted to take down DAN for treason and espionage. They wanted to take down Qazi for material support for terrorism. They wanted to disrupt this silent cell. The letter wasn't enough for the United States Attorney to convene a grand jury and win an indictment for such serious federal charges. They needed to catch both of them with their hands in the cookie jar.

On the pretext it being part of his job, Fahim stopped by the hospital and discovered that Vic's son, Karim, had been discharged.

He stormed out of the hospital, telling himself that this now had as much to do with his mission. As it did, he desperately wanted to know the truth about Karim, had he flipped? Thoughts of Jennifer followed and Fahim cursed them as the work of Satan. He prayed as hard as he ever had asking the blessed Allah for forgiveness for his weaknesses and for his failures.

"OK, people, listen up," SSA Floyd announced as he started the situational briefing. Fifteen minutes earlier the offices at the JTTF echoed with his voice stating he expected everyone in the large conference hall in fifteen minutes. Everyone was there. "I don't need to remind you that the information you are about to receive is classified as Top Secret. That means you don't discuss this with anyone outside this room. Not your wives, your wives' sisters, your girlfriends, your drinking buddies, or your drinking buddies that are banging your wives' sisters and their friends." There were a few chuckles in the room. "There is a major operation going down back east. It's a counter terrorism case out of Virginia. We are assisting with multiple simultaneous search warrants, takedowns, interviews, and processing."

"Is this related to the 'Virginia Jihad' case?" one of the senior agents interrupted.

"From what limited info I have on it, yes." SSA Floyd continued giving a brief background on the subject. "Washington has tasked JTTF's across the country to assist, including the LA JTTF. We're sending twenty people out. If you are on the list, cancel all of your appointments for the next week. I need people to help cover those that are travelling. Those tasked for this operation, go home and get your things together. Pack for one week, including tactical gear. We are meeting at 1400 hours at the offices in Westwood. We will load up and bus out together to our flight. We have a C-130 transport for all of the gear and personnel. Any questions?"

No response. The agents who had gathered in the conference room were anxious to hear if their names were on the list. They waited and wondered how they were going to cancel not only their appointments but family engagements, parent-teacher conferences, soccer games, and on and on.

"Special Agent Dawud Ali Nazari. Dan, you are going for language skills," Floyd announced.

"Yes, sir" the young agent responded.

Floyd continued reading the list of names, most of whom were volunteers as assigned secondary duties on the FBI's LA Office regional SWAT team. They were all tactically oriented and trained in basic SWAT operations. The FBI uses regional tactical teams to conduct high risk search warrants on local targets. The regional FBI SWAT teams, although well trained, are different from the more prestigious FBI Hostage Rescue Team, an elite special operations unit who are internationally recognized among the world's top hostage rescue and counter terrorism tactical forces.

There wasn't much time. Dan raced out from the JTTF. He had to get home, pack his things and cancel and re-schedule appointments. Such was the life as a Bureau Special Agent. He had been warned that he could be reassigned on a moment's notice depending on the needs of the Bureau. This was one of those times and while inconvenient, it gave him access to information which he could use to further his cause. He also had to do one more thing. He had to get warning out to Qazi that his close friend in Morgantown, who he had spoken so highly of, was in danger.

The young agent picked up his issued phone and started dialing.

Wrong phone. He picked up his personal phone and re-dialed his business partner's number.

Time constraints create pressure and stress which sometimes cause careless mistakes. It's what the Counter Intelligence agents were counting on.

"Hey JC, Floyd here."

"Yeah, I know. What's going on?"

"Can your guys put eyes on the Islamic Center for me and keep them on all day?" Floyd needed LAPD assistance in the surveillance of the Woodland Hills Center. He could not have anyone miss anything.

"Something going on?"

"Can't talk on the phone." It was a violation of protocol to discuss operational and national security matters over an open unsecured phone line. "Can you and Steve be in Westwood at 1500 hours?"

"Shouldn't be a problem. Captain Wade will want to be there also."

"Of course, that's fine."

"What am I looking for in Woodland Hills?" JC asked, fishing for more specifics. It was a reasonable request. They had to know what they were looking for.

"Anything unusual. Things should be business as usual. Can you make sure you have direct contact with your surveillance team?"

"We do. See you this afternoon."

Dawud, Dan, arrived early at the Westwood FBI Los Angeles offices wearing a pair of comfortable 511 tactical pants and a polo shirt which had been tucked in. His gold FBI shield was clipped his belt buckle on his right side just in front of his displayed sidearm which was also holstered on his right hip. Dan was summoned into a room to update some of his personnel records.

When he exited, SSA Floyd was waiting for him in the hallway.

"There you are, Dan," Floyd said.

"Sorry, they had some admin forms to update."

"We still have time. Everyone is up the hallway waiting for you." SSA Floyd, walking with a sense of urgency, led the way. He arrived at a double door and reached for the handle as he stepped back to allow Dan to enter first. As Dan stepped in front of the senior agent, Floyd suddenly and violently pushed Dan into the room. Surprised, Dan stumbled in and caught his footing, only to look up at a roomful of guns pointing at him.

"Don't you fucking move," the only voice, from the senior agent, commanded as he moved in and grabbed Dan. Two other agents joined him, each taking a hold of one of Dan's arms while SSA Floyd disarmed the traitor.

The room was silent as ratcheting sound of the metal handcuffs clinched a little extra tightly around Dan's wrists.

"Dawud Ali Nazari, you are under arrest for espionage and treason," Floyd began. "You have the right to remain silent. You have the right to an attorney before and during any questioning. If you cannot afford an attorney, one will be appointed to you free of charge by the government of the United States. Do you understand these rights?"

Dan did not respond. He was still shell shocked. He didn't understand what was happening and what had gone wrong.

"You fucking disgust me." Floyd growled through his clenched teeth. "Get this piece of shit out of here."

Dan was escorted out of the room by the agents assigned to Counter Intelligence. It was not gentle.

Floyd needed to splash some water on his face. "We are not going to Virginia! Repeat, we are NOT going to Virginia," his booming voice echoed. "Briefing in ten minutes. Right here. Someone go downstairs. LAPD is waiting. Bring them up."

"RACR Division," the voice on the other end of the line at the LAPD's Command Post Center answered.

"This is Detective John Carter from Anti-Terrorist Division. I'm going to need an emergency SWAT call out." JC had a map spread out across his lap and the front seat while Steve drove. He was providing details and discussing staging areas. Steve wondered when the searing heat and high winds would stop. They were on their way to Woodland Hills to assist the FBI on service of federal search warrants on the Islamic Center. While LAPD SWAT was as good as they get and generally better trained and equipped than the local FBI team, this was an FBI case and warrant. LAPD SWAT would be there to provide assistance and take over if things went sideways. As a matter of practice, LAPD is against intermingling agencies during tactical operations as the training and response is varied between departments.

Captain Wade had met them in Westwood and was also heading out to the Islamic Center in her own car. She would make the necessary notifications to the Chief of Police. He would want to know about this before it actually happened and what exactly the Department's role was in case he had to answer questions from the Mayor's Office or local press, who would quickly pick up that something was going down. She would also need to notify the LAPD Topanga Division, who was responsible for patrol in the local area.

"I understand the FBI wanting to take the guys down themselves. It's probably better that way," JC finally said after hanging up the phone.

"And that didn't take long at all," Steve responded with a new admiration for his federal counterparts.

The Counter Intelligence team of special agents had gotten approval to put wire taps on all of Dan's phones, Qazi's phones, and who knows who else's phones. The FBI had the federal authority to use National Security Letters (NSLs) and the FISA courts under the expanded authority of the Patriot Act to conduct emergency electronic eavesdropping on both DAN and Qazi and probably a couple of others. They had overheard and recorded first, DAN's warning to Qazi of the impending Virginia operation, a counter intelligence ruse, and then Qazi's subsequent phone call to Virginia warning of the same and to destroy all records and contacts.

"I guess I'll have to stop talking shit about them," Hudson continued. "At least for a couple of days," he said laughing.

"No. I wouldn't stop, they deserve it. Well, maybe you could lay off for a day or two…but that's it! And that is an order." They both laughed, knowing that the inter-agency rivalry was good and that neither agency would have gotten to the point they were at now without the resources, assistance, and professionalism of both agencies.

Qazi was furious and ready to burn down the city. He exited the house, upon the orders of the FBI entry team leader. Assault weapons were pointed at him from the endless agents dressed in black heavy ballistic armor.

His family was directed at gunpoint to lie on the hot pavement.

Qazi refused to comply and the imam pulled out a large saber from under his robes and began swinging it wildly while screaming at the federal officers. Suddenly, a single shot silenced the area as a bullet travelling slightly left of the intended target ripped through the preacher's right shoulder tearing flesh, muscle, and bone fragments with it.

The impact of the bullet flung the saber from the crazed Imam's grip as Qazi fell to the ground screaming.

"How dare you!" the Imam exclaimed. "You dirty apostates. YOU are the Taliban!" Qazi lay on the burning pavement, shot, stunned, and filled with a debilitating rage and disbelief. The police and FBI raiders began to pour into his mosque.

"Get out of my holy mosque, you sons of infidel whores. I claim sanctuary. How dare you!"

"This ain't exactly the middle ages, padre," Ryan said as a warrant was shoved into Qazi's hands. He and other squad members had entered the grounds on the heels of the initial raiding party.

"Abomination," he shouted.

"You're charged with the material support of terrorism," JC told Qazi and SSA Floyd read him his rights.

Two of his younger students who had just arrived struggled with a uniformed officer in an attempt to assist the preacher but they were easily shoved back down by the police.

Everyone on the grounds of the mosque was stunned and bitterly angry. Some grew nauseous as they watched Qazi, the Imam, their sacred most holy man, get manhandled and shoved into a police car and driven off. At that moment, the blind, searing faith in which many had gained, died.

Once the entire mosque, Islamic Center, and adjoining house were cleared, scores of agents entered, began searching and seizing anything and everything they could, files, computers, books, photos, and mail.

A Bureau video and photography team had also arrived.

Searching any religious grounds or places of worship had significant First Amendment implications. They had to ensure everything was done by the book and documented correctly. They were sure to take heat from the ACLU as well as some of the other public Muslim outreach organizations who oftentimes served as public relation groups, lobbyists, and political action committees furthering the Muslim agenda. Many of these groups have been shown to be fronts and acting on behalf of organizations directly linked to terrorism around the globe.

Captain Wade, JC, and Steve made their way through the yellow crime scene tape and uniformed officers who were guarding the outer perimeter of the scene which was bustling with agents searching for and collecting evidence.

"Look at this," someone exclaimed. "This will make your blood curdle." It was a copy of Afghani Taliban laws. Jennifer took hold of them and was visibly angered as she finished the first few words.

Attention women:

You will stay inside your homes at all times. It is not proper for women to wander aimlessly about the streets. If you go outside, you must be accompanied by a mahram, *a male relative. If you are caught alone on the street, you will be beaten and sent home.*

You will not, under any circumstances, show your face. You will cover with burqa when outside. If you do not, you will be severely beaten.

Cosmetics are forbidden.

Jewelry is forbidden.

You will not wear charming clothes.

You will not speak unless spoken to.

You will not make eye contact with men.

You will not laugh in public. If you do, you will be beaten.

You will not paint your nails. If you do, you will lose a finger.

Girls are forbidden from attending school. All schools for girls will be closed immediately.

Women are forbidden from working.
If you are found guilty of adultery, you will be stoned to death.
Listen. Listen well. Obey. Allah-u-akbar.

Jennifer was too stunned, too angry to comment.

"Yeah, Captain, I felt the same way when I read it. Here's the rest of it. Applies to both men and women."

Word of the Imam's arrest spread immediately through the Islamic Center community, the senior council, and Qazi's students. Soon, it would travel throughout the country and then back to Pakistan.

Mahmood was at the warehouse taking an inventory when a breathless Fahim gasped out the news on the phone. Mahmood dropped his phone and it took him several seconds to pick it up.

"Fahim, I need you to get the word out. Do you remember where the warehouse is?"

"Yes, I think so."

"It is safe here. Gather everyone. We will regroup here as soon as everyone can get here. Limit the cars and make sure everyone knows not to be followed. We do not know what the police know and what they do not know."

"Brother Mahmood, the time for action is now," Fahim growled in bitter anger.

The young, Imam-trained mujahedeen were in danger of disintegrating as a group. Indeed, all but dead without their head. Mahmood would not allow that to happen.

Less than a minute later Mahmood was on the phone starting a phone chain with the other council members: Husyan Helmandi,

Habib Khan, and Ziya Gokalp. The Imam's arrest left the council members grieved, puzzled, frightened, unsure, and confused.

Mahmood's heart was racing as he paced back and forth across the warehouse floor. It would be at least another two hours before everyone would arrive at this hidden location. Not everyone was informed about the function of the warehouse but it didn't seem to matter. Mahmood would ensure that the wrath of Allah himself would avenge the injustice that had befallen them. He would need to start planning and he would need….

"My Mexican friend, it's me. How many guns can you get? Money is not an issue. I want them tonight."

Friday morning brought a slew of procedural legal issues to the detectives and agents working counter terrorism. The Bureau would be working through the weekend sorting through the evidence and ensuring the charges could be presented by the United States Attorney's Office on Monday morning. Detectives from LAPD and LASD would see what state charges could be filed ranging from conspiracy and murder to interfering with police investigations. The detectives wanted a back-up plan to keep both arrestees in custody in case the federal charges were dropped or otherwise delayed, causing a release from federal custody.

A team of high powered and expensive lawyers rushed to Qazi's defense, only to learn that someone arrested under certain antiterrorism laws could not be sprung from jail quite so easily.

Qazi was held in a single cell at the federal Metropolitan Detention Center (MDC) in downtown Los Angeles with around the clock guards. His phone calls would be monitored and recorded and he would not be allowed any contact with other inmates. Security was heightened throughout the federal detention center and off-duty officers were alerted to expect mandatory extended overtime shifts.

The police had hoped to delay the media's learning of the arrest as long as possible but Qazi was barely a block from the Islamic Center before word leaked out.

Immediately, the Imam's arrest became a lead headline, not only in Los Angeles but, across the country and the world. Not all of the resultant comments were positive. Some were ominously threatening.

The police brass, while maintaining a soft but firm posture for the media and public, was lavish in their praise for the anti-terror unit.

PART IV: THREE FOOTED

During the previous night's meeting, the group of students had previously thought of Ziya Golkap as a respected, wise, detailed, and cautious aide of Qazi's senior advisors. After last night's meeting, which was more of a war dance, the accountant left looking like a coward not worthy of being a member of their group. His faith was openly challenged by Mahmood and he responded by calling Mahmood a blood thirsty fool who would die by the sword he insisted on swinging. He cautioned the younger students to follow Mahmood at their own peril, and then stormed out.

The remaining council members followed in a sign of unity. They had too much to lose by the rash actions that Mahmood and the brainwashed group were preaching and intended to do. They knew that it was just a matter of time before agents from the FBI would come knocking on their doors, asking questions about their connections to, and involvement with, Qazi. Now was a time for caution.

Qazi was apparently the only one who could control and organize this group and if they couldn't get the imam released, they would clearly have to start distancing themselves from the students.

Fahim didn't have the maturity or insight to see what the senior council members saw. His anger had him in a blind rage as he drove around various Reseda and Canoga Park neighborhoods.

Many of the inner-city Los Angeles neighborhoods were littered with metal grocery shopping carts. Many residents didn't have cars and had to walk to local grocery stores. As a result, they would push their shopping carts full with their groceries home. Carts were left along the streets and sidewalks to be collected later by the local markets. It was a huge issue of contention as many homeowners blamed illegals for creating the eye sore.

These carts were the focus of Fahim's efforts on this hot and windy summer day.

Mahmood spent the day purchasing as much ammunition as he could collect. He didn't want to draw unwanted attention so he purchased only reasonable amounts from every gun and outdoors store and gun range he could find. He purchased enough for the variety of firearms he had acquired the night before from associates, who he knew were both unsavory and criminal. As he drove around the City, he also stopped at several auto parts supply stores and purchased several five-gallon gasoline containers. By the end of the day, the passenger compartment of his white Mercedes was stuffed full with them.

Muhammad and Mustafa spent the morning alternating between praying and reading and re-reading an article Qazi had provided them from Inspire Magazine. Inspire magazine is an English online publication reportedly published by Al Qaeda, which provides instruction on numerous topics including bomb making. This article provided instruction on the use of pressure cookers as improvised explosive devices. They would need to take a trip to Walmart by the end of the afternoon.

Meanwhile, Yunnus Banah and Nassim al Waqqas spent the day at the Los Angeles Zoo. They walked around, not paying particular attention to the attractions but instead becoming acquainted with the grounds. They collected and studied the maps, routes of travel, entrances, exits, and crowded exhibits. To the casual observer, they looked like anyone else at the zoo.

Rachel was not the casual observer.

Her heart stopped when she saw the same two men from outside the warehouse that first night with her new boyfriend. "What are they doing here?" she said out loud to herself.

She called Steve immediately, but her call went straight to voice mail. She remembered his involvement in all the news stories. He must be busy and what would he be able to do, anyway?

But seeing them sent shivers up her spine. Something inside of her told her not to let them out of her sight. She started following the two men.

Saturday passed routinely in Los Angeles... The usual traffic snarls and motorists' curses, some domestic violence, the usual robberies, burglaries, murders and gang shootings, and traffic collisions kept the LAPD busy, while the vast variety of entertainment, the myriad of restaurants, parties, beaches, mountain hiking trails, filled with locals and vacationers.

The weekend's weather was far from routine. Extreme summer temperatures were predicted in the upper 90's, and well into the triple digits in the valleys and high desert areas. Humidity was well below fifteen percent and the "Devil Winds" were expected to continue at 35 m.p.h. with gusts reaching over 60 m.p.h.

Both the Los Angeles County and City fire departments as well as the National Forest Service fire services were on high alert.

For several thousand Los Angelinos, those who lived to tell the tale, this Saturday would be the most momentous of their lives.

Most wouldn't know that they had been chosen by fate or chance, until the sun set. Only a handful knew the disaster the City was about to see.

Qazi, languishing helpless in the infidel jail, believed himself to be calm and serene, because he truly believed Allah blessed him. An examination of his body and nervous system would have revealed higher blood pressure and tension. He could only wait.

Saturday was Reagan Stancill's fifteenth birthday, and the tall, freckle-faced girl was elated beyond words. Two days earlier, the doctor had told her that the cancer that had her at the gate of death when she turned fourteen was now in remission. She had grabbed one of the panda bears that decorated her bedroom. It was the one that she had clung to during some of her sickest moments, finding some small comfort while enduring the treatments and sickness from the medicine no young girl should have to experience. She now danced around the room with it excitedly when her parents told her they were going to the zoo to see the new panda exhibit that had just arrived from China.

Justina Gallardo was excited for the weekend. The twenty-four year old single mother had endured a number of life's challenges. Despite having been in an abusive and controlling relationship when she was younger, she had managed to graduate from college with a Bachelor's degree while becoming an all-star softball player. Her hard work and sacrifice had earned her a scholarship.

Now the young woman had finally found someone worthy of her million-dollar smile. She had been born and raised in the Los Angeles area and by default was raised as a diehard Los Angeles Dodger's fan.

Her newfound romance had surprised her with Dodger's tickets to the Saturday evening game. The Dodgers were in first place and things looked promising for a strong post season run and possible World Series presence. They were playing the Boston Red Sox, who were dominating the American League East. The whole town was excited for this matchup and baseball fans hoped for and even predicted this series was a prelude to the post season championship.

So they could enjoy a few beers at the game, they were planning on taking the Metro Link train into downtown Union Station and then a quick shuttle into Chavez Ravine in Elysian Park.

Mark Notterman and his wife were celebrating their eighth wedding anniversary. He had arranged for his parents to watch the kids so he could take her to a nice dinner in Pasadena's Old Town area. As a restaurant manager who was working his way through school, he and his wife didn't yet have much, if any, time to themselves. His late work schedule and demands of school placed a lot of responsibility on his young wife. They both knew that one day all of their hard work would pay off. But until then, night's like this every few months would have to do.

Eric Orlando was a single father of a beautiful seven-year old daughter, Emily. Emily's mother had suffered severe depression after the birth of her only child. Abuse of prescription medications soon led to crystal meth addiction. After endless months of doctors, wards, and now jail, Eric had taken full custody of Emily.

Emily was involved in Brownie Troop No. 143 and her dad volunteered every chance he could. He wanted to be involved as much as possible.

The troop was using some of the money they earned from fundraising to spend the day at the new panda exhibit at the zoo.

Roger Amie was a preacher. His church engaged in student exchange programs with other churches around the country and sometimes internationally. Families from the parish were currently hosting a group of low income children from outside Atlanta, Georgia, many of whom had never seen the ocean before.

Today, they were planning to visit Hollywood. The pre-teenagers were excited and hopeful to see a movie star or two.

Rena and Roy Christensen had been married for some 40 years. A few weeks earlier, no one would have bet that they would be celebrating a 41st wedding anniversary. Rena had been seeing a younger man and Roy had found out about the affair.

The strain, an incipient hatred, could be felt in every corner of their 14-room, 5 – bathroom house. The worst seemed about to happen when Rena came home early one evening and announced that she had been a fool and that the affair was over.

It wasn't quite that simple, of course, but within a week, they were sharing the same bed again. Their former love had returned and burrowed in deeper. They wanted a special occasion to celebrate their rekindled love.

Over a late breakfast in bed that Saturday morning, Rena said, "Oh, Roy, this is the first day of the rest of our lives."

The first call came in via cell phone just before 3:00 p.m. to the California Highway Patrol dispatch.

"911, what is your emergency?" the dispatcher quickly rattled off.

"Looks like a forest fire…" the caller responded.

"What is the location?"

"I'm on the 101 Freeway, near Las Virgines. There is some billowing black smoke right over the ridgeline…."

The County Emergency response plans were put into alert. Fire and police were dispatched to the northwest portion of the County. As always this time of year with this weather, the fires would spread quickly, fueled by dry brush and high winds.

Fahim pushed a bouncing shopping cart along the Metro Link train tracks along San Fernando Road in Pacoima, a neighborhood in the San Fernando Valley within the Los Angeles City limits. It was easy enough to park off of Pierce Street and Sutter Avenue and fit right in. Just another homeless person, drug addict, or mentally ill person in an area, where all were common. He didn't even draw a second look from the residents or passersby on the streets. He pushed the cart right onto the tracks as he walked between San Fernando Road and the fence line of the Whiteman Airport, a small general aviation airport which catered to small private owners and news station helicopters, as well as housing the 35th Squadron of the Civil Air Patrol.

When the front right wheel of the shopping cart turned becoming jammed in between the loose gravel and wooden rail road tie, the cart easily tipped over onto its side. Fahim left it as planned and walked back to where he had parked.

Mahmood was used to driving like a crazed mad man through the City streets and freeways. He had to make a conscious effort to remain calm. He could not afford to be stopped with a car full of gasoline cans while fires began to burn throughout LA County. He had travelled from the 101 freeway to the 405 southbound to Sepulveda Boulevard, He now turned right onto Mountaingate Road and followed it until he reached Promontory Road. He took Promontory all the way until it dead-ended at a locked fire road gate.

He parked his white Mercedes and walked down the fire road, which was three ridgelines of steep, dry terrain, north of the Getty Museum. This one was personal. The fire was sure to burn quickly with the heat. He hadn't expected to see anyone, so he didn't count on a pair of hikers walk by as he attempted to cover the five-gallon can of gas can he was carrying. He drew quizzical looks as they passed on the isolated trail and his scowls quickly told the hikers not to interact with him.

The second brush fire call was called into LAPD 911 Dispatch off the Sepulveda Pass. It was moving quickly and fanned by the winds. It immediately posed a threat to nearby homes. Callers described a suspicious white Mercedes and a description of a possible arson suspect.

LAFD and LAPD were dispatched to the scene as well as an LAPD helicopter. LAPD Air Ships, as the police helicopters were called, had regular coverage over the skies of Los Angeles. An Air Ship was dispatched to the area in order to provide a better estimate to the LAFD Command Post as well as to the LAPD's RACR Division.

Justina sat next to her date on the Antelope Valley Line, both wearing Dodger Blue baseball hats. Her tight-fitting Dodger blue t-shirt stretched tight across her well-endowed chest. She drew several glances from her date. She didn't mind at all. The young had a happy smile on her face. They sat closely, teasingly, and intimately next to each other and butterflies danced in her stomach.

The passenger train sped towards downtown Union Station carrying the new couple and the engineer did not see the shopping cart which had been laid on its side between the rails. He was unable to stop the train in time before running over the metal cart. As the shopping cart broke apart and its pieces lodged in the undercarriage of the train, it severed one of the locomotive's air-hoses. The train's wheels rolled smoothly over the metal rail track but with the mangled metal cart being dragged under the speeding passenger train, one of the wheels was guided over the rail causing a derailment.

Feeling that the train was leaving the track, the engineer tried to bring the train to an emergency stop only to learn that the air brakes were not functioning. The train started to tip as it veered off course and down the slope and into oncoming traffic.

The excitement and butterflies in the stomachs of the young couple quickly turned to terror as they felt the train take a sudden change of course and start to roll onto its side. The screams from the passengers as bones were breaking was drowned out by the sound of scrapping metal. The train began to roll onto its side one car at a time. Bodies, blood, and personal belongings were strewn among the passenger compartment as the train slid into the heavily travelled traffic along San Fernando Road.

Fresh smoke and debris covered a path of total destruction and devastation that lasted several hundred yards. Small explosions and fires started as diesel fuel spilled into the streets. Survivors wandered aimlessly in shock deafened temporarily by the noise as others tried to climb out of and escape from the derailed train.

Police radios crackled throughout the City, "All Units, this is a City-wide tactical alert due to two major incidents in the San Fernando Valley. This is a City-wide tactical alert. RACR Division is hereby activated as the Emergency Command Center."

City wide tactical alerts enabled the Department to better manage available resources during emergency situations. It freed up Patrol response from having to handling minor disturbance radio calls and held all on-duty personnel for re-deployment anywhere throughout the City. It also enabled on duty command staff to recall off-duty officers and order them to report back to duty. It was the first stage of a Department mobilization to deal with any unusual occurrences or events.

Alert notifications were simultaneously sent to cell phones throughout the various commands. RACR was monitoring a major brush fire in the far western San Fernando Valley, another major brush fire in the County area just outside the City limits, and now a major train wreck.

As the Commanding Officer of Anti-Terrorist Division, Jennifer Wade received the Blackberry notifications.

"Hmmm," she thought out loud as she pushed the auto dial button to JC's cell phone. Her unit was not on duty or on-call but their dedication to the assignment overrode other petty issues and her people always had their phones nearby.

"Hey, Captain," JC answered.

"You seeing any of this?"

"I'm seeing it on the news. It's all coincidence right now and at best circumstantial."

"We had no evidence to support any attacks but…"

"We've both been in this game for far too long to know that there are no such things as coincidences," JC agreed with her.

"Why don't we start to see who is available...."

JC's phone buzzed for another caller. It was Steve.

"That's Steve now. We are not the only ones sensing something else here."

"OK, I'm heading to the office."

The first explosion ripped through the black duffle bag which was left on Hollywood Boulevard in front of the legendary El Capitan Theatre. The famous strip in Hollywood is the location of the Dolby and the Oscars, as well as other well known venues. The blast immediately killed several people who were within 100 feet of the duffle bag on the crowded sidewalk across from the Dolby Theatre. Homemade shrapnel consisting of ball bearings, nails, nuts, and bolts whipped through every open space impaling into or through whatever they made contact with. Wood, metal, concrete, skin and body tissue all were shredded open. Blood filled the streets as people with partial limbs tried to pick themselves off the ground in a dazed, confused, and deafened state, trying to figure out what just happened through the white smoke which had filled the street. Car alarms were sounding. A street actor dressed in a Spider Man costume walked in a dazed circle in the street, he was missing an entire arm. Those not in the primary or secondary kill zone started screaming and in a panic ran in any and all directions from the initial blast. Soon the sounds of sirens started approaching.

Roger Amie felt the shock wave as the ground and everything around him seemed to contract and then expand. His equilibrium had been affected by the blast and he saw a white cloud engulf the street a couple blocks away. Through the smoke and haze he saw a panicked crowd running towards him and his group of exchange students. There was no time. He quickly huddled the kids together and pressed them up against the glass of the storefront on the corner of Hollywood and Highland, shielding them with his large round body. It was all he could do to get them out of the way of the rushing mob and to keep them from getting trampled on the sidewalk.

Exactly thirty seconds later, the heart of the rushing panicked mob reached the intersection of Hollywood Boulevard and Highland Avenue where the preacher was huddled over his children to protect them. A black and white police car with lights flashing and sirens screaming was in the intersection attempting to locate the blast scene. Panic was everywhere in this highly populated tourist location. Just then, ninety seconds later, the second pressure cooker exploded at the intersection of Hollywood and Highland sending death, destruction, and devastation indiscriminately through the crowd. The bomb was cruel in its selection of victims: Old, young, male, female, white, Black, Hispanic, Asian, happy, sad, married, separated, and divorced.

There was nothing fair about any of it or the countless lives and shattered dreams and hopes that would be ruined this day.

However, the cruelty of this attack didn't stop there. Exactly two minutes later, a third and equally devastating homemade improvised explosive device (IED) detonated across from the famed Pantages Theatre located just a couple of blocks east from the Hollywood and Highland intersection. Hollywood Boulevard was a war zone. No one, almost no one, knew what could come next.

"Sorry Steve, I was on the other line with Captain Wade."

"Ok, so I'm not the only one....HOLY SHIT! JC, I've got my radio here and there were just three explosions in Hollywood. Frequency is going crazy! Two major brush fires, one train derailment, explosions in Hollywood. JC, this is NOT a coincidence! THIS IS AN ATTACK!"

"I'm on my way in…"

"NO!" JC screamed. "DON'T GO IN. Repeat. DO NOT GO IN."

"What?" Steve questioned.

"They are selecting targets. Police Headquarters may not be safe."

"Shit! You are right. Good call. Where to?"

"Call everyone. We need somewhere central……The Academy at Elysian Pa…"

Steve cut him off, "Dodgers are at home tonight. Traffic will be bad getting in and out….How about the parking lot at the LA Zoo? It's nearby. I have a friendly contact there. Plenty of room, facilities, food. We can make it a temporary ATD Command Post."

"Perfect. Make it happen. I'll start the emergency phone chain. Steve, make sure you have all your equipment. Vests, guns, ammo, everything."

"Boss, I'm ready for anything," he responded as he hit the lights and sirens on his City issued blacked out Ford Expedition and sped towards the LA Zoo from Pasadena. What he had left out with JC to the urgency was that he had a friendly contact in Rachel at the zoo. He knew he would be happy to see her, but more importantly he would be happy for the help he could get from his team.

Meanwhile, countless couples like Mark Notterman and his wife and Rena and Roy Christensen were strolling through the shops, restaurants, and coffee houses lining Pasadena's Old Town.

As Steve sped Code Three towards downtown Los Angeles, he passed several Pasadena Police cars and fire engines heading towards Colorado Street in Old Town Pasadena. Had he also been monitoring the Pasadena frequency, he would have learned that identical improvised explosive device attacks had just occurred along the heavy populated Colorado Boulevard, the shopping and business center of the popular Los Angeles suburb.

After placing the shopping cart along the tracks in Pacoima, Fahim placed three more on tracks heading east and south from Union Station. Unbeknownst to him, the derailment of the Metro Link passenger train brought all the surrounding rail traffic to a halt. There would be no more movement on any of the regions' railways until the tracks could be inspected. Officers from Amtrak and the Pacific Western Railroad Police Departments were immediately dispatched to the area.

Steve dialed Rachel on his personal cell phone, "Hey Rachel, listen…"

"Thank God, it's you," she interrupted out of breath.

"What's wrong?" he asked sensing a panic in her tone.

"They're back!" she exclaimed.

"Who is back?" he asked.

"Those two Muslims from the warehouse are here at the zoo. I saw them yesterday and they're here again. Something isn't right. I tried to call you yesterday but you didn't answer."

Steve was already driving Code 3 but he increased his speed as he headed towards the zoo.

"Ok, Rachel, listen. I am on my way. Do you see them?"

"Yes, they just showed up."

"Ok, stay calm. Keep your distance but not too far as that you lose sight of them. Are they carrying anything?"

"No, but they're both wearing heavy clothing. Steve it's too hot out here."

"I know." He did not know if she was aware of the events around the rest of the city but he didn't want her panicking. He needed her calm. He had to keep her talking. "Tell me where they are and what they are wearing." He muted his phone as she continued to ramble on and dialed up JC on his city phone, quickly explaining the situation to him and said that he had possible suspects at the Zoo. Steve was five minutes out and he would be switching to the ATD tactical radio frequency. He couldn't juggle two cell phones. JC would have to advise the others that they were possibly responding to the next incident which very well may be about to happen.

Smoke came from his tires and the smell of burning brake pads filled the SUV as Steve took the merging ramp from the 110 freeway onto the 5 freeway which would lead him into the Griffith Park area of the city, where the LA Zoo is located.

Muhammad and Mustafa had placed their homemade pressure cooker bombs inside black duffle bags they bought at a local swap meet in an effort to keep law enforcement from tracking them. They filled the pressure cookers with a variety of ball bearings, nails, and nuts and bolts. Regular timers were unpredictable so they detonated the bomb by wiring "pay as you go" throw away cell phones they purchased with false names.

Pressure cooker bombs had been used for years and their use was widely published in white supremacist circles and literature over the past forty years. According to the Department of Homeland Security, construction of these IEDs has been taught extensively in

Afghan training camps for years. In July 2010, Al Qaeda published a "how to" article in its propaganda filled *Inspire* magazine.

They had made the 6th and final call as they drove away from Pasadena, which set off the final pressure cooker bomb in Old Town Pasadena. The phone had been used as a trigger. They broke up the phone into pieces as they drove and they sporadically threw the fragments out the window and into the street. No one would be able to physically trace them to the phones now. They were committed to the cause and aware of the risks but were not intent on a suicide mission. The plan was to get away and not get caught. They were not set on martyrdom just yet.

This phase of the plan was complete. Now they were on their way to the Holmby Hills Mansion to join the others.

"So be it," Mustafa said. "Let the apostates die without mercy."

Saturday. 1620 hours.

The third brush fire call came in to the LAPD's 911 Emergency Center located off of Roscoe Boulevard in the western San Fernando Valley.

"911, what is your emergency?" the Police Service Representative (PSR) , or emergency dispatcher, said as she answered the emergency line.

"I live off Boulder Ridge Terrance. We have a brush fire coming towards us from the Santa Susana Pass."

This part of the city was rural horse property with open property bordering a mountain pass separating the City and County of Los Angeles from nearby suburban Simi Valley in Ventura County.

Mahmood fled the scene of the third fire he had started. He was nervous, for the first two but this one became easier. His plan was to surround the entire City in a wall of fire and spread emergency resources thin before joining the others later in the evening for the grand finale. They would get away with it, too. Already, police and fire responses were being spread across the city. He smiled at the sweet revenge they would take for the arrest of Qazi. The infidels would pay a hefty price. The police should have left them alone. He would ensure they would regret the day they tried to stop them and the coming of the new age of Islam. The time was upon them to literally rise-up from the ashes.

He sped up the 118 Freeway to the 210 Freeway. He passed a mobile home park in Sylmar which had been almost completely destroyed by an undetected brush fire that swept through the sleeping park in the middle of the night.

"How fitting to dispatch this area into a blazing hell," he said out loud. "They should have learned to pay homage to Allah the first time." He turned his car into the Stetson Ranch Park.

His concentration drifted into thoughts of getting his hands on his whore of a wife. He would make her pay immediately, then send her back to from where she came to live out her life in shame and misery.

Mahmood was unaware of the LAPD Air Unit which had responded to the call of the third brush fire. The officer pilots observed his white Mercedes speeding away from the area and matched it to the description of the possible arson suspect seen in the area of the second brush fire, which was now dubbed, "The Getty Fire." The two-man crew of the helicopter consisted of sworn police officers – one pilot and one tactical flight officer. The pilot was responsible for flying the aircraft while the tactical flight officer was responsible for navigating the city's landmarks and communicating with police units on the ground.

The pilot pulled up, increasing air space, so their presence would go unnoticed by the driver of the Mercedes. They started broadcasting for additional units when they observed the arson suspect pull into the dry Stetson Ranch Park and they began a wide aerial circling orbit. The patrol response was delayed due to everything else happening in the city. Typically, officers in the Air Ship were in a support role which consisted in observing and directing responding ground units from the air, providing a bird's eye view advantage. When the pilot saw Mahmood exit the car, holding a five gallon gasoline can, he knew that they had to act. They still wore their Department issued handguns outside their jumpsuits and they had to take action. The pilot came in for an emergency landing into the park as the tactical flight officer broadcasted an "Officer Needs Help" radio call.

Mahmood felt the blast of whipping air and deafening roar of the helicopter blades and engines before realizing that the helicopter was on top of him.

"Shit! You fuckers will not stop me!" he yelled out loud and he started running. He unscrewed the cap of the gasoline can and began pouring out a trail of gasoline as he ran over the uneven ground. Gasoline was spread over the dry brush but also spilling on his legs as he ran.

The tactical flight officer jumped out of the aircraft and hit the ground running. The officer was in foot pursuit but Mahmood had a good head start on the man.

Mahmood turned to see the officer in a full sprint after him. He stopped, threw the gasoline can, and fumbled for his lighter. Mahmood had practiced with the device and was confident he could set it off without trouble.

The officer saw Mahmood trying to ignite the fuel-coated brush and drew his service weapon. His verbal commands went unheard under the wash of the helicopters rotor blades but his facial expression said it all.

Mahmood ignored the officer as he turned and bent over to shield the flame from the wind long enough to grow and spread a flame. Instantly, the flame roared onto Mahmood's hands and clawed over his clothes. The fire ran down his legs and then the rising flames engulfed him. Screeching in agony, Mahmood ran along the path like a fat torch before falling into the high grass consumed in the very anger and fire he created.

Mahmood had become the first martyr of the day.

The fire created a small brush fire around the fallen terrorist, which was quickly snuffed out thanks to the quick thinking of the air crew officers and standard extinguishers which were kept on the aircraft.

Young Regan was standing in the crowd and drinking mineral water to cool herself from the afternoon heat. Her gaze was focused on the panda in its huge cage. The panda looked scared. Regan wondered how the bear was really feeling about his new home. Was he nervous? Did he miss his friends or old home? Was he happy? She was lost in thought when she faintly heard several quick popping sounds.

"Who is setting off fireworks," she thought without looking. "Don't they know they are going to scare the new panda bear?"

Regan's thoughts were turned to confusion when a crowd started running and screaming. The rushing mob knocked her forward and back as the bottle of water was ripped from her hand. She cried out in terror for her parents who suddenly disappeared behind a moving wall of panicked people. She stumbled trying to keep up with the mob but only lasted a couple of steps before falling beneath the pounding feet. The crowd acted like a scared heard of bulls, moving on instinct and unaware of where they pounded and on who. A frightening amount of energy was created. The fear and will to survive will smother the weak and young. Regan was both. She stood no chance.

Fahim had placed half a dozen carts on railroad tracks surrounding the City but he did not realize that all train service had stopped. Two of the other carts had been discovered by responding police and security officers.

He drove down a street lined with fast food restaurants. All the fried and greasy food the infidels ate was slowly poisoning them. In reality, they would kill themselves in due time but he wanted a painful and quick experience. Americans had become flabby and weak. They were certainly no match for the strong, lean, young men of the Taliban.

Fahim listened to the chaos on the local news radio station. Emergency response teams were stretched thin between multiple explosions in Hollywood and Pasadena, the train derailment in Pacoima, and the three raging brush fires: the Los Virgines Fire, the Getty Fire, and, now, the Chatsworth Fire.

He wondered what the delay was on the other planned targets but dared not use his cell phone. It would not matter. It would not change the outcome of the next target, a worldwide symbol of western decadence. Tonight's actions would serve as a battle cry for repressed Muslims around the world, leading to the dawn of a new age of Islam.

Steve arrived at the zoo just in time to hear the first gunshots echo across the concrete lined paths winding through the hills of the Los Angeles Zoo.

"Shit!" he screamed as he exited his SUV and ran to the rear hatchback and instantly donned his black tactical assault vest marked **POLICE** in bold white lettering. Steve kept his vest in a ready state equipped with ammunition magazines, d-ring clips, and multi-use 550 cord. He released his police issued urban assault rifle (UPR), a police version of the AR-15, and started running up the hill towards the sound of gunfire. He jammed his hand-held police radio into a front pouch of his vest and felt his heart racing. He had to force himself not to sprint but to run quick, smooth, and steady. Deep controlled breathing. He needed oxygen to his brain so he could think clearly. He scanned the panicked fleeing crowd ahead of him for any sign of a threat as he ran. He was all alone. There was no room for error.

Steve didn't see or hear Gonzalez who was 50 yards behind him, also in tactical gear.coming up from behind trying to catch up with him.

Jennifer did not divert to the zoo. She also did not go to police headquarters. Instead, she drove straight to RACR Division, the Department's emergency command and control center. She knew that all the information would be directed and coordinated there and wanted the information fresh as it came in.

Coordinated explosions. A train derailment. Brush fires being reported, a suspicious encounter with a possible arson suspect. This was definitely a coordinated terrorist attack. Now, the question was who, why, was this it, and, if not, what else? She hadn't heard from Steve before the reports of the Air Unit's interception of the possible arson suspect came in.

The suspect was burned badly and the car DMV records had returned to a closed dealership. A cursory check of the Secretary of State's online business records revealed the business owner as Mahmood Erdogan.

"How do I know that name?" she said aloud to herself. She dialed Steve to see if the name was related to Operation Q-Tip. No answer. "That's weird," she thought again out loud.

She had a gut feeling that Fahim was somehow involved in this. Next, she scrolled through her Blackberry contact list and pulled up Fahim's cell phone number.

Things were frantic at RACR and the assigned weekend personnel were scrambling around trying to coordinate and track all of the incidents. She found a senior detective and identified herself as the Commanding Officer of ATD.

"Listen, I know things are crazy. I have a lead. I need a desk with a computer and a phone."

Rachel was on the line with Steve but the phone line disconnected when she heard the distinct sound of gunfire, followed by screams and mass panic. She had been following the two and describing their location to Steve when she saw them both reach for their guns and began shooting into the crowd. She couldn't believe her eyes. This wasn't some third world country overseas where she completed her military service. This was right here in the United States.

As soon as the shooting started, the orderly crowd transformed into a panicked mob. Rachel saw a young girl fall and start to get trampled. Without hesitation, disregarding her own safety, she sprinted towards her and into the gunfire.

The gunman indiscriminately continued to spray the crowd with gunfire as Rachel pushed her way against the thinning crowd to reach the girl. She could see her now. Only a few more steps when suddenly, a searing and burning pain shot through her left leg. One of the gunmen's bullets ripped through her left calf. She stumbled forward and was able to fall on top of the girl. She screamed out in pain but was also instantly relieved to discover that the girl was still alive and conscious as she shielded the girl with her own body.

"What's your name?"

"R-R-R-Reagan…"

"It's going to be all right, Reagan"

Suddenly, the gunfire stopped. Rachel looked up to see that the gunmen were fumbling with their magazines in an attempt to reload. She made a mental note that they were not very well trained. Their delay created an opportunity to escape. If she could only get the both of them around the corner, she had a key to an employee entrance at the back of the exhibit. Rachel could lock them in there and wait for help.

"Let's go," she said as she grabbed Reagan's tiny hand. Rachel tried to stand but instantly fell, stumbling forward. Her left shin had been shattered. Rachel's survival instinct kicked in. She would not just lie there and wait to be killed. She started crawling towards safety, pulling the frozen and terrified girl with her.

"How much time do I have," she thought as she glanced over her shoulder to identify the threat. She glanced just in time to see the first gunman's head explode as she simultaneously heard two quick gunshots from the distance. The first gunman instantly fell to the ground clearly incapacitated.

Rachel looked in the direction of the distant gunfire and saw Steve moving toward the first gunman with his sights looking on, scanning the area. His movements were precise, smooth, and methodical.

She glanced over and saw the second gunman, who was obstructed from Steve's view, bring up a rifle but it was not pointed at Steve. She frantically looked in the direction where the second gunman was focused and saw a second policeman coming up to the side of Steve.

"*WATCH OUT!*" she started screaming, but it was too late.

Steve jerked his head to the right, reacting from the quick burst of fire only to see Gonzalez fall to the ground. He immediately identified the second threat and unleashed several controlled three-round bursts. An immediate rage and desire for revenge at the sudden loss of his partner and friend filled the detective. When the second gunmen fell, he let loose one more three-round burst, just for good measure. There would be no arrest or fair trial for this one.

Steve advanced on the shooter to confirm he was dead before running over to Gonzalez just as Ryan and JC arrived, having sprinted up the hill. Gonzalez had been directing them in while trying to catch up with Steve. JC was out of breath but he managed to call for help and direct a medical response over the radio. It was necessary for the civilian casualties but the "*Shots Fired, Officer Needs Help, Officer Down,*" radio transmission was a drill in futility.

Gonzalez was already dead.

Jennifer was standing over a desk in a back office when her phone rang, it was JC.

"Hey, Captain. It's bad," JC said.

Jennifer's face went pale as she swayed backward and then

forward. The detective who had been helping her saw the change in her body and jumped up in front of her just as her knees buckled and she fell forward. She fell into his chest and he guided her into a chair. She never fainted or lost consciousness, just got weak in the knees. She couldn't believe she had lost one of her officers. This was what every commanding officer dreaded.

"I can't process this right now," she said aloud.

"Captain, are you there?" JC said into the phone.

The detective helping her picked up the phone and spoke for her. "She just lost her balance," he said. He didn't know Captain Wade, but the detective quickly developed a respect and liking for her over the past half an hour, while they worked on the tactical emergency.

"I'm OK. Are you?" She had to be sure JC could still function.

"I'm not hurt. Steve and Ryan are with me. Everyone is uninjured."

"This isn't done yet. We need to stay focused or more people are going to die."

"We have South Bureau units coming to hold the scene. Ryan recovered some papers from the pocket of one of our shooters here. We found directions to the Playboy Mansion and maps to the grounds. Steve remembers some of our players working security there."

"Shit! I have an emergency ping on Fahim's phone. He's there now."

"Ok then boss, we have an identified and operational cell *and* in our info, seems to me a credible threat to the Playboy Mansion. We are on our way there now."

"I'm calling SWAT and West LA Division. I'll meet you there. JC...."

"Yeah?"

"Stay safe."

Against her will, Steve escorted Rachel into one of the ambulances that were arriving on scene.

"I'll be fine," she pleaded, not wanting to be seen as a victim.

"No way," he insisted. "You are going to get this checked out." He was concerned about her loss of blood and chance of infection. With everything going on, Steve was sure that the hospital would bandage her up, give her some medications, and release her within a few hours. Also, his job wasn't over yet. The hospital would keep her out of his way where he wouldn't worry about her.

"But it's only a flesh wound…"

"Are you always this stubborn?" one of the firefighters interrupted her. "Don't worry, the real heroes are here now," he said jokingly. The tone and urgency of the surrounding situation quickly over rode the moment's lightness and joke. "We are taking her to California Hospital over on Grand Avenue. She'll be in good hands."

"I know where it is. Thanks, guys."

He tried to force a reassuring smile to ease the concern he noticed on her face just as the rear doors slammed closed and the ambulance sped away, lights and siren.

Fahim, Abu, Tony, Muhammad, and Mustafa faced the east and knelt on their prayer mats in the cramped security guard shack.

"My brothers are soldiers in Allah's arm…" Fahim began as he led the group in a pre-attack prayer session. Everyone in the room already had blood on their hands from the day's events, "… let the apostates die quickly or slowly but die they shall without mercy….."

It would be a couple of more hours before guests began arriving for the party at the mansion. Fahim knew they had to stay focused and prayer would be the best way to accomplish that.

The other three would join them soon. They would continue

praying, planning, and preparing for the last, and most impressive, attack of the day. When the infidel whores who would be parading around with no respect for themselves, when their minds were clouded with alcohol and drugs, when hedonism flourished...then. Then, and only then, would the small band of holy warriors descend upon them and deliver their souls to redemption. The symbol of everything that was wrong with the West would be an example for the world to see. The time was now, before the apostates arrested and persecuted any more of their brothers.

"The arrest of our beloved imam was a sign, no, a call, from the prophet into action. And, we will deliver unto the graces of Allah. We will not fail you. We have cleansed our souls, our minds, our hearts..."

Damn, who is calling me now, "Hello," the woman said answering her cell phone.

"Is this Maria?" the caller asked.

"Yes..."

"Maria, this is Detective Hudson from the LAPD."

"Oh, yes, I remember you," she said hopefully. "What is happening? You must be busy."

Steve cut her off, "Listen, Maria. This is important. Where are you right now!"

"Well, Detective," she said annoyed at the bluntness and forcefulness of his tone. "I'm actually working. I'm at the Mansion. We are having a rather large event tonight and I'm very...."

"Do you see your security staff," he demanded.

She started to respond with an attitude but the urgency in his voice told her otherwise. "N...n..n...no. I don't. Now that you mention it, I haven't seen them in a while, which is strange. They should be out and abou..."

"How many people are on the grounds right now," he said again, cutting her off.

"The regular staff, a few of the bunnies lounging around and getting ready, but the guests won't start arriving for another couple of hours."

"Listen, I need you to gather everyone on the grounds. Is there somewhere secure in the main building you can lock everyone in to? Somewhere hidden and safe."

The Playboy Mansion was known for hidden passages and rooms.

"Yes, I think so."

"Ok. I need you to gather everyone and do it. Do not alert security. Stay away from any of your security staff."

"What is going on?" she now demanded.

"We have information that your security staff has been compromised and we have, what I believe, an immediate credible threat against the Mansion. You are going to start hearing sirens. Do not come out. Keep your cell phone with you. I will call you directly when you can come out. I need you to do this and I need you to do it now. This is not a joke."

Everyone in the news media was in a frenzy. People were being called in during days off. Something big was happening in Los Angeles, something huge, but they had no idea yet what it was. None of them wanted to miss one of the biggest stories of their collective careers. Already, speculation suggested a series of terrorist attacks. Various stations tried to create a minute-by-minute timeline of the day's events, and put the pieces together, so to speak.

Images of the carnage and confusion interrupted every local television channel. Train wreck, fires, explosions throughout the city, and an armed attack at the zoo. Cell phone videos and photos were starting to come in to the news stations from citizens on the ground. Images were saturating social media sites such as Facebook, Instagram, and YouTube. Media teams were scouring these sites for images. Careers could be made or destroyed over event coverage such as what they were witnessing. And in news media, sadly, ratings and "headline news" ruled the day at the expense of accuracy, privacy concerns, or common decency.

Qazi's bail requests had been denied and he was sitting in the intake block at the Federal Metropolitan Detention Center in downtown Los Angeles. The intake block was an open bay style dorm room crammed full with bunk beds. There were two small sitting areas with televisions. Everyone new to the facility was placed in intake until they were classified for a housing assignment. Classifications were done to identify security threats and concerns, mental illnesses, addictions, keep aways, general population inmates, and other special needs.

One television was unofficially designated by the inmates for sports and the other for movies. Today however, both televisions were glued to the local news stations. Inmates sat in helpless shock and disbelief over what was happening in the outside world. In the world where most of them had family and loved ones.

One young inmate whose loved ones and family had long ago abandoned him sat on his bunk alone. He was filled with anger and hate fueled by white supremist philosophies. These ideals were clearly tattooed across his body. Horns were tattooed across his forehead which he kept freshly shaved. Teardrops were inked underneath his eyes. His arms and chest were covered with a variety of hate images including Nazi swastikas, crossed hammers, iron eagles, the numbers "666", and most notably, "NLR."

Nazi Low Riders, a prison gang, created by the Aryan Brotherhood to carry out the will of the "Brand" after its members were removed from the general population and immediately sent into administration segregation in institutions across the country. NLR had grown and become so big, they were now their own major prison gang.

The young hate-filled inmate didn't need much, if any, reason to resort to immediate violence. Images of women, young children, elderly, and other innocents injured, scared, panicked, and being rushed to waiting ambulances, were more than a sufficient outlet for his rage. His gaze shifted back and forth from the news broadcasting to Qazi. Images of the dead shooter at the zoo coupled with speculation of Islamic terrorists put the imam on the gang member's radar. He clutched a plastic toothbrush concealed in his pants pocket. The toothbrush wasn't a regular toothbrush. The brush had been removed and the plastic handle had been ground down in a pencil sharpener to form a typical prison weapon or "shank" with a deadly point. The handle had been taped to prevent slipping from sweat and blood. He watched and waited.

When Qazi got up and walked to the bathroom against the back wall, the young Nazi Low Rider followed him. Seasoned inmates sensed something and heads were on a swivel.

The correctional officer was preoccupied at his desk. His attention was divided between his telephone conversation, the television, and a magazine on his desk. He was uninterested in the activities of the inmates.

Qazi turned from the sink and was surprised to bump into the other inmate. He was more surprised as he felt the hard plastic pick puncture his chest repeatedly. It had happened so quickly, the imam didn't have a chance to react. His body instantly went into shock as he slumped forward onto his attacker and then was pushed backwards, falling onto the floor. All he could do was lay on the cold, hard concrete floor and listen to the sucking sound from the open wounds on his chest, as a general alarm was sent out.

The sound of approaching sirens sent the praying group into a panicked rush. They scrambled towards and hastily grabbed their weapons and whatever extra ammunition they could grab in the moment's instance. They ran outside confused as the sirens descended on top of them. They were now on the psychological defensive. They lost the offensive surprise and initiative. They were not ready. It changed everything and they ran back and forth and in circles, like lost lab rats.

As the first black and white pulled up to the Mansion's driveway, it was met by Mustafa, who quickly fired a three-round burst from his assault rifle. The rounds slammed head first into the engine and windshield. The officers quickly exited and returned fire, sending Mustafa back out of sight into the cover of the heavy vegetation.

The fight had begun.

Jennifer skidded to a screeching stop behind the back of the row of black and whites that had descended on the Mansion. The radio was screaming with officers sharing gunfire with an unknown number of heavily armed suspects inside the Mansion grounds. They had no idea how many suspects they had inside but it was a very active and developing scene.

Jennifer quickly found a field sergeant who was trying to coordinate command and control over the chaos. When he saw Jennifer arrive at scene with a Captain's badge, a sigh of relief came across his face.

"You accepting command of this situation Captain?"

"No, Sergeant. You're doing fine and have a better handle on it. My people are arriving now and I will coordinate with them."

Just then, Steve came running from around the corner. He was in a full sprint with all of his gear.

"JC and Ryan are right behind me," he said, trying to catch his breath.

"Steve, you've been here before. Can you give us a layout," Jennifer said noticing the relief on the young patrol sergeant's face.

Steve grabbed the white board which was laid out on the trunk of the Sergeant's black and white. He quickly sketched a map of the grounds as best as he could remember from Maria's tour a few weeks earlier. Uniformed patrol officers were already formulating a contact team where the initial shots were exchanged.

"We can't wait for SWAT. This is an active shooter scene and we can't let them fortify their positions. We have friendlies inside hiding. I have direct phone contact with them."

"I agree," Jennifer stated not giving the sergeant a chance to object.

"Ok, this is what I suggest…"

JC and Ryan arrived. Ryan's age was catching up with him and he was winded. Steve continued, "Patrol will continue up the front entrance and overtake the security shack which is here," Steve explained as he pointed to the hastily drawn sketch of the grounds. "There is a hidden service entrance over here by the zoo area. Our team will enter here and secure this side. This outbuilding here is Hugh's game room and movie theatre. Both teams will meet here. From here, we will have control of ingress and egress of all emergency vehicles from both directions. Once we secure this area, we'll call for support teams. Start forming up additional teams as they arrive. Once we get the perimeter grounds under control, we can deal with the main Mansion. Hopefully, SWAT will be here by then."

"We'll have to watch the cross fire as we converge on the game room and theatre building," JC added, agreeing with the plan.

"What tactical radio frequency are you on?" Jennifer asked.

"All the city wide channels are tied up. We are on West Bureau Channel 142," the sergeant responded, confidence returning to his voice with the arrival of solid support from seasoned and veteran officers.

"Brief your contact team," JC stated.

"Give us four minutes to entry at this point," Steve said.

Jennifer turned towards the patrol sergeant, "You got this. I'm going with my team."

"*LET'S DO IT!*" JC called out and they were off.

Four minutes in and the team of ATD detectives made entry through the discussed gate. Right on time. They moved quickly but cautiously. Steve took point, flanked by JC and Ryan. Jennifer took rear guard. As the four man team covered ground, they heard a series of gunshots from the other team. They were making contact.

"Stay alert," JC whispered. "They may be sending some our way."

Just then, a figure appeared out of the shadows and crossed directly in front of Steve. He had a long beard and was wearing dark military style clothing. He was reaching for something…

"Drop the gun! It's over, Fahim!"

There would be no compliance on this day. The two guns fired simultaneously. One round slammed into the Detective's chest knocking him off his feet. His tactical vest complete with steel plates absorbed the bullet. The impact would leave a pretty good bruise but he was not seriously injured. He was lucky.

Fahim wouldn't have the same luck. One of Steve's bullets found their mark as did one of JC's bullets. Both bullets tore into Fahim's stomach and slammed him backwards. His gun went flying away as he grabbed his stomach and hit the ground. Writhing on the ground, he screeched with a pain like none he had ever felt before.

"Damn you all to the fires of hell," he cursed.

Jennifer advanced a couple of feet until she stood over the bearded, bleeding boy who had failed so miserably at playing soldier. With obviously great effort, his eyes found Jennifer. Fahim tried to control his heavy breathing. He wiped his mouth and an odd smile spread across his angular face.

"Help me, you stupid cunt. Allah…Imam will never let me die and…" His eyes grew cloudy, feeble rocking the ground, trying to hold in his guts as blood trickled out.

"Your beloved Imam didn't train you very well. How's the old fellow doing in jail, by the way?"

Grimace turned into hatred and Fahim's face showed it. "How dare you speak of him in such a way. You…female infidel. I'm a man. A mujahidin blessed by Allah. Look at me when you talk, woman…."

Jennifer twisted her head around slightly, "Oh you poor little boy. Left all on your own and making every mistake possible…"

"Shut up! You stupid pig of a whore!" Fahim's body was trembling and going into shock.

"Fahim, you are too dumb and too slow to play with the big boys."

The only sounds were his groans and wheezing breath. She thought about just letting him lie there and let the life just ooze out of him but she wasn't that person.

He was too livid with rage to speak as he drifted in and out consciousness.

Thirty-seven minutes later, Fahim bled out and died in an ambulance.

The other contact team had neutralized the remaining attackers. Mustafa and Muhammad had gone down shooting it out with the uniformed officers.

When push came to shove and actually faced with life or death, Abu and his sidekick Tony, the Italian convert, had given up and surrendered to officers. They were handcuffed and led away. Both cooperated and were talking to officers at the scene. Additional contact teams had entered the Mansion to secure those hiding inside and bomb squad K-9 dogs would sweep the area out of precaution.

It was over. ATD had averted another tragedy but not without loss.

Members of the city administration and police hierarchy were all scrambling for cover and trying to come up with excuses for the rapacious media. There would be recriminations, demotions, resignations, firings, investigative committees and panels, articles and TV reports. Books would be rushed into publication.

And the detectives sitting at Justice Cafe couldn't have cared less about any of it. Like an army unit in and just out of combat, they were concerned only with their own squad.

Steve, JC, and Ryan all sipped their beers while Jennifer gave an update. Casualties from the LA Zoo, Hollywood Boulevard, and Old Town Pasadena were still coming in but preliminary reporting had at least a dozen people dead and scores seriously injured. The winds were expected to die down overnight but the fires would take another week before they would be fully contained. Thankfully, no homes had been lost yet from any of the fires. Emergency rooms and trauma centers were full across the region. The city's police services remained on tactical alert. The Department was mobilized to twelve hour shifts and was supported by the Los Angeles County Sheriff's Department and California Highway Patrol who had set up Command Posts to coordinate their response. LASD and CHP wouldn't really do much but the extra police presence was designed to reassure the public that everything was under control. Perception really was nine-tenths of the battle. The neighboring county sheriff's departments from Ventura, Kern, Orange, Riverside, and San Bernardino were also put on heightened states of alert. The governor declared a state of emergency and activated the National Guard.

ATD would have its work cut out for them over the next couple of months with reports, timelines, case debriefs, and on and on. There would be a lot of questions asked that would need to be answered. Roles of the various agencies involved would be scrutinized about who knew what and when. But right now, that was the least of their concerns as they had the task of burying one of their own.

JC started going through the events that led to Pedro's death. When he was done, they all raised their glasses in his honor. There were no tears at the table. Those would come later. For these men, those usually came when they were alone and lost in thought, such as when they were driving. They would miss their friend dearly.

It was all bittersweet. They had lost one their own along with all of the innocent lives lost. But they all also knew they had uncovered a greater plot and disrupted a legitimate silent terror cell. They had stopped an evil from happening which was much worse than what had happened. Pedro Gonzalez had not died in vain.

Rachel hobbled on crutches through the door at Justice Cafe and was assaulted by the smell of hard liquor. She also quickly realized that everyone in the bar had turned to look at her. A big and intimidating patrolman stood up and blocked her path.

"Closed party, lady."

"Do I look like a member of the fucking media?" she shot back instantly.

JC had seen her now and he walked over. "It's okay, Vernon. She's here with us."

Rachel continued to stare down Vernon as she was led in by JC. "What's happened to Steve?"

"He's fine. We're all over here. He's having some deafness in his ears from all the gunfire."

Steve jumped up at the sight of her and gave her a warm embrace as Ryan immediately called out for another round on the double and the mood at the table instantly changed.

After the day's events, Justice Cafe wouldn't give out any bills for this group of officers.

"Those look disgusting!" Rachel exclaimed noticing the wings and blue cheese on the table.

"But the smell is better than anything you'll find at the zoo!" Ryan said and they all laughed as Detectives Rivera and King from Robbery Homicide Division walked over. They were old partners of Steve's from previous assignments and without speaking, they dropped an RHD challenge coin on the table.

"You did not just do that…" JC started.

"OH Hell No!" Ryan called out as everyone at the table reached into their pockets for their ATD coins and in unison slammed them on the table. Everyone laughed as Jennifer explained the concept to Rachel, who was already well versed in the military tradition.

Elite units kept a unit challenge coin and when challenged by another member or another unit, the tradition stated you had to respond with your own coin which was supposed to be with you, at all times. Tradition called for the loser of the challenge to buy the next round of drinks.

Rachel picked up one of the coins, admiring the ATD logo. "Nice design but what does it mean?"

Ryan began explaining the meaning of the eye, the shield, the chessboard, the scales of justice, the lightning bolts, and the sphinx.

"The riddle of the sphinx," Ryan continued. "JC there designed it."

"I'm afraid I don't remember that one from high school," Rachel said.

Steve continued, "What has one voice, four legs in the morning, two legs in the afternoon, and three legs in the evening?"

Rachel looked on puzzled.

"Man," JC finally answered. "Man has one voice throughout his life. He crawls on all four as a baby, learns to walk on two legs, and then uses a cane later in life."

"You guys really are smarter than you look," she responded. As they all laughed, she whispered into Steve's ear, "I could use a good man. Take me home."

And he did.

Larry Alvarez is a police detective supervisor (ret.) with the Los Angeles Police Department. He has worked patrol, gangs, vice, counter terrorism, organized crime, intelligence, undercover, night watch detectives, surveillance, officer-involved-shootings, internal affairs, and a host of other investigative assignments. Detective Alvarez holds a Juris Doctorate degree, a Master's Degree in Criminal Justice, and a Bachelor's Degree in Criminology. He is a criminal justice professor, and has been published in the Counter Terrorism Journal and the F.B.I. Law Enforcement Bulletin. This is his first novel.

CREDITS

Cover Original Concept: *Internet Open Source: Free for Commercial Use & Redesign*

Cover Design: *Joe Lozano*

ATD Logo: *Robert Boyd, used with permission.*

Editing: *George McNeil, Laureano Alvarez, Mark Alvarez*

Made in the USA
San Bernardino, CA
05 October 2018